HOW
Maya
GOT
FIERCE

ALSO BY SONA CHARAIPOTRA

Tiny Pretty Things
Shiny Broken Pieces
Symptoms of a Heartbreak
The Rumor Game

HOW Maya GOT FIERCE

SONA CHARAIPOTRA

FEIWEL AND FRIENDS
New York

A Feiwel and Friends Book
An imprint of Macmillan Publishing Group, LLC
120 Broadway, New York, NY 10271 • fiercereads.com

Our books may be purchased in bulk for promotional, educational, or business use. Please contact your local bookseller or the Macmillan Corporate and Premium Sales Department at (800) 221-7945 ext. 5442 or by email at MacmillanSpecialMarkets@macmillan.com.

Library of Congress Control Number: 2020919624

First edition, 2022
Book design by Aurora Parlagreco
Feiwel and Friends logo designed by Filomena Tuosto
Printed in the United States of America

ISBN 978-1-250-76213-9 (hardcover)

10 9 8 7 6 5 4 3 2 1

To my darling Kavya Kaur Dhillon—
and all the other girls like her who are writing
themselves into the narrative.

1

THERE'S SOMETHING ABOUT A CALIFORNIA SKY THAT MIGHT just make you stay.

Maybe it's in the hues—all pinks, blues, and purples, with the occasional rage of orange streaking through like a flame. Maybe it's the way the afternoon sun dips to meet the moon, impatient and petulant, like star-crossed lovers fated to never quite connect. Or maybe it's that occasional waft of jasmine, demure and seductive, beckoning with long, nimble fingers.

That is, if you can smell it at all over the stench of garlic.

Because that's all I can smell, 98 percent of the time. Garlic on my skin. Garlic on my clothes. Garlic in my hair. Living in the heart of Gilroy, the Garlic Capital of the World, I can't just wash it right out. It is there, ever present. Tragically, perhaps, forever.

It's not that I don't like garlic. I mean, I'm brown. Indian. Punjabi, specifically. We put garlic in *everything*. (Except for our chai.) Also: My parents are pretty much the King and Queen of Garlic, literally, at least in Gilroy, where most of the commercial production and distribution happens these days. Our home sits at the edge of about twenty acres, garlic plants as far as the eye can see. Endless fields of lush green garlic, ripe for the picking. Well, almost ripe. Harvest will be mostly the end of July through August. But there's a lot to be done before then.

This year, for the first time in my life, I won't be here for it.

Is it weird that I miss it already? The scent still lingers in the oven-baked June air, the gray faux leather of my mom's '98 Toyota Camry, and even in my hair, though I washed it twice this morning with the strawberry shampoo my best friend, Cherry, ordered me from Ulta—which I forgot to pack in my mad dash out the door.

But there's no time to worry about that now, because I'm decidedly late and Mom is ridiculously slow. She insists on driving—doesn't trust me, even though I've been running the tractor since I was ten—so a forty-minute car ride will take sixty. Which is fine, because I've got work to do.

I have to capture this moment, the one when I leave the only world I've ever known behind. A car selfie won't cut it. I stretch out through the sunroof, elbows propped on the edge as I try to get the perfect sunset shot with my phone. I can still see Cherry in front of the house, waving.

I slide back down into my sticky seat and examine my handiwork. Not bad.

There's something about a California sunset that might just make you stay.

Hmm, too Insta-poet.

Fire in the sky? Time to say goodbye!

Cherry would laugh at that one.

Gonna miss that blazing Cali sky. East Coast bound, baby!

Too humblebraggy.

Maybe another angle? I leap up through the sunroof again, my mom tugging at my jumpsuit, trying to pull me back down to earth. But there's no stopping me now. Not when I'm so close.

The raging fires in the hills have finally given way to a controlled burn, but the sky is definitely putting on a show today. As it should be.

After all, this is the moment I make my great escape from Gilroy and garlic and Geras. The moment when Maya Gera, California farm girl, books it from here all the way cross-country, to the city that never sleeps, the place dreams are made of. My dreams, at least. In New York. And for once, it's not just me making up stories. This is real. The moment—

"You almost made me hit that deer!" Ma yells as the car swerves, nearly sending me flying right out the sunroof. I thwack my elbow hard as I slink back into the passenger seat. My mom grips the steering wheel, trying to regain control of the car. I rebuckle my seat belt and rub at the bruises already forming on my thigh.

"They're quick, the deer," Ma says, all casual, as if she didn't practically kill us both. She glares at me as she pulls back onto the road, like I'm to blame or something.

"That could have been bad, Ma," I say as she picks up speed—which for her means doing thirty—on the empty two-lane highway. Peering out the window, I note a few trampled plants and a dented fence pole on the right side. "The Berrys' mailbox is a definite goner."

Ma frowns as she peers over the dash. "Don't worry. I'll take them some chutney. Will go well with all their fancy cheese." Chutney's her signature solution for every occasion, even when you accidentally kill your neighbors' fence.

We inch onto the freeway, and—as suspected—traffic has halted. I reshuffle the chaos in my backpack—laptop, tablet, and magazines—checking again for the printout of my itinerary and boarding pass, and instead discover a little toiletry pouch Cherry must have sneaked into it. It holds rose skin mist, extra-moisturizing sunblock, and hair serum, along with a note in her familiar, loopy scrawl. *For the frizz. Don't do anything I wouldn't do. Or anything I would.*

Homesickness hits me with a pang. Cherry's like my sister, my conscience, my voice of reason. And the little devil on my shoulder sometimes. Maybe that's why I've been such a mess this week. We've never really been apart, not in seventeen years. Every summer, when we're not busy with the harvest (which is most of the time), I help her work on a capsule collection for her future fashion line, Suite Cherry Bombe, which she sells at her dad's Very Cherry fruit stand and through an Etsy shop. It's a retro mishmash of Bettie Page pinup

3

vibes and old-school '70s Bollywood à la Zeenat Aman. This year she'll have to do it without me.

But she insisted on helping me pack, which means my suitcase and carry-on are stuffed with teal silk rompers, bright, poppy-striped scarves, and mod print dresses, all ultraglam gear that's decidedly not quite ready for Cow Camp. Which is where I'll be spending the summer.

The Linden Institute Precollege Agriculture Program is a must for any self-respecting farm boy or girl (read: heir or heiress) these days. Housed on the Rutgers University campus, it's known for giving a broad-scope overview of the agriculture industry as a business, as well as a hands-on education in the down-and-dirty stuff. Like milking cows. What do cows have to do with garlic? Beats me. But off I go, at Papa and Dadoo's insistence. As the oldest of the three kids—and the next in line to the Gera Garlic throne (sigh)—I am supposed to be the guinea pig *and* set the example.

This summer's the first step in the rest of my life, at least how my family has it planned for me. That includes agriculture undergrad at a respectable UC campus and an MBA in management and administration before I settle in and take over the family garlic farm (tiny now, but ideally growing) one day. Along with delivering a suitable husband and two-point-three kids, ideally boys. Dog optional.

Sounds flip, but a lot is riding on this summer. Like everything. This is where we're shipped off to make critical connections, to find strategic alliances (read: potential parent-approved brides and grooms, preferably Sikh), and to learn how to actually grow our empires.

Is that how I envision my ideal future? Hell no. But I will endure Cow Camp and even aim to thrive. Because that's what a good Indian kid—especially the oldest—does.

The silver lining? I'll be an hour away from New York City. And in the center of Manhattan, in the glitter of Times Square, stands the towering McIntyre-Scott Media Inc. building. Home of my bible, my road map, my lifelong guidebook. *Fierce* magazine. The secret dream. The one that lives in my head—and on my vision board. If I'm lucky, I'll manage to sneak in a trip or two into the city.

"Make sure you take good notes," Ma says, tapping the steering wheel, her pace quickening as anxiety arches her brows, thick and unruly. I text Cherry to remind her to wax them. Then Ma's commands start, firing like garlic pellets shooting out of the dehydrator:

- "Call Chacha's cousin Bhaljinder, too. He lives in Maplewood. Or Montclair. Or Morristown. Or something. Lots of *M* towns in New Jersey."
- "Try not to eat too much junk food. Buy groceries. But don't put too much on the credit card."
- "Papa said Guru Pathak will be there. His parents have a garlic farm in Madera."
- "Study hard. Have fun. Maybe you can visit New York. I've heard it's beautiful. But we never stopped. Only saw the airport. LaGuardia?"
- "If you make a good impression on Dean Maxwell, he'll write you a college recommendation. Papa will be so happy."

We're finally moving again, so Ma carefully veers into the carpool lane. She'll stay there the whole ride, straight shot, because she hates changing lanes. My stomach squeezes as the sign for the airport passes out the window. And there are the rolling hills. Weird. Feels like I might miss them.

I pull out my phone again, indulging the urge to commemorate. Summer means all dry yellow grass and bare trees; random dark, scorched patches; and the occasional horse or cow strolling. Cows. Hmm. That could be perfect. Hashtag #CowCamp or whatever. I wonder if I could get a better shot.

5

"Don't you dare," Ma says, tapping my leg lightly with her right hand to keep my butt firmly planted in my seat. "I put chai stuff in your bag. I don't know how much Roop cooks, but you know the basics. You can teach her a few things, henna?"

Ugh, Roop. The couch. Family bonding. Not ideal. But worth it, I guess, for the proximity to New York City. I'll be crashing with my cousin, who used to be my fave but is now a stranger, pretty much. She's a pediatrics resident at this big hospital in New Brunswick, New Jersey, which is where Rutgers is, too.

"Go see Sukhi Mamiji, acha?" Ma says. "Bring Roop. Mamiji says she hardly sees her."

Family drama. Not my thing. "Ma, I'm going to be so busy, milking cows, husking corn, and all that," I say. We don't really know what went down with Roop and her mom. But I know it's not my job to fix it.

I look at my phone again, posting the picture and the finalized caption:

To New York, the place dreams are made of. But damn: That fierce Cali sky just might make you stay.

Not bad. Bright smile, right side (best side!) forward, windblown hair, and that show-off sun kissing the rolling hills. Idyllic, even.

Ma's starting with the orders again, so I click open my music app and load her favorite playlist. Works like a charm. Her rules are replaced with her soft, breathy humming, words that have floated in and out of my head since I was a baby, those classics Ma used to listen to with her mom when she was little. "*Yeh raat bheegi bheegi,*" she sings, off-key. "You know, maybe it'll rain there. I miss the rain."

California's been burning for as long as I can remember. But she means New Delhi. She hasn't been back to India in nearly a decade, not since her mother died. "There's no point," she always says when I ask why. "Everyone I love is here."

The words hit me hard. *Everyone I love is here.*

It's true. I've never been this far away from home before. I've barely even left the state.

Maybe the flutters in my stomach are a sign that I'm headed exactly where I'm supposed to go.

"You'll call me every day?" Ma presses again.

"We can video chat," I mumble. "Watch *Mahi Way*."

"Make sure you eat the paranthas. They'll be okay, even late."

I pat my bag, comforted by the carbs that will soon fill my belly. Stuffed with potatoes, love, and high hopes.

Even though my brothers—twins, fourteen now—will be home to keep her busy, Ma'll miss me. Cherry will help. Her dad is the farm foreman, and she pretty much moves into my room every summer. But she's not great with house stuff. Her dad just dotes, ever supportive. Even joined the local queer community center with her, and does Suite Cherry shipping runs every week.

My father is pretty much the opposite: rules, expectations, obligations. But he lets the boys get away with everything. Their whole summer will be one endless video game marathon. Well, that and harvesting garlic or whatever. "Make them do dishes," I say, trying not to count the likes on my phone. "Don't do everything yourself."

She sighs. "Sometimes it's just easier . . ."

"Ma."

"I know."

She pulls into the terminal and up to the curb, and I can tell she's worrying about her solo drive home already. She's safe on the road. Plots her lane switches miles in advance and sticks to the local routes, mostly. It makes me want to race ahead, to push back, to plow forward. As far as I can go.

But I'll miss her, too.

As I pull on my backpack and grab my suitcases from the trunk, she reaches down for something else, smiling sheepishly. A giant jar of her signature fire orange, delicious, soon-to-be-patented (if only I were joking) garlic chutney. It's bigger than my head twice over. "For RoopKiran. Remember how she loved it?"

"Ma, I can't carry that. It's liquid."

"No, it is solid." She's got that stern, straight-line mouth thing happening. A battle I'm not about to win. I take the giant jug, wondering how I'm going to manage it and my baggage.

"Okay, Mama. Chalti hoon." Before I can step away, she snatches me up to her quite large bosom for an all-encompassing hug, one that will have to get the two of us through the next few months. "Love you," I mumble into her flowered salwar kameez, inhaling Charlie perfume. Sweet. Safe. Familiar.

"Love you, too, beta. Behave. Don't forget to call!"

I feel her teary eyes watching me all the way up through the security gate, beyond which snakes an endless line. I snap a pic from overhead, already dreaming up my perfect caption.

Got it.

Here goes nothing. And everything.

After arguing with security about garlic chutney for forty minutes, I stumble onto the plane just as the doors close, locking my hand around the little Ganesh key chain Ma stuck on my backpack. We're Sikh, but Ma's family is a mix, and her best friend Veena's auntie in Delhi sent it from the mandir near their old house in Shakti Nagar. And this trip is off to an auspicious start. They filled my seat because of the delay, which meant the only one left was 3A. In first class. I can't wait to document my good fortune on social.

"Excuse me," I say to the guy sitting in 3B. My age. Brown. Cute. And—

"Late much?" he asks, like he's not even surprised to see me. It's Ranbir. Dhillon. *Of the Sonoma Dhillons.* He smirks. His teeth are perfectly straight and white, like a Desi toothpaste ad, and his skin a sun-bronzed brown. Shaggy dark waves frame a cut-glass jawline. Ma would be swooning.

Okay, I'm swooning, too. "What are you doing here?" I say, my voice squeaking.

He holds up his phone. "I saw your post. Dude, you nearly missed the plane." He's got that Brown Prince Charming grin pasted on his face, and I don't know if I want to punch him or kiss him. "I'm going to Cow Camp. Your mom told my mom you were coming."

I can hear Ma's voice in my head now: *Same flight, henna? Thoda company, thoda safety.* Blah, blah, blah. But she couldn't have plotted for first class. Right?

The flight attendant shuffles our way, gesturing for me to sit. Ranbir stands and stashes my roller overhead. "Guess I'll be your chaperone, young lady." He smiles down at me, then falters. "Dolly's on her way. She made a pit stop in Texas."

I thought they broke up. That's what the auntie network's been reporting. But maybe not.

He grins again, his eyes crinkling at the edges, and motions toward my seat, offering to scoot. But I want the window. I squish my way past him, his hands on my waist, steadying.

"Are these pajamas?" he asks, and the heat shoots straight to my cheeks.

"It's called a jumpsuit." Cherry's idea. Of course.

"Like for a toddler?" His eyes are laughing, but his mouth is serious. Except for the one quirk on the left side. Like he's trying not to crack up. "What'll you do when you have to pee?"

Good question. I plop down in my wide leather seat. I shrug. "Cherry."

He nods. Everyone knows Cherry. Or knows *of* her anyway. "We should plot another dance-off in New Brunswick." Ranbir leans toward me as I settle in. "I need a chance to redeem myself."

I don't know what got into me at that wedding. Maybe it was the freedom I felt as one of the bridesmaids, or the twirl of my blue bandhani silk lehenga. Cherry did my makeup, and I

9

felt pretty, like for the first time ever. When the dholi banged his drum, the rhythm got under my skin. Then there he was. I liked it. And him.

But Cherry went on and on about how truckbois are trouble. All these rich farm kids are big-time players. Money, power, looks. Way out of my league. Because of Dolly. And I haven't actually ever dated a boy. Or kissed a boy. Or anything else. Plus, I need to focus. And I think my dad has his heart set on Guru Pathak, heir to his own mini garlic empire in Madera. Sigh.

Ranbir flashes his phone at me. "Heard about these after-hours bhangra throw-downs in the city."

"You're asking to get your ass kicked." Because I totally won that dance-off. And will again.

I feel his eyes on me as I shove my backpack and the satchel under the front of my seat, pulling out only essentials: my iPad, water bottle, and the latest issue of *Fierce*, of course.

"Is that—" Ranbir wrinkles his nose, adorable.

"Garlic. Chutney."

"Oh, your mom's famous—"

"Gera Garlic, yup."

"That explains it." He takes the satchel with the jar inside and tucks it securely between a few suitcases overhead. I'm instantly relieved to be garlic-free. At least temporarily.

I focus on adjusting the window shade, my heart racing at the thought of sitting next to him for seven whole hours. How am I going to survive this?

"You excited about Cow Camp?" he says, leaning back in his plush leather seat.

I shrug, looking down at my iPad. "Not how I would've planned to spend my summer."

"But it is the Critical First Step to the Rest of Your Life," he says, one bushy brow perched.

He's probably had his whole life plotted out for him, too. "The plan is UC Davis, maybe, for agriculture management; MBA; then back to the farm. How about you?"

"About the same. After all, I've got an empire waiting." He's grinning, but it doesn't hit his eyes this time.

I nod. "Me too." Sort of. Gera Garlic is a tiny island nation compared to most of the continents these kids will inherit.

"Speaking of which." He looks around sneakily, then pulls a few small bottles out of his bag. "Dhillon Estate Bespoke Wines. Courtesy of my dad." Ranbir's family owns a sprawling winery in Sonoma, and they've been all over the press lately because they launched a new hybrid: Proscato. With a screw top. Elegant.

"How'd you sneak that in?"

"First class, baby." He offers me a bottle and opens the other.

I've never actually had wine. A few sips of my dad's whiskey, yes. But proscato? We clink bottles, pose for a selfie, and I take a sip. It's sweet and fizzy and goes down easy.

"Here's to milking cows and scooping shit, right?" He laughs. "Though what that has to do with grapevines, I'll never know."

None of us really do. Last time I asked, Papa went on and on about instilling work ethic and business sense. It's the Cult of Desi Farmer, transplanted from India to here, dozens of agricultural empires run by old-school Punjabi families, each with its own legacy and legend. My grandpa, Pindi Das Gera, owned a thousand acres outside Lahore, lost to partition—the way the Brits divided the subcontinent into India and Pakistan in 1947, a wound that's still fresh. But in the wilds of central California, he's made Gera Garlic a real contender. There's Raisin King Batth in Caruthers and the Randhawa clan, spices in Stockton. And, of course, the Sonoma Dhillons, Ranbir's family, the most well known and wealthy. And here I am. Drinking wine with the family's heir, who's headed to Cow Camp, too.

I take another sip, and he grins. This summer might not be so bad, scooping shit and all.

First class is fun. After a dinner of chicken with goopy mushroom sauce, the attendant hands out care kits with sleep masks and headphones. Ranbir starts a movie, then zonks out, so I spend a few hours journaling and reading magazines, listening to him snore, this light, soft, hiccupy thing. I'm staring again, so I decide to focus on a *Fierce* quiz instead.

Do They Covet You? *Fierce* Shares 7 For-Sure Swoon Signs

BY XANDER SANTOS

Here's how you'll know.

1. **They can't stop staring.** The look of love? It's all in the eyes—and if they can't take theirs off you, they're definitely swooning. Be bold! Stare back!
2. **They want to be where you are.** If they show up at your book club, yoga class, and crash movie night with your friends, you've got a fan.
3. **They stalk your social media.** Cuz pressing the little heart button is easier than confessing how they really feel.
4. **They give you a nickname.** Terms of endearment? Aw!!
5. **They ask your friends about you.** Admiring minds need to know!
6. **They're dying to touch you.** We're not talking space invaders here, but it's any excuse to get a little closer— because you're simply irresistible.
7. **They think you're hilarious.** If they laugh at all your jokes—even the duds—you know they're a keeper.

2

A FEW HOURS LATER, THE PLANE COASTS DOWNWARD, THE city lights glittering in the distance.

"Have you ever been to New York?" Ranbir asks my reflection. His eyes are drowsy, his hair a sleep-rumpled halo.

I shake my head, grabbing my copy of *Fierce* off the tray table. Greta Thunberg and Malala pose together on the cover, the future in all its glory. "I want to check out the Met, MoMA, and definitely the Mac Media Tower." I hold up my magazine. "Home to *Fierce*. I wonder if they do tours."

"You're the only person I know who actually still reads magazines," he says, our hands grazing as he swipes it from my hands.

"It's a habit now." That's not quite right. "Almost a ritual."

He raises a brow, amused.

I shrug. "My cousin gave it to me. Roop, the one I'm staying with. When I was ten, she visited with her mom, and handed it to me and Cherry like it was nothing. But it was a whole new world inside. One where girls and women could be and do anything—become astronauts, authors, maybe even president. One where we could be creators, run businesses, shatter ceilings and expectations."

It was full of this firebrand spirit I'd never witnessed before. "It reminded me of Roop, too," I say. "I idolized her. She knew she wanted to be a doctor and she wanted to go to Princeton and that she would pull it off, no matter what her mother or anyone else said."

Sukhi Mamiji—my mom's brother's wife—is totally old-school Punjabi, even more than Ma. Salwar kameez and weekly gurdwara seva and a life running the household. When Roop's dad died—heart attack—their little family fell apart. "They stayed with us for the summer, and Roop filled my head with ideas about goals, not dreams, and going after what you want," I say, mostly to my reflection in the window. But I can see Ranbir grinning behind me. "When she left, she gave me a subscription to *Fierce*. Even though I haven't seen her in seven years, the magazines keep coming."

Inside, every month, I find a window into what my world could look like. Instead of the insular one I live in: picking garlic, keeping the books for Papa, doing homework, practicing random new stitches, working the farm stand with Cherry, learning to cook and run the house alongside Ma.

He shuffles through it, but I can tell he doesn't see what I see. Hardly anyone does. "Looks like a lot of fancy clothes and makeup to me," he says.

"It's so much more than that," I say, turning back to face him. "My favorite stories are the ones about the girls who look like me. Like Malala, yeah, but not always on a mission to save the world or whatever. There's this Muslim Instagram artist who draws cartoons calling out the stalker aunties. And this enby dancer who's reinventing kathakali by blending it with hip-hop."

He taps my hand with his, startling me out of my *Fierce* fixation. "I could see you doing something cool like that. We should see if we can check it out."

I lean back into the window, catching my first real glimpse of New York. All twinkling lights, close enough to touch, and I can't help but let my fingers linger on the glass. Ranbir leans in, too, heat radiating off his skin, the lemony sharpness of his shampoo so bright I want to inhale it. I catch a hint of garlic. Which would be me, of course. "That view never gets old, does it?"

"I've never seen it before," I say, staring at the skyline, gripping the armrest as we zip toward the ground. As we land, Ranbir's hand sits lightly on top of mine, reassuring and electrifying all at once.

Blushing, I resist the urge to pull mine away. I focus instead on our faces smiling back at us in the reflection on the glass, scattered with a constellation of city lights.

New York.

Or, well, Newark. Then New Brunswick. Whatever. I'm so ready for the new.

The overhead lights come up then, indicating that the plane's about to touch down, and suddenly we're here. "I can't believe it."

"Cow Camp awaits." Ranbir yawns, his cheeks puffing and his eyes crinkling as he tries to stifle it, sort of adorable. "I'm beat. What is it, like two A.M.?"

A gazillion notifications pour in as I reboot my phone. A few texts from Cherry, shouting about the proscato selfie Ranbir posted right before takeoff. Endless messages from Ma.

> **MA:** There yet?
> **MA:** Did you eat?
> **MA:** Call me.
> **MA:** How's Roop?
> **MA:** Don't forget the chutney.

"Who's that?" Ranbir says, leaning over, nosy. I flash my phone at him. "Of course."

We grab our luggage, and then there's a long awkward moment. Ranbir shuffles, unsure, running his hand through his curls, stepping close and then away. He looks at his phone as it buzzes, once, twice, but slips it into his pocket. "Need a ride?"

"My cousin's picking me up." I look around, wondering if I'll even recognize her. "But maybe you can hitch a ride with us?" He grins. "Roop should be here any sec."

I check my phone. Nothing. I try calling, but it goes straight to voice mail. I send another text. No response.

My phone's lighting up, so I check to see if it's Roop. It's not.

MA: Roop mil gayi? Call me.

MA: Cherry says Ranbir is on your flight? He's cute, nah?

Guess she saw his post. But no comment on the wine. Thank god.

MA: Papa says hi. Phone kar. Call before bed.

MA: Maya! Where are you?

MAYA: Ma! Getting a cab. I'll call you from Roop's.

MA: Theek hai.

Then one from Cherry.

CHERRY: I'm taking her phone away. And remember: #truckboisaretrouble

Ranbir watches me, eyes amused, as I laugh.

"I can call an Uber," he says. "You ready?"

I nod. Guess this is it, the start of things, either way.

Forty minutes later, the cab drives away, leaving me on the corner of Somerset Street in New Brunswick. Alone in the dark. With Ranbir.

The streetlamps cast shadows. There's an intersection, the bustle of a busy downtown street on one side, shops and restaurants catering to college kids. There's a bookstore about a block away and a sign for the train station, steps leading up into a tunnel under the bridge. With trains to New York. Like actual New York City. Right there! Beckoning.

"Maya." Ranbir steps closer, worry in his voice. "What's the address?"

"It's 121 Somerset," I say. Inked in my brain.

"It's this one." He takes my big suitcase and heads up the stairs to the stoop. I follow him up with my roller and the chutney.

"I'm right across the street," he says, shuffling again.

The streetlights shine in his eyes like flecks of gold.

"You should go," I say, though I'm grateful when he doesn't move. I lean forward and hit the buzzer. Fourth floor. Once, twice. Three times. Nothing. I look at my phone, hoping for some kind of clue. I try calling. Voice mail. Again.

"Did she text?" He's standing right behind me now, peering over my shoulder.

I shake my head. I will not cry. But who forgets to pick up their little cousin on her first ever trip cross-country? At three in the morning?

"Maybe there's a key?" He rifles through the mailboxes, then looks under the doormat.

I double-check the address in my texts. Definitely 121 Somerset. Apartment 4. Yup. But no answer.

I sit down on a step, settling in. "I'm okay." Ranbir hovers, unsure of what to do. "She'll be here in a minute."

He plops down next to me. "Then I'll go in a minute."

We sit in awkward silence as my phone lights up again.

MA: It's getting really late.

What should I say? What can I say? That I'm sitting here on a strange stoop in a strange city because my cousin clearly Forgot I Exist and couldn't be bothered to pick me up? Nope. Not that. I type a few words and hope for the best: *In New Brunswick. Safe.*

That should do it. My phone rings. Roop, finally.

It's Ma. Shit.

I click it off, frantic and violent, nearly dropping the phone on the brick steps. But Ranbir catches it, smirking again. "Not Roop?"

17

"My mom." I frown down at my phone. "She'd freak if she knew Roop was MIA."

"You could tell her you're with me."

I grimace. "She'd freak if she knew I was with you."

He laughs. How does he still smell good after seven hours on a plane? Like mint and earth and something else I can't place. Sweet and sharp and familiar.

"Nimbu." It just slips out.

"Nimbu?" he asks. "Like lemon?"

"That's what Roop used to call me when I was little." My voice sounds weird, like I'm about to cry. "I was always climbing the lemon trees in our front yard." I don't mention that he smells like home. "I can't believe she forgot me." I'm blinking fast, trying to stop the tears, my face hot. "Am I that forgettable?"

"I don't think you're forgettable at all," he says, and my heart does a little leap. "Maybe she's on call?"

I shrug. "Ma's pretty on top of things. I know she bullied Roop into this. But how do you just—" My voice cracks.

"Tired, huh?" He loops an arm around me, tucking me closer, so my head rests on his shoulder. It's so comfortable and familiar— too practiced, like he's done it a million times before—and part of me wants to leap away. I probably have coffee-and-garlic breath, and my hair is frizzing in this heat—who knew New Jersey was so humid?—and where the hell is Roop? I need a shower and maybe some chai and actual pajamas. But most of me just relaxes into it, despite myself. Still, I have to ask.

"Dolly's already here, huh?" I say, probably too sharp.

"Got here this afternoon."

"She's staying in the dorms?"

"Yup."

"Shouldn't you go catch up with her?"

He shrugs. "I'll see her when I see her." He takes a deep breath, his arm slipping off my shoulders, creating a gaping space between us. Or maybe I did that. "We broke up two months ago. It didn't go well. Been awkward ever since."

"Why?" My heart is pounding now, and I don't know why.

"She's having . . . some trouble letting go."

"You're not?" I focus on my feet, kicking incessantly, sticky and sweaty in my sneakers.

"It's time to move on." He shrugs, running a hand through his hair. "I mean, we've been together since we were, like, fourteen. We're different people now."

He seems so far away, I kind of hate myself for bringing it up. "Maybe you'll get back together." I clear my throat. "If that's what you want."

He kicks my foot with his. "It's not." So low I barely hear him. "Can't you tell?"

My stomach flips. He slips his arm around my waist again, pulling me closer.

Just as he's about to lean in, a shadow falls over us. Two women, kissing as they climb the stairs, stumble forward as Ranbir grabs my arm to pull me up, out of the way.

"Oh, sorry, I didn't—Maya?" The voice is incredulous, familiar. Slightly annoyed. Definitely Roop. Even in the dark, I can tell she looks leaner, her brown face gaunt and tired, like she hasn't been sleeping enough. Her familiar curly mop is pulled back, her standard-issue jeans and T-shirt worn and comfortable. The pixie-haired woman, tiny and bright-eyed, wears a flapper-esque dress and heels. She holds Roop's hand, casually possessive.

Wait. How did I not know this? "Hey" is all I can manage.

Roop shudders, like she's trying to shake off her confusion. "Oh my god, I forgot."

I want to say: *You sure did.* Or: *How could you?* Or anything at all. But I just stand there on the stoop, silent. Guess I'm all out of words after *Hey.* Especially when Ranbir takes my hand. Like he knows I need it.

"I thought you were coming next week," Roop says. It sounds like an accusation.

"Definitely this week," the other girl says in a British accent, looking down at her phone. Roop's phone? From where I stand, I can see my name on the screen, and a long string of messages. "You put it on do not disturb again, Roopie."

"Because my mom kept texting. I didn't realize she meant Maya was coming. Today."

The other girl picks up my backpack, smiling warmly. "My fault." She's elfin and brown, her sharp nose pierced, a little diamond glinting in the light. "I had her phone in my purse. Been waiting awhile?"

I shrug. "About an hour."

Roop looks at all the bags piled on the stoop with a frown. "At least you had company," she says, like I'm the one who blew her off.

"I'm Rana. Uh, Ranbir." He drops my hand to offer to shake hers, awkwardly. "I'm in the agriculture program with Maya."

"Sorry we kept you waiting," Roop says, Oscar the Grouch forced to apologize.

I shrug again. I have to stop doing that. "We're still on California time. It's not that late there."

"I'm sure you want to get settled," the other girl says pointedly. "So Maya will see you on Monday. Ranbir, was it?"

"Or maybe tomorrow?" Ranbir asks, looking at me. "I'll be around if you want to do something."

I give him a tight smile as he grabs his stuff. We watch him cross the street in silence.

"Looks like we interrupted something," the girlfriend says, grinning. "He's cute."

"Yeah." My cheeks flush. What an introduction.

"Come on," Roop says, taking my big bag, while the other girl grabs the small one.

I follow them up the staircase, my pace slowing, slowing,

slowing to a snail's by the time we get to the fourth floor. Don't they have elevators in New Brunswick?

"The rent's cheaper the higher you go," Roop says, hoisting the bag up the last few steps. "Med students don't make much."

"Are you going to be a doctor, too?" I ask the other girl, huffing and puffing to catch my breath.

"Nope. I work in the city," she says, peering back at me with a grin. "In fashion. Cute jumpsuit."

"Thanks." I can't keep the hope out of my voice. New York City! Fashion! Like, actual, real-life glam. "Anywhere I'd know?"

"The closet at *Fierce*. It's a women's magazine. Have you read it?"

"Oh my god! You're Shenaz Shah." I totally recognize her from the style pages in the magazine. "I love your Found Fashion pieces."

I thought this summer was going to suck. But here I am, two hours in, meeting someone who works at *Fierce*.

Roop flips on the lights. The apartment is small and cluttered, with a big fluffy couch shoved against one wall, a small flat-screen TV against another, and a kitchenette in the corner. Even the fridge is mini. There are two doors off the living room.

"Our bedroom," Roop says, pointing. "Kitchen. Bath. Living room." And finally, the couch, a faded blue corduroy. "Your room." She sets my big bag next to the sofa and walks toward one of the doors. "I've got an early shift tomorrow. Shenaz will show you where to park your stuff."

Then she's gone. Seven years. And not even a hug.

"She's been like that . . . pretty much as long as I've known her," Shenaz says sheepishly, rubbing the back of her neck. "But she's cute. Like that guy."

My cheeks flame. I look at my phone. There's already a message. Brunch tomorrow?

I write back immediately. Yes please. Let's do 11:30.

"Is it him?" Shenaz putters around, clearing out the living room, and leans to look.

I nod and she laughs. "You've already got it bad." She lifts the rice satchel, still sitting where I abandoned it. She sniffs. "Is this food? Smells like—"

"Garlic. Chutney. My mom made it. For Roop. She loved it the last time she was in California, and Ma's definitely a feeder. You don't have to eat it all. Or any of it. If you're, like, a vampire or something."

Shenaz laughs, plopping herself down on the sofa. "I like garlic."

I tentatively take a seat beside her. I wonder if she knows I didn't know. About her and Roop. But I can't ask that. Besides, we have more important things to discuss. "I can't believe it. *Fierce!*"

I've read her Found Fashion pieces a million times. She's one of the reasons I devour the magazine religiously every month— and Shenaz is Cherry's idol. Wait till I tell her! An actual, real-life brown person at the center of the culture creation capital of the world. And now I'm sitting next to her.

"It's a really fun gig. The pay's not great, but you can't beat the perks."

"What kind of perks?" I can't keep the excitement out of my voice.

She laughs again, this tinkly thing, and I can tell why Roop would like her. I just met her, and I might be a little in love myself. At least an Official Girl Crush.

"It's pretty awesome. I get paid to obsess about the latest and greatest from your favorite designers before it even hits the runway," she says with a wicked grin, then waltzes through the place to a rack in the corner, piled high with haute couture. "And even get to keep some of it." She rests her cheek on a random sequined ball gown lovingly, petting it. "Definitely need more closet space."

"I've read *Fierce* since I was ten," I say. "I've actually been published in the magazine."

She turns to peer at me, curious.

"When I was twelve. They had this fashion spread in the print mag called Indian Stunner, Desi-inspired designs, like lehenga skirts paired with T-shirts and kurtis with cutoffs and stuff. My friend Cherry—the one who made this jumpsuit—and I were really excited."

"I remember that one," she says, drumming her fingers on her chin. "It was a few years before I started working there."

"I was disappointed that they did this gorgeous spread with all these amazing clothes—and every single model was white."

"I remember that, too." She's smiling now.

"So I wrote a strongly worded letter. Sort of yelling about why they'd leave us out of our own story."

"The whitewashing. Happens all the time."

"Still?"

"Still." She taps her lip thoughtfully. "Though hopefully that'll start to shift with Dulcie St. Claire at the helm. So you wrote a letter?"

"And they published it. With my name. In print."

Maya Gera. In ink. In *Fierce*. I still have that issue stashed away in my keepsake box. Something in me shifted that day. Like a dream solidified, a little bit. Something to reach for. If I were someone else.

"Not long after that—not just the letter, but a couple of blowups—they brought a few people of color onto the staff," Shenaz says. "Legend Scott, Ericka Turner. Didn't solve everything, but it was a start. Dulcie will push it even further."

The shakeup that brought Dulcie St. Claire in as editor in chief has been all over the press. She's one of the first Black women to run a magazine at Mac Media—and in media overall, actually. And she's like thirty, pretty young for such a big leap. But she's going to kick ass. "She seems amazing," I say. "Do you get to work with her?"

"She helped me get my start." Shenaz grins, her eyes far away, lost in a memory. "Bedtime for you, Maya Memsahib. You must be exhausted."

She stands and pulls a blanket and some sheets out of the coffee table, a giant, wood-carved Indian-style trunk, kind of like the one my nanima had at her old house in Delhi. (Wait, it *is* the one Nani had at her old house in Delhi. I'm instantly jealous.) We spread the lavender sheets on the lumpy couch, and she tosses me a pillow.

"I'm off. There's water in the fridge if you need it. Maybe we can grab dinner tomorrow or something, all of us."

I nod. "That would be great. I haven't seen Roop in years."

"She told me all about it." I think she's going to say more, but she yawns, and it reminds me of a kitten. Small, playful, sleepy.

"Thank you for letting me stay. I know it's a lot. But I'm super excited. I mean, *Fierce*! I'd love to hear more about it sometime."

"'Night." She heads toward the bedroom, then pauses. "You know what? I have to work tomorrow. Closet inventory. I do a few Sundays a month. It's quiet at the office. Peaceful, even. Plus overtime."

She's going in. To the *Fierce* office. In New York City.

"Wanna come?" she asks. "I could use the help. And pay you an intern stipend, since I don't have one yet. Twelve bucks an hour. Not bad."

"YES!" I leap off the couch and into her arms—the apartment is that small. "Yes! Yes! Yes!" Then it hits me. "Oh, but I don't—what would I wear?"

Shenaz waves toward the rack near the bathroom. "Feel free." There are handbags, dresses, shoes, thousands of dollars' worth of swoonworthy couture. "I need my beauty sleep. Sweet dreams, Maya Memsahib."

As she shuffles off toward the bathroom, I pinch myself. Just in case.

When we got here and no one was home, I thought I was

doomed. Truly. Roop certainly hasn't been reassuring. But Shenaz has given me hope. People come here to chase their dreams, to make them a reality. She's doing just that. A brown girl, like me.

Cow Camp may not be my calling. But I've been here for less than a day, and tomorrow I get to go to *Fierce*. I'm so close to my dream, I can taste it.

And truth be told, it does not taste like garlic.

MAYA: Ma, look at Roop's place!

MA: It's quite small, huh?

MAYA: It's cozy. And charming. Did you know Roop's roommate works at Fierce magazine? She said she'll give me a tour.

MA: That's nice, beta. But you should prepare for Monday! Big day! Love you.

CHERRY: You totally made out with him, didn't you?

MAYA: I don't know what you're talking about.

CHERRY: Fess up.

MAYA: YOU WILL NEVER BELIEVE!

CHERRY: WHATTTT!

MAYA: Roop's girlfriend works at FIERCE!

MAYA: Oh, and Roop has a girlfriend.

CHERRY: At Fierce? That's awesome. I'm totally jealous.

CHERRY: Also: Don't be mad. I knew. About the girlfriend.

MAYA: What do you mean?

CHERRY: I've known since that summer they visited. That Roop's gay.

MAYA: How?

CHERRY: Because I knew I was, even then. So we talked about it.

CHERRY: Maya?

MAYA: She never told me.

CHERRY: I know. Things are rough with her mom.

MAYA: Did she not think I'd understand?

CHERRY: You should talk to her.

3

SUNDAY SUN STREAMS THROUGH THE SINGLE LIVING ROOM window, an early A.M. wake-up call whether I want to sleep in or not. Not that I got much rest on the lumpy couch. I kept thinking about yesterday. And today. About New York City. And dreams come true.

And about what Cherry said.

I look around, taking in the space in the sunshine. It's cramped and cluttered, but there's light at least, hitting my face and warming my arms. The window's open, the air thick and hot. I'm sticky and slick, the humidity making my hair frizz and T-shirt cling.

At home, right about now, the sky would be pink enflamed with orange as the sun started its morning blaze, loud and intrusive and amazing, the heat slow and mellow as it rose, like in an oven. A wave of homesickness washes over me. I want to pull out my phone and call Ma. But it's only five thirty there.

I smile to myself, thinking about the day that lies ahead.

New York City. The *Fierce* office. Still can't believe it.

Shenaz bustles out of the bathroom, a towel turbaning her head. "Come on, Maya, hustle," she says, dropping a few eggs in a pot to boil. "We gotta catch the nine A.M." She gives me a quick once-over, taking in my messy hair and sleep-rumpled clothes, then waltzes over to the rack, combing through options. "This will do."

She hands me a soft, floral-print wrap dress and a small tub. "This stuff works miracles," she says as I look at the hair mask. "LeLabo. Hinoki, spirulina, and coconut oil. Leave it on for three minutes. You'll smell delicious. Be ready in ten."

The water's barely tepid, but it doesn't even matter. I can't believe I get to see the *Fierce* magazine offices. To walk those hallowed halls. To breathe that rarefied air. To feel the energy of all those critical, culture-making voices coming together, shaping the way we think and feel and dress. I can't wait to tell Cherry about it. The thought makes me happy dance as I climb out of the shower.

I'm dressed and ready a few minutes later, hair braided in two pigtails for easy maintenance. Way too excited to eat. But when we're about to leave, it hits me. Sneakers. And flip-flops. That's pretty much all I've got. And so not *Fierce*.

"What size?" Shenaz says, looking at my feet in dismay. "Sixish? Too small for anything here." I look at her feet. Definitely bigger, even though she's two inches shorter than me. She shrugs. "Guess these will have to do for now. We'll fix it when we get there."

I feel like a dork: designer summer dress, carefully crafted pigtails, flawless barely-there makeup, and ratty old Chucks. Oh well. Off to a stellar start.

Or we were. But as I buckle my sequined fanny pack—a gift from Papa—onto my hip, Shenaz stops short. I nearly plow right over her.

"What is that?" she says, one brow sharply raised. "And why is it trying to eat you?"

I frown. "I don't understand."

She steps forward tentatively and tugs at my waist. "Kill it! Kill it." She manages to snap the buckle, and the fanny pack hits the floor.

"Papa got it for me. So I'd be safe carrying my wallet and stuff."

"You cannot wear that thing to the city. And definitely not to Mac Media. LuLu would have you arrested. And me fired."

She struts toward the rack, combing through until she finds just what she's looking for. A small, structured leather bag in this deep blue patent leather. "Perfect."

Ten minutes later, we're on New Jersey Transit. The train's

nearly empty, so Shenaz and I grab a four-seater, with two seats facing each other. She's got her laptop out, prepping for inventory, so I stare out the window at what is apparently the Garden State. The landscape shifts from the shiny urbanness of downtown New Brunswick to grassy swamps and then smaller cities with older, graffitied buildings and boarded-up windows.

I'm dying to ask Shenaz how much longer, but I don't want to be the annoying kid sister, tagging along and overeager. I commemorate my adventure by taking pictures of the more interesting graffiti that marks our path—a birdman dressed in a tracksuit, a random rainbow of om symbols, and a repeated motif: a girl riding a lion, fierce like Kali. Because I'll want to remember this forever, I post a few shots to social.

Cherry comments instantly: *Please eat a bagel for me.*

"Nearly there," Shenaz says, looking up as the train descends into a tunnel, darkness surrounding us on either side. "The office is in Times Square, about eight blocks, okay?"

She stashes her computer and grabs her stuff, and I follow her off the train and onto the platform. Penn Station is a maze of tunnels and stairs, busy and bustling even on Sunday. I can spot the tourists by the way they pause and point, confused. I follow Shenaz as she pushes forward, weaving in and around the crowds, mad dashing through. We take an escalator up, and when we step off, we're there. In actual New York City.

I pause to breathe it all in. The sky is bright above, but the blanket of blue is carved up by the towering buildings all around us, stretching toward it like endless fields of corn reaching for the California sun. The air is thick, like the sky will burst any second, even though there's no sign of rain. The humidity holds the scents of roasting meat and maybe BO and is that pee?

I can't help gaping at the sights even as I race to keep up with Shenaz. Everything is so much bigger here. There's this energy, electrifying and bold, that pulsates through, like you have to keep moving or you'll miss it all. There are more people than I've ever seen in my life—tourists strolling, while others bulldoze forward, no time to waste. By the time I'm done taking another breath, Shenaz is half a block away, and I run to catch up.

"Is that the Empire State Building?" I ask. I'm dying to take a picture.

She speeds ahead. But the city's got ahold of me—the street vendors, the nonstop honking and traffic, kids my age running around by themselves like they own the place.

"You gotta keep up," Shenaz shouts behind her. My fancy dress is damp with sweat. But sleeveless, so no pit stains. "We're almost there."

I stick as close as I can for the next few blocks, and at some point Shenaz reaches back and grabs my hand, like I'm a small child she's in charge of, weaving us through the crowds at warp speed.

We pause under a towering building, all steel and glass and magic, the way it shoots straight up toward the sky. The McIntyre-Scott Tower. I'd recognize it anywhere.

Shenaz pulls out an ID card, slipping through revolving doors. I race to follow. Inside is an oasis, cool and calm and cocooning, all white and gray marble and glass. She's already at the reception counter, waving me over. "Tony, this is my girlfriend's cousin Maya. She's helping with inventory today."

I give the clerk a big cheery smile, waving, and he nods politely. "ID?"

"Oh." I fish it out of my purse, knocking out my pink tortoiseshell Target sunglasses.

"I don't think those would be allowed in the building," Tony says as I tuck them safely back into my bag. "Definitely don't let Jude see them."

Jude McIntyre, the scion of the Mac Media empire. He actually exists. Right here in these hallowed halls.

"Is he here today?" I ask, excited. Panicked.

"Sometimes he's in on Sundays. If he's working on a big scoop." Shenaz frowns, looking down at her clothes, and then at mine. "But, man, I hope not."

Tony nods, printing out a little pass and handing it to me. Emblazoned on the top is my name, in black and white, along with Shenaz's, and the words *Fierce* and *32nd floor*. I can't even believe it.

I follow Shenaz into the elevator bank for floors thirty to forty. Forty floors? Surreal. Everything looks so elegant and specific, like the movie set version of a magazine office tower. But it's all real. And I'm here.

The elevator zooms up thirty floors in five seconds flat, my stomach whooshing like it did when the plane took off. It slows as it hits 30, then 31, and then comes to a smooth stop at 32, the doors opening magically like a portal into another world. That's what it is, really, because as soon as I step out, I'm in a place I never thought I'd see in my actual lifetime.

It doesn't look quite like I'd imagined. Yes, there's a neon-pink *Fierce* sign lit on the wall. (And of course I pose for a selfie.) But where's the reception desk, the endless lobby of images they always show in the editor's letter?

"That's on thirty-four," Shenaz says, reading my mind. "The fancy floor. For editorial and video. We've got three floors. This is where the fashion and design wings are. More functional and practical, less showy, less grand." She slashes her ID at the door, and I follow her through the darkened halls, trying to mask my disappointment. "I'd give you a tour, but nobody's here on Sundays unless something's breaking."

I follow her through another set of glass doors, and the room lights up, dramatic and instant. Magic. "Welcome to the fashion closet."

It's not really a closet at all. More an endless series of rooms, each hopelessly devoted to a particular type of clothing or accessory, as reverent and worshipful as Nanima's mandir in her old haveli in Delhi. The walls are lined with pristine white lacquered shelves and custom racks. Every inch of carefully designed, fully usable real estate is occupied by the latest (and greatest) in modern American (and international) couture. On one rack, there's the new Prada jumpsuit line everyone's been coveting. On the other side is a whole season's worth of peacoats. I recognize Burberry and Versace, along with a Kate Spade black-and-white-striped one that makes me swoon.

I snap a quick picture for Cherry, but Shenaz's eyes are a warning. "No sharing. LuLu would murder me."

The next room has shoes in every style imaginable, "all in size six for in-house shoots," Shenaz informs me. Too small for her, but maybe just right for me. There's a giant box full of leather boots all tossed in like they're headed to Goodwill. Ball gowns fill the next room down, and there's another just for T-shirts. The rooms flow from one to the next, open ended and infinite, like one of those shotgun houses we read about when we studied New Orleans. I imagine rifling through the gowns and donning them all, one after the other, Shenaz my fairy fashionista godmother as I prepare to run off to the grand ball, careful not to lose my Louboutins or whatever. I really wish Cherry could see this place.

"All right," Shenaz says, clapping her hands to get my attention. "Let's get to it. Can you start with the boots?" I peer at the box—nearly as big as me—and raise my brows. "Go through them all, pair them up, then check each pair off this list," she says as the printer spits something out. "Then pack them up and get them ready to ship back to the designers. After that, you can do fall accessories." I follow her gaze to the corner of that room. There must be like two hundred boxes. "I know," she says with a deep sigh. Then grins. "But lunch is on me."

She disappears, and I get to work. Not the glam I imagined, though I can't help but try on a few pairs here and there.

Thigh-high cherry leather, little ankle booties that Ma would love, alligator with four-inch heels that make me all of, well, five six.

"Need help?" a male voice asks, startling me out of my daze and nearly making me topple in my pencil-heeled snakeskin Valentinos. Well, not *mine*. But they fit like they should be. "Shenaz said there was a lot today."

Behind a pair of giant rolling carts stands a guy about my age, maybe a little older, with light brown freckled skin; short, floppy brown hair; and a crooked grin that causes this magical, delicious dent to appear in the center of his left cheek. I can't stop staring at it, at him, and he doesn't seem surprised. Not one bit.

"You new?" the dimple asks.

"I'm—uh—"

"Freelance?" He starts piling one of my batches of boots into a box. "Gucci, right?"

"I came in with Shenaz. Are you in fashion, too?"

He turns back to smile at me. "Nah, I'm the EA. Editorial assistant. For features." He knocks my elbow in greeting, the box in his arms. "Been here about a year. But sometimes I help out on weekends. Extra cash."

"Oh, I thought—"

"That I was an intern? I always get that. I'm a sophomore at Columbia, but managed to pull this off with night classes. Xander, by the way. Santos. You?"

This is it, Maya. The moment to not embarrass yourself. By forgetting how to speak. "Maya. Malhotra." Wait, where did that come from? "I mean, Gera. But, like, it's a—" I lose it again, my train of thought, any actual logic left in my head.

"Pen name?" He's grinning again, the dimple distracting.

"Yeah, that." The name I would have had, maybe, if this was a life I could actually live.

"Cool. I thought about it, too, for anonymity or whatever. But I kinda like my name."

Xander Santos. I've definitely seen his name on the *Fierce* site. But where? He keeps moving full speed ahead, piling boots into boxes, sealing them up, putting them on carts.

I'm so out of breath by the time we get to the last one, my heart is pounding. He sets the box down, then heads toward the door. "I'll drop these off. Then accessories, if you want to get started."

When he disappears, I text Cherry and sneak a pic, because I can't not send it.

GUESS. WHERE. I. AM!!!

She sends me back an endless row of exclamations and a GIF of herself bhangra-ing. I'm recording one to send back when Xander appears in the doorway, dark eyes amused.

"Are you—dancing?"

Oh god, my cheeks. I try to smile, but it feels like a grimace. "Texting a friend. It's bhangra, this Punjabi—"

He grins again. "I know. Careful, though. Cameras everywhere, especially here."

I nod and look at the task list, annoyed he's ruining my fun.

We work in silence for a couple of hours, logging fall accessories. Every so often I peek at Xander. He's living my dream. And pretty much my age. How? I have a million questions. Like: What do you study at Columbia? Or: How did you end up at *Fierce*? Or: Did you know that the dimple that dents your cheek is absolutely riveting?

"Where are you from, Maya?" he asks, shocking me out of my brain spiral.

"California." I log another pair of sunglasses—my thirtieth. Who knew sunglasses were such a big fall must-have?

"Far from home," he says, and there's that dimple again. "Los Angeles? San Francisco?"

People always think those are the only real cities in California. "Gilroy," I say, trying not to sound annoyed. "Near San Jose. Best known for—"

"The garlic festival." His voice is quiet. "And the shooting. That's rough."

I shrug. "Most people have forgotten already. But it definitely left a scar."

On the town. On my family. On me.

"I can imagine. What brought you to New York?"

"I've got family here." I can't help but ask. "How'd you end up at *Fierce*?"

"Ramon brought me in. In entertainment. I interned for him when he was at the men's rag *Dashing*, and when he moved here, I started writing for the website. For the He Said column." He grins. "Been doing it for like two years. So when the EA spot opened up, I applied."

"Wait, you're Mr. X?"

"Guilty." He logs another belt, avoiding my gaze.

My cheeks heat, like I know way too much about him. And his love life. "But you're still in school?"

He leans forward, grabbing a bunch of belts from a box. "Yeah, had to change my whole schedule and life around to make this work. And fight with my parents, who were furious when I went part-time. Immigrant parents, you know the deal. But I couldn't pass up the opportunity. People spend years doing free internships and still never get in the door."

I sigh knowingly. "Yeah." I mean, at least that's what I imagine.

"This is what I want to do after I graduate anyway. So when the chance came up, I had to ask. They didn't take me seriously at first, of course."

I turn to look at him. "Why?"

"I'm a guy and it's a women's mag, for one thing. And Ericka thought I was too young. Had to work really hard to prove them wrong." He shrugs. "But here I am. It's a good time to be here. Dulcie's really going to change things. Or I hope so anyway." He stands, sealing up another box and adding it to the cart, now piled high. "Shenaz wants me steaming this week's picks in the studio, so that's a wrap for me." He grins, gathering his stuff. "Nice meeting you, Maya."

Then he's gone, like I made him up in my head.

I can't stop thinking about what he said. About going after what you want, no matter what the cost. I don't know if I have it in me. But I wish I did.

Two endless hours later, all the shoes and accessories are sorted, accounted for, and ready to return, pristine and neatly labeled in their boxes, heading back to downtown Manhattan or all the way to Paris. Without me, of course.

"The fashion closet can be fun," Shenaz says, like she's reminding herself. She stands in the doorway, looking at the newly cleared space with satisfaction. "But days like these, man, I wonder why. Good job here, by the way. Everything went down already?"

I nod. "Xander—"

"Forgot to mention him." Her eyes sparkle. "Charming, huh? Has all the editorial ladies swooning."

She combs through some stragglers, then she holds up another pair of shoes—maybe one I missed? They're strappy, cobalt-blue leather low heels, with a brown trim, super cute. "A new designer, Lisa Lee. Keepers. Five and a half. Wanna try?"

I look down at my decidedly unglamorous, still sneakered feet. Would they be wasted on me? Maybe. Am I going to say no? Nuh-uh! "Yes, please!" I snatch them away, pulling them on while Shenaz orders lunch from an Ethiopian joint. I wonder if I like Ethiopian food.

Shenaz waltzes up again, beaming, hiding something else behind her back. "I found you another treat." Her whole body vibrates with excitement. "You'll never believe."

She holds the object out, and I examine it carefully, tenderly. It's a black leather fanny pack, quilted, clearly hand stitched. Prada. "Oh my god," I say, leaping up. "It's perfect."

I hug her, and we jump around in glee for a minute before she makes us compose ourselves. "There are eyes everywhere," she says, all dramatic, and I laugh as she shuffles off.

I'm deep into logging peacoats when Shenaz comes back with the food.

"Can't eat in the closet," she says, waving me out. Then she frowns. "Dude, I think your phone's going." My phone peeks out of my purse, pulsating violently. I grab it and follow Shenaz and the food into a conference room called Vera Wang. Which makes me grin.

My phone buzzes again. Maybe Ma. Or Cherry. But when I look at the number, it's a 707. Ranbir. Five missed calls in the past two hours. It's one thirty. And we were supposed to meet at the apartment for brunch at eleven thirty. Shit.

Guilt envelops me like a cloud of fancy perfume. I call him back, but it goes to voice mail. Once, twice, three times. I text that I'm sorry, that it slipped my mind, that I'm here in the city with Shenaz. At *Fierce*. He'll understand, right? He has to. But he doesn't respond.

"You okay?" Shenaz asks, unpacking paper boxes filled with food.

My stomach rumbles, but I'm not sure I can bring myself to eat. "I forgot about brunch. With Ranbir."

She shrugs. "I'm sure he'll understand."

She digs in, and the rich, earthy aromas beckon, strangely familiar, making my mouth water. There's saucy, spicy chicken and lamb and lentils and greens, all scooped up with injera, a sour, fermented crepelike bread. For a minute Shenaz watches me as I taste everything, excited about my excitement. "The flavors feel very Indian," I say, going back for more.

"Berbere uses a lot of similar spices, kind of like a Desi masala," she says, mouth full. "That's one of my favorite things about living here. So many different cultures and experiences. Food is a great way to explore. You're going to love trying all the new things." She looks wistful for a minute. "Sometimes I get so busy, I forget to enjoy it."

How can that possibly be true? This miraculous place? Seeing my words, my name on the page, the way I did with that letter to the editor, it changed something. Today cemented that feeling forever in my mind. I'd be grateful for every moment, breathing this air, seeing how it all works, getting to be a part of shaping the way people think, feel, and especially what they wear. If only I could. Even in the smallest way.

"How'd you end up at *Fierce*?" I ask her.

She looks up and smiles, staring at her reflection in the endless windows, which look down into the bustle of Times Square. "It's a long story," she says. "I was always the black sheep of my family. My parents are from old-school Desi England. Crawley, originally, by Gatwick Airport. South of central London."

I nod, dipping injera into the lamb and greens. I could drink the sauce.

"They were pretty traditional. Even when I was little, I drove my mother batty, cutting up my kurtis and redoing them in mixed-and-matched swatches. Making lehengas out of curtains." I grin. Like Cherry. "I get it from her. She's the one who taught me how to sew in the first place. We moved to London after my dad died, Southall, and she set up a little stall, taking in mending and stitching for extra dosh. Pop was a barrister, so it wasn't like we were destitute or nothing. But it was tough."

She's lost, far away, like the story's replaying in her head. "Then I fell in love with my best friend, Misha. We were inseparable. Until Mum caught us making out one day in my room." She looks down at her food again. "Things were different for a long time after that. But eventually she let it go. Then I moved here. Met Roop. Mum was so happy that I had someone who loves me and takes care of me. Like a little piece of home." She takes a deep breath. "She even reached out to Sukhi Auntie—your mamiji. She's not responsive." She looks up at me, shrugging. "Guess you know about that already."

I don't, actually. But if it was my business, if they wanted me to know, I'm sure I would. So I focus on fashion, as one does. "And *Fierce*?" I ask, dying of curiosity. "It's such a dream."

"Dulcie St. Claire found me." She can't keep the grin off her face. "I was working for Meera Khanna Couture, and Dulcie came in. Back when she was at *Epic*. She asked for a quick fix on one of the pieces they planned to include in a fashion spread. I started freelancing for her. When LuLu was looking for an assistant, she recommended me. Been here ever since. I worked my way up in the closet for the past four years, and now I edit Found Fashion, along with some accessory pages and some shoots. Though I still haven't quite made it out of the closet." She giggles. "No pun, of course."

I smile, thinking about her and Roop and my family and the way things work out. I wonder how much my mother knows, what choices she made. Or would have made, if she had known. Would she have stepped in?

When Cherry came out, her dad didn't make a big deal of it. None of us did. Even though there's been gossip and nonsense among the auntie set. Cherry doesn't care about that.

Maybe things are different now. As much as I'd like to believe Mom would have and could have fixed things for Roop, I don't know if that's true. Now I'm here, and the gap between me and Roop might be impossible to close. Like she might just be a stranger. Especially if Cherry knew and I didn't.

"Give Roop a minute," Shenaz says, reading my mind again. "The past few years have been a lot. For a while, we thought her mum would come around. She hasn't called us in months. Just texted about your visit and family and priorities."

I swallow hard. Maybe I do need to step up and do something. But what can I do?

"Did Ranbir text you back?" Shenaz says. "Maybe you guys can grab dinner."

Can't hurt to ask. I send another message, but he doesn't respond. Not the whole train ride back. Not when I get home and find a little gift bag with fruit and Dhillon Estate Bespoke Wine—proscato—tucked into the vestibule, warm and waiting.

"Uf," Shenaz says. "He seems like a keeper." Then she grabs my stuff and hands me a check. "Intern stipend. You definitely earned it."

"I don't know how to thank you enough for today." I hug her again. "It was a dream come true."

"Well, you cut my day in half. Maybe you could come again another Sunday." She takes the wine and treats, then waves me off. "Now go get that boy."

4

I UNBRAID MY HAIR AS I CROSS THE STREET, LETTING IT cascade in long waves. I check my reflection in the glass doors at Easton Avenue apartments, making faces, ready and determined.

The building is huge, twelve stories of pink stucco, dwarfing the brownstones across the way. College kids mill around at the main door. I flash my ID at the security guard and head toward the elevator.

As the doors open, I fight the urge to turn around and bolt. Dolly and her BFF Jiya step off, all pretty and pink in summer dresses and sandals. Dammit. Of all people.

Dolly's flawless, as usual, her hair braided into a prim crown atop her head, highlights shimmering like gold, her makeup light and lovely. Jiya's a mirror image, a little fuzzier. A yes woman, the sidekick. Like me with Cherry. Has been since I've known them. Which is pretty much forever, from gurdwara events and weddings and Central Valley Vaisakhi festivals. While their practiced indifference is well worn by now, the actual disdain that flashes on Dolly's face when she sees me pinches.

"Hey," she says, eyes curious, taking in my dress, my shoes, my hair, already starting its inevitable frizz. "I thought you weren't staying in the dorms."

"I'm not. I'm across the street. With my cousin." She waits for more, but I don't owe her anything.

"Here to see Ranbir?" Jiya snorts. "Heard he was your chaperone. Such a big bhaiya type."

"Guess you guys would know." I shrug, trying to take the edge off. "Ready for orientation?"

"Can't wait," Jiya says, sarcasm dripping like sweat. "We're about to hit the mall for some 'farm gear.'"

"Yeah," Dolly says, peering over her sunglasses. "Cute dress. Mandira Wirk?"

"Good eye." I hit the elevator button. "See you tomorrow."

By the time I get to the sixth floor, my heart is racing. I take a deep breath, wondering if I should text Cherry. She'd say this is a terrible idea. She'd be right.

I find 605 and knock a few times. I'm about to send another forlorn text when the elevator opens again and a bunch of wet, rowdy, half-naked guys exit it, sloshing water across the hall. Ranbir is one of them, his curls slick with chlorine, sunglasses perched on his head. His skin is dark from the sun, the muscles in his arms and chest rippling and glistening. I'm staring, but I can't help it.

"Hey," Ranbir says as they head toward the door to their suite. "What are you—who let you up?"

No one, really. But nobody stopped me either.

"How'd you get past the dorm guard?" Guru Pathak asks. Madera Ranchos, also garlic—the kid Papa keeps bringing up. I try not to cringe. "Impressive."

The guys shuffle past, whooping a bit as they head into the suite. Ranbir folds his arms across his chest, and I look away. My cheeks are all hot, and I can't speak. I shouldn't have come.

He shrugs, like he's about to head inside, too. Like he can't be bothered.

"I'm really sorry I bailed," I say as he walks toward the door. "I meant to make it to brunch. Then Shenaz asked me to go into the city with her, and she works at *Fierce* and it was like a dream come true and I was so excited and it's like everything just whoooooooshed"—my hand flies above my head—"right out of my brain." I take a breath, steadying myself. "Anyway, I'm sorry. I know I suck. But I didn't mean to blow you off."

His hand is on the doorknob, pushing it open, heading inside. Guess that's it, then.

He leans back out. "Give me ten minutes to shower?" he says. "I need to put some clothes on, clearly. You're totally drooling." He's grinning, that crinkle thing going again. "And I'm starving."

He disappears behind the door, and I hear more rowdy boy noise inside.

I lean against the wall, my cheeks burning, my heart pounding. I was staring. Ogling, even. But I'd definitely do it again.

A few minutes later, Ranbir steps outside. His hair is damp and he's wearing jeans and a PURÉ PUNJABI T-shirt, along with flip-flops. "Thanks for waiting." There's that clean lemon scent again as he hugs me—and that back note. Earthy and familiar. Sandalwood?

He pops something in his mouth, then offers me a piece. Not gum. Cardamom. I take it, crunching as the floral flavor fills my mouth. That's what it is.

"Lachi." He grins. "We grow a small patch on the farm. It's my favorite."

"I'm really sorry," I say again, and he laughs.

"It's okay. I get it. I'm kind of itching to get to the city, too." I follow him as he heads to the elevator. "But it'll have to wait." He hits the button. "You hungry?"

I nod. Right now I'd follow him anywhere. "Good, because I know a place." He grabs my hand, and we head outside.

Twenty minutes later, our cab pulls up to a sprawling, golden-domed gurdwara. Cars parked as far as the eye can see, kids playing on a swing set just outside the temple. The sinewy tones of harmonium and dilruba pipe through a loudspeaker, a masculine voice booming out a shabad about honoring family and community. For the first time in about forty-eight hours, I feel like I'm home.

"I heard they do chole bhature all day on Sundays," Ranbir says

43

as he climbs out of the car and runs to my door, opening it for me. "Come on. I hope we didn't miss it."

We put our shoes in the gender-divided shoe closets, and he grabs a scarf to cover his head. I feel a bit awkward in my summer dress with bare shoulders, so I pull a chunni around them and over my head. It's bright blue with gold trim and little embroidered flowers, so it clashes with my dress, but it's so pretty I can't resist.

We duck into the main hall, where the evening services are wrapping up. There are about a hundred worshippers sitting, heads bent in prayer. I follow Ranbir up the main aisle, and we both kneel and bow our heads to the Guru Granth Sahib, the living and breathing Sikh Holy Book, which sits esteemed in an awning-covered bed up front, being fanned with a large pankh feather by a Gyani as the others sing the shabads. Ranbir drops some cash into the donation box, grins at me again, then heads off to sit on the men's side of the congregation.

My stomach grumbles as I settle into a spot on the floor in the women's section. Most of the ladies are older, dressed in salwar kameez with colorful chunnies on their heads, children tucked into laps or running around like my brothers and I used to. Someone's grandma smiles at me; the little girl in her lap eyes me suspiciously, sucking her thumb. The dadima strokes her hair, and the girl starts to drift off, the gurdwara as comfortable and familiar as home. They're all like this, gurdwaras, everywhere across the world. Warm, welcoming, a place to fill your belly and your heart. Exactly what I need before I venture off into the real world tomorrow.

I bow my head, lost in the prayers. The notes cue the final shabad, one about finding your path, and a voice rings out, strong and low and clear, as the dilruba and harmonium hum in the background. It's Ranbir, standing at the mic, his hands folded in front of his chest, his eyes closed as he sings.

I can't stop staring again, but this time it feels different. His voice brings a richness to the words that locks me in place. He finishes the song, and the Gyanis wrap up the services with notes about opportunities for service and Sunday School. An old man passes around the prasad, doling portions of steaming, sweet, greasy halwa into outstretched palms. I slurp mine greedily, the ghee slicking my hands and my mouth, then realize Ranbir is towering over me. Smirking.

He offers a hand. "Ready? I can tell you're hungry."

The ghee coats my teeth, so I just raise my brows and follow.

We hit the line for the buffet, my chunni drifting down slowly from my head as volunteers hand us shiny metal divided plates, ladling in the chole bhature—lip-smackingly spicy curried chickpeas and fried fluffy bread to dip in it. Cool yogurt lands in another one of the slots, while a salad of pickled onions and achar hits another. In the center circle, last but never least, a round, golden ladoo made of besan, sweetly studded with pistachios.

"You might be an actual genius," I say, my mouth already full as we settle down on one of the mats on the floor. Ranbir plops down next to me, too close for Auntie Approval, our knees touching. "Beats pizza any day."

He slurps a spoonful of chole. "Figured we might as well treat ourselves before we start hauling hay and milking cows. Ready for Cow Camp?"

I shrug. "Can't get excited, even though I know it's the Very First Step in the Rest of My Life." I look down at my plate, thinking about *Fierce*. How it finally felt like I was in the right timeline for once. "Might be fun, right?"

"We'll make it fun," Ranbir says, dipping his bread again. "Pooper-scooper!"

"Not if I can help it." I want to mention Dolly, to deflate the tension. But I leave it alone. "I didn't know you sing."

"Only shabads at the gurdwara," he says, looking down at his plate, suddenly shy. "And in the shower. It would be kind of fun to learn more, to maybe take a few lessons. But I—"

"You could totally do that." My mind races with possibilities. "Maybe at the arts school? I'm sure they have something for the summer."

"I did think about it." His face flashes with anxiety as he twirls his bhatura into the chole. "But it's just too hard. To find the time. To do my own thing."

"Like what?" I polish off my ladoo, instantly craving another.

"I mean, maybe I'd really study music." He looks up from under a thick fringe of dark lashes, one any beauty vlogger would kill for, and sighs. "There's this class I thought might be cool—on modernizing raag. It's at NYU. At night."

"That sounds amazing. Why don't you sign up?"

"It's a seminar. They might not take a high school kid, even if I am a senior." He shrugs. "Plus, I'd be MIA two nights a week. Someone would notice."

Dolly would notice. "And tell your parents," I say.

He sighs. "Dolly thinks it's a silly idea."

"Because of your family's plans for you." And maybe her.

He grins, finally looking up at me. "Yup."

"It's time you start making some plans of your own," I say, reaching for his ladoo. I take a little nibble, then turn back to him with what I hope is a mischievous grin.

He grabs my hand, stealing the ladoo back and chomping dramatically. Even though there are like twenty aunties watching. "Maybe I will."

We walk back to campus, exploring the neighborhood as the sun sets.

"So Roop's girlfriend works at that magazine?"

As we cross the street, he takes my hand again, like I'm a kid. I'd be offended, but I'm kind of thrilled when he doesn't let go. "The one I've been reading forever. The one I've always sort of dreamed of working at."

He grins down at me. "Now's your chance."

I shrug. "She said I could help out again. Another Sunday."

"They probably have internships."

"They definitely have internships. But you have to have experience and connections to even get in the door."

"You're already in the door."

I pause. He's a few steps ahead, still holding my hand. He's right. I do have a real connection now. Maybe I could do this. "But Cow Camp."

It's why I'm here. My purpose. To set me on my path.

He tugs me forward. Closer. "Here's the thing," he says, and I step closer still. Close enough to kiss, if he just leaned down. But he doesn't. "The magazine will be there. And there's always next summer. I, for one, am looking forward to scooping shit with you." He grins, then walks ahead again. "It's getting late. We should get back. Orientation tomorrow."

5

AFTER ANOTHER NIGHT TOSSING ON THE COUCH, I'M STILL bleary-eyed (and jet-lagged) when we get to Cook Campus the next morning. It's a stark contrast to downtown New Brunswick, all trees and winding paths, with random patches of farmland that almost, not quite, remind me of home. And this underlying earthy smell—one that's decidedly not garlic.

"Manure," Ranbir says, that smirk playing again as we stumble off the bus. "That's it."

It's 6 A.M., and the student center is quiet but buzzing with an influx of teenagers ready for anything. The air is supercharged, almost electric. Especially with Ranbir right next to me, his arm casually pressed against mine.

The sun is starting to peek out, the air thick with humidity. My hair—in two braids, farm ready—is frizzing despite being washed literally twenty minutes ago, complete with argan oil conditioner. My part of California is oven hot in the summer, but Jersey is humid hot, so short-alls were a smart idea. Cherry trimmed them with her signature print, bright and poppy.

But as we settle in with the group, eyes poke like daggers. Dolly and her clique, all ferocious energy. Like they want me to explode or something.

"Ready?" Ranbir says, leading the way. His hand hovers near mine, pinkies touching, and I want to lock it in, but I can't quite bring myself to do it. There's something crackling between us, fresh and intoxicating, and even the waft of manure can't bring me down. Neither can Dolly, who openly stares as Ranbir leans down and whispers into my hair. "These shorts are fun. Perfect for Cow Camp."

He's so close I could reach up and kiss him. I defuse it by pulling my Papa-not-Prada fanny pack around, grabbing my water bottle. I don't know how we're going to manage this humidity out in the cornfields. "Thanks. A Cherry Bombe original."

Dolly leans in, casual in her eavesdropping. Turns out her version of "farm gear" is not mine. Most of the Desi crew—and of the twelve girls and twenty guys here, at least half are brown—didn't read the orientation manual, because they're rocking summer dresses and too-short skirts. And the sun hats are amazing. Definitely expensive. I want to snap a pic for Shenaz, who could probably ID every designer they're wearing. But that would be rude.

"Welcome to the Linden Institute Precollege Agricultural Summer Program," a surprisingly booming voice announces. It's coming from a balding, forty-something white man wearing khakis, a polo, and a beige baseball cap, marked with a grinning brown cow. "Or Cow Camp, as some call it. I'm Dean Maxwell, supervisor of your summer session." He seems quite fond of his bullhorn. "Expect a lot of hard work and practical experience. And fun." He grins, awaiting applause, but we stand in sweaty silence. "All right, let's get you geared up."

Maxwell halts in front of a field of small green trees with a bright red barn off in the distance. He stands tall and stoic, then lifts the bullhorn. "Today is the first day of the rest of your lives. Here, you will learn the techniques and strategies you need to know to get down and dirty—and I do mean dirty," he says with a smirk, which prompts some snickers, "in a variety of agricultural settings. We'll be doing morning sessions on animal husbandry—yes, even if your parents own a winery—and fieldwork exploring crop cultivation and management. In the afternoons, we retreat to the classroom for workshops on animal science, farm finance and capital growth, and a few very special lectures on topics like hybrids and ethics, and branding and marketing in the agricultural arena."

I wonder how he can breathe; he's droning on and on. And I can't stop thinking about the fact that I'm going to be here, scooping shit, while Shenaz sorts through the winter collections that are supposed to arrive today. I can picture myself there, oohing and aahing over all the velvet and cashmere.

"Hope you're in my group," Ranbir whispers into my hair, knocking me right out of my daydream. "This seems like it's going to be intense."

The more Maxwell talks, the further the fantasy retreats, the reality of sweltering sun and stalkery ex-girlfriends settling like an anchor. "You'll study with top agricultural experts and are expected to be serious students worthy of their attention." I regret not bringing chai with me. I really need the caffeine. "By summer's end, you'll be well prepared to enter any agricultural program in the United States." He looks dramatically from student to student. "Some of you anyway."

He's right. Some of us were not cut out for this life. *Like me*, I realize with a start. Even though I'm probably the one with the most firsthand farming experience here. *I should be at Fierce.*

The thought flits away as soon as it hits, too quick to catch.

Maxwell takes a breath, then lifts the bullhorn again. "Agriculture is a team sport, which most of you know. But if you don't, you'll come to learn that intimately this summer. Go forth and prosper."

He takes a bow, then waits for the applause again. Nothing. "Time to break into groups." He looks down at his clipboard, checking off an endless list of names. "Ranbir Singh Dhillon, Guru

Pathak, Jiya Sharma, Marcus Hernandez, Dolly Kaur Randhawa."
He pauses, scratching his beard, and the moments tick by, slow and
painful. "And Maya Gera, group two."

I don't hear a word he says after that. I'm in Ranbir's group.
But when I turn to find him, he's all the way on the other side of
the lobby, Dolly's arm looped through his, her palm lightly on his
chest as she laughs, tossing her head back so the golden streaks in
her dark cascade of waves catch the sunlight. He offers her that
toothpaste-ad grin, and something implodes inside me, like my
heart has dropped right into my sneakers. This is going to be the
longest summer ever.

"Gather with your teams and prepare for your assignments,"
Maxwell booms into the bullhorn, waking everyone up. Team
two's on livestock. Lovely.

There's a frantic scramble as the students—many strangers—
attempt to find their groups. But I know exactly where mine is. It's
formed around Dolly and Ranbir, with Jiya hanging close, Guru
shuffling his feet, and this other guy who looks as confused as I feel.

"I'm Maya," I say, like they're all strangers. Even though they're
mostly not.

"Hey, Maya," the new dude says with a big smile. He's tall,
brown, and freckled. And he's wearing actual overalls. "I'm Marcus. From Georgia. What about you?"

"She's from California. Gilroy," Dolly interjects. "Garlic country, isn't that right, Maya?" She wrinkles her nose, like she can smell
it or something. Like she's the one person who doesn't actually love
garlic. Guru looks at me, confused by the jab, too. Oblivious to the
politics, I guess.

"Gilroy," Marcus says, grasping. "That's where the garlic festival was, right?"

"Is." I try not to bite. The yearly garlic extravaganza was a major
event for the community, but a shooting a few years ago has made

it shrink and shrivel, like an overripe bulb left too long in the sun. The rest of the world has forgotten, like they do every time a shooting happens. There'll be another tomorrow. But it hit our little community hard. "They still do it. It's just smaller."

"I've always wanted to go. I love garlic," Marcus says, beaming. "What about the rest of y'all?"

"Dolly and I are from Stockton and Merced. Guru is from the Madera Ranchos, also garlic, right?" Jiya chimes in with a droll smile, intrigued. I can almost see him blushing under that beard. "And Rana—I mean, Ranbir is from Sonoma. We're like half the California farm community right here."

Ranbir grimaces, but Marcus smiles, brows raised. "That's awesome. My parents don't own a single acre, but I've been working farms since I was five. Figured I might as well learn how to run one."

Dolly smiles so sweetly in my direction, I almost choke. "You'll have to teach us all about garlic," she says. "You know, since we'll be collaborating and all."

"What?" I don't get it.

"Maybe she doesn't know," Jiya says, sharp as a sickle. "Your parents did say—"

Dolly's hand flies to her mouth, all dramatic. "I forgot. Never mind, Maya. I'm just so glad we finally get to connect."

Me too. Or whatever. But clearly I missed something.

"We should really get to work," Jiya says, pulling the schedule from the folder. "We're supposed to orient ourselves to the animals by feeding chickens and meeting some of our four-legged friends."

We're all assigned tasks—endless, tedious, down and dirty, as promised. Jiya and Dolly, of course, choose to go deal with the chickens and eggs—the cleanest and easiest of the tasks—and Guru follows along, quiet but determined. I get stuck on horse duty with Marcus and Ranbir.

"When are we going to the city?" Marcus says as he uses a curry comb to start shaking out the dust on Princess—who's pale gold, very pregnant, and cranky. "Y'all been yet?"

"I've been a few times with my parents," Ranbir says. "My uncle lives in Queens."

"I got to go yesterday," I say proudly as I start sudsing Princess up. Wilbur neighs in the next stall, eager for some attention. "My cousin's girlfriend works in Times Square. So I spent the day at the McIntyre-Scott Tower."

"Mac Media? Thought it was shutting down," Marcus says, sweat already glistening on his brown, buzzed head. "My cousin works for CNN. She says nobody reads magazines anymore."

"Maya does," Ranbir says. His hand keeps nudging mine as we groom Princess, and there's this twinkle in his eye, like he has big plans. "What's that magazine called again? The one you were reading on the plane?"

"I thought you were asleep on the plane?"

He shrugs. "You were so into it, like rewriting the articles. It's her dream job."

I look down, a puddle of suds at my feet.

"What?" Marcus says. "Writing articles?"

"For *Fierce*." I don't even know why we're still talking about this.

"You could totally rock it," Marcus says. "Although my cousin says there's been a lot of upheaval there."

"They just got a new editor in chief," I say. "One of the few Black women to run a major magazine. And one of the few Black women editors in publishing, period."

"That's cool," Marcus says, grabbing a dandy brush to run through the horse's wet coat.

"It's, like, groundbreaking." My voice squeaks. "I got to work in the fashion closet with my cousin's girlfriend. It was pretty fucking awesome."

Marcus looks surprised. "Grab it, girl."

Ranbir grins. "You should write something. Get it in front of the right person."

"Like they'd take a pitch from a teenager."

Marcus shrugs and grins. "Worth a shot. Youth rules these days."

"Fanny packs and all," Ranbir says, tugging at my Papa-not-Prada pack.

"My dad gave it to me." I shrug. "And I'll have you know I scored a Prada belt bag yesterday. Super coveted, and directly from the *Fierce* fashion closet."

"You definitely know how to work it," Marcus says. "Very few people could pull off that ensemble. What does this dude know about fashion anyway?"

Ranbir laughs. "Not a lot, clearly!" Then he turns the hose on Marcus, splashing me and Princess in the process, too.

"Hey!" I leap away. Even Princess neighs with disgust, shivering despite the 90-degree heat.

Ranbir's phone buzzes, and he steps away to answer.

"What's with you and Ranbir?" Marcus says, smirking. "You guys hooking up or what?"

"Or what," I say with all the indignation I can muster. "I know him from home. All of them, actually. Desi farm kids. It's a thing."

"I heard. Rich kids. I've experienced my fair share, but none like this clique. The dorms are intense." He stares off into the distance. "Bespoke Wine? He seems nice, though." He cocks a brow, his broad brown nose crinkling. "And you do garlic?"

"My family does. I'll bring you some of our famous chutney. But we've only got twenty acres. That's why I'm here. My parents want it to be bigger—like Guru's family. They have like ten thousand acres."

"And Dolly—"

"She's the Spice Goddess. Spices and packaged goods." I lean closer, conspiratorially. "She and Ranbir . . ."

"I could tell," he says, laughing as Princess shakes and splashes.

"The way she draped herself on him before she headed over to the chickens, like she'd never see him again." He leans in closer. "That dude, Guru? He's interested. In her. Not you."

I make a face. I'm not into Guru anyway.

"But Ranbir? He's got his eyes on you." I follow Marcus's gaze, and he's right. Ranbir is watching us, phone still to his ear, sun haloing his head. "You dig?"

"Only if he can get with my fanny pack," I say, doing my diva strut again.

Marcus laughs. "Rock it." He steps back, heading toward the next stall. "Gonna work on Wilbur. You got this?"

I nod and start drying Princess off with a grooming rag. She sort of purrs under the warm fuzz of the towel, sighing contentedly as I rub her coat with some balm. It's like she's grinning, big square teeth and a hee-haw honk. We don't have horses at home, but they seem like lovely creatures. Mostly.

A shadow falls over me. "I'm in!" Ranbir says. "NYU will make an exception. My class starts in two weeks." He's grinning down at me, his eyes doing that crinkle again, slightly irresistible. "We should celebrate." His voice is low, hopeful. "Like maybe that Thai place down the block?"

I grin back up at him. "Definitely. The spicier the better."

CHERRY: Dude, the gurdwara? Making me look bad over here. Roop take you?

MAYA: No, actually. Ranbir.

CHERRY: Like with Dolly + crew?

MAYA: Just us.

CHERRY: MAYA. ☹ #truckboisaretrouble

CHERRY: How was your first day? You gonna send me video from Fierce?

MAYA: Shenaz kiboshed it. "Eyes everywhere." ⓦ

MAYA: I'll FaceTime you next time. Just for a minute. Pinkie swear. Okay, bedtime. Early start tomorrow.

CHERRY: Break a leg! Or, uh, milk a cow? ☺ Call me after. And Ma, too!

6

BY THE END OF THE SECOND WEEK OF CAMP, WE'VE SETTLED into a routine. We start at dawn, hitting the farm for "experiential learning" tasks till lunch, usually subs and potato chips from food services. Then it's class time until five, with some of us (guilty) nodding off in the air-conditioning. By the time the bus drops us off on the corner of Easton Avenue and Somerset Street, everyone's fried. But Marcus says the dorms are wild after hours, all drinking and hookups and shenanigans at the pool next door.

I haven't been, with good reason. Ranbir and I always part at the P.M. bus, all casual. Then he texts and we meet up for dinner, his treat. We've done Thai, Chinese, Malaysian, pizza. Yesterday was Mexican, and definitely, uh, different from the California version.

We end up talking for hours—about his family and mine, my brothers and their *Minecraft* obsession, visits to Punjab, grapes and garlic and petty auntie antics. He still hasn't kissed me, though. Maybe I'm misinterpreting things? Or maybe it's Dolly. She follows him around like a shadow. Which sucks. But I get it. Three years is forever. After she mentioned my parents, acting like she knows them, I'm sure she has an agenda.

Friday evening, I get out of the shower, put on pajamas, and wrap my hair in a towel turban to let Cherry's antifrizz serum set. I make myself a cup of chai, then FaceTime Ma, since we haven't talked in days. Gotta admit: I've been avoiding her.

She picks up immediately, and seeing her lined brown face— mostly forehead, until she pulls back a teensy bit—makes my stomach swoosh with homesickness. She's wearing a purple flowered salwar kameez, sandalwood powder collected at her cleavage, even though I always tell her to go easy. "Finally, puth. I've been waiting forever. Is Roop there? Show me the home. Where is your room? Why do you have a tholia on your head?" She takes a sip of chai. "Dolly's mom told me that you've been hanging out. Dolly and Jiya seem like good girls—"

"I wouldn't say hanging out, but they're in my group. And—" I want to ask her about what Dolly said, about collaborating. I also kind of don't want to know. I collapse onto the couch, still strewn with sheets and this morning's clothing chaos. "It's definitely intense. I'm learning a lot. Horses, cows, corn, some lectures. It's a pretty long day. But Roop and her roommate are still working." What do I tell her about Shenaz? "It's so humid here, it wrecks my hair." I wave my phone around the room. "And this is pretty much it, the whole apartment."

"You must be so tired, bacha," she says, but she's the one who looks exhausted. Her face is a deep brown from the fields, the smile lines sharper, her eyes bloodshot. "So small, henna?" I can see her peering, like she can 3D herself into the space, see into the corners. "Kitchen dikha. That's the fridge? What have you been eating?"

Good question, but I can't tell her the truth. I maybe manage a bagel and coffee before the A.M. bus, then we have those bland sandwiches at lunch. And dinners with Ranbir.

"Why are you making that face?" Ma says, bringing me back to the moment, the sofa, my chai. "Eating okay?"

"We don't cook much. We're hardly here." I take another sip. "I've tried a few places nearby. Lots of Asian food. Mexican here is terrible. I got to go to the city with Shenaz. She got us Ethiopian—you'd love it."

"Careful in the city, beta. Mamiji says it's dangerous, drugs, prostitutes. We don't know Shenaz."

"It's perfectly safe. Shenaz is awesome. She's British. You'd like her."

"How are the other kids there?" Ma asks. "Guru seems like a good boy."

I do not want to talk about Guru and garlic and strategic alliances. "And Ranbir, and Marcus, who's really cool, from Georgia. His family works on a peach farm."

"Like Manjit's." Ma grins. "Good program. All these connections will help expand the business."

She tries to hide it, but her face cracks a little. I know the farm's been struggling since the shooting, but also because of the constant droughts and fires. A lot of garlic production has shifted farther into the Valley. I've heard her and Papa argue, late at night, about payments and equipment and the employees they laid off two summers ago and couldn't afford to bring back. That's why the harvest is all us—including the twins, now that they're a little older—and the few men Cherry's dad can bring in on a measly budget. That's why the fruit stand sales are so necessary, and Cherry pitches in with her Etsy stuff, even though she's hoping to go somewhere fancy to study fashion.

My path is set of course. *But maybe it doesn't have to be.*

I stifle the thought. "I'm definitely learning a lot." I don't tell her about the dozing, or Dolly's daggers, or how much downtime I'm spending with Ranbir. Even though she thinks he's charming.

"The gurdwara seems nice. Good you went. But make a plan to go see Mamiji," Ma says. "She keeps calling. You didn't even text to say Sat Sri Akaal."

There's a huge clang, like pots and pans falling. Ma frowns. "Cherry's here. She won't go home," she adds, lowering her voice and making a face. "Such a mess. Keeps burning rotis. She's learning, but she will need a good Indian wife."

Cherry's head pops forward onto the screen, all nostrils. "What's so funny?" she asks as Ma putters off to the kitchen to assess the damage.

"Get ready, Ma's gonna find you a strategic alliance, a Good Indian Girl. One who doesn't burn rotis."

She shrugs. "My rotis aren't burnt. Just crispy. I'll be making them better than you by the end of the summer."

"When's Ava coming down?" Cherry's been seeing this stunner she met at her summer design camp last year at UCLA—which she paid for herself through Cherry Bombe sales. They don't get to hang much, but they talk a lot. I know, because I've lived through nonstop FaceTime sessions during some of our sleepovers. They're annoyingly adorable together.

She frowns, looking at her nails, cherry red. Avoiding my gaze. "Ava's at UCLA again." Here comes the pout. "Seems there's a new love interest."

Uh-oh. "You could drive down. It's only like five hours."

She shakes her head. "Things are different. And your mom needs me. She really misses you." She frowns. "I do, too. It's weird here without you. Especially the fruit stand."

"Weird here, too. I wish you could be here. New York was so cool. You'd love it."

And *Fierce*. I loved it.

"Go see FIT for me. It's right by Penn Station. And that giant needle-and-button statue. And there's a Bollywood fashion exhibit at MoMA. You. Have. To. Go. Please."

"Definitely." I drain my chai. "I'm so wiped, though. Cow Camp is exhausting and endless."

"And then there's all those late nights with truckboi." She makes a kissy face.

"He's not a truckboi."

"He's so a truckboi." More kissing noises. I wish I could throw something at her.

"He hasn't kissed me yet."

That stops her cold. Her eyes glitter—literally, gold glitter shadow or whatever, but also a glint of mischief. "Has he had the opportunity?" One look and she knows everything. "Maya."

I shrug. "Dolly's definitely still into him."

"Let her have him." She grimaces. "Your dad keeps talking about Guru, though. He does seem like a lovely, tall, strapping Punjabi boy with much garlic expertise."

I gag. "He's fine. But barely talks. And when he does, it's about garlic."

"Well, maybe you should try talking to him." She makes a face again. "Things are bad here, Maya. Like half the crop is white rot. And the other tractor broke again. Pop's stressed, and your dad's been gone a lot, 'taking meetings.'"

"What do you mean, meetings?" *Like what Dolly said.*

She shrugs. "That's all I got from my eavesdropping. But I'll nose around."

I nod. My phone beeps. Ranbir. I send it to voice mail.

"Who's that?" But she already knows. "Careful, kid. You can't hack a rebound romance. Not built for it."

"You should talk, Miss Social Media Stalker."

She sighs. "Have your fun, if you must, get it out of your system. But don't say I didn't warn you." Even wags a finger, hand on her hip dramatically, faux pained.

"Okay, Auntieji." A bunch of text notifications pop up. "I should go. I'm starving, and there's absolutely no food in this apartment."

"Yeah, yeah. Go find truckboi." She blows me a kiss, then disappears.

I check my texts, and it's him, of course.

> **RANBIR:** Have a surprise for you. Meet me in front of the dorm? Eight-ish?

I really like hanging out with him, but I'm also super tired and don't know how much longer I can keep up this pace—a couple of hours' sleep on a lumpy couch, the lack of chai all day, the jet lag that hasn't quite faded. As I text him back, Cherry's warning echoes in my head.

Maybe it is a bad idea. Clearly. But the way my heart surges at his name on my phone, the way my pulse races when he smiles at me, it seems inevitable. Might as well enjoy myself in the meantime.

Ranbir's already there when I get to the building. It took me a minute to figure out my outfit—the shoes I got from *Fierce* and a sleeveless, V-neck palazzo number from Reformation I swiped from Shenaz's rack because it's meant to be calf length and wasn't too long for me. But maybe a little low cut, now that I see the way his eyes take me in. He grins and pulls me into a hug, then leans back a bit, pondering the outfit. "Romper?" he asks, quite serious. "Jumper?"

"Jumpsuit," I say, laughing. "But close. The wide legs are called palazzos."

"Pants that look like a skirt."

"Shenaz would definitely appreciate your interest."

He laughs. "Here comes the Uber," he says as it rolls up. He opens the door, then scoots in after me.

"Where are we going?" I ask, but he shakes his head, and we're there in like ten minutes.

He helps me out of the car and leads the way to a place called Destination Dogs.

I stop short and double over, laughing. "Wait, what?"

He grins, one brow perched high. "You don't like hot dogs? They have veggie options."

"Not what I was expecting." I follow him inside.

"My sister Simi told me about it. From *Diners, Drive-Ins and Dives*. She's Food Network–obsessed."

"Ma loves Guy Fieri!" I'll have to tell her all about this. Maybe even about Ranbir.

We grab a high-top table for two. "Want to order a bunch and share?" I ask him, and he nods, pulling my stool closer so we can scope the menu together. "Let's try the Veg-Dog Meal-ionaire." Samosa topped and spicy? Bring it. "And the Conquistadog? I love chorizo."

"Sim says the Patatas Ridiculas are a must," he says, pointing at the menu. Then he grins, wicked. "How do you feel about python?"

I lean in closer to look. One Bite in Bangkok promises snake sausage, pepper jelly, cucumber relish. "Do you think it's, like, actual python?"

He wags his brows, and I bust out laughing. "We could find out."

"Okay, and a chili cheese dog for sure." Because we haven't ordered enough. "That's a lot of food."

Ranbir shrugs. "My kid sister is expecting a full report."

As the waiter walks away with our massive order, I'm suddenly nervous, like we'll run out of things to talk about.

But Ranbir stands and grabs my hand. "Ready for the surprise?"

I frown. "I thought this was the surprise."

He leads me to a room filled with pinball machines and game booths. "The best part," he says solemnly. "And . . ." He does a *Price Is Right* strut that Ma would appreciate. "Skee-Ball."

I nearly jump with excitement. "You do not even know what you just got yourself into. I'm pretty much the actual Skee-Ball champion of the world. Or at least of the Gera family."

"Challenge accepted," he says, and slides a credit card through the slot on each of the machines.

The little balls thunder down, and we start rolling, eyeing each other meanly as we play. His style is casual, haphazard, and decidedly entertaining, swinging and sliding the ball any which way and hoping for the best. Mine is precise, measured, contained, with a slingshot roll that ensures max points—50s and 100s every time. We play five rounds—and I win all of them—until he finally just plops on the floor in defeat.

"Okay, champ. I bow down." Then he does.

"Come on, loser, let's eat." I offer a hand, and he scrambles to his feet, following me back to the table.

Ranbir starts splitting up the dogs while I dig into the fries.

"Tell Sim two thumbs-up," I say over a mouthful of potato and cheese sauce. "Crispy, light, cheesy."

"Cheesy all right," he says, snapping a picture as I stick out my potato-covered tongue. He clicks a few buttons.

"Wait—" I say. "Don't . . ."

"Too late. Sent to Simi. I'm sure she'll appreciate it."

Then he pulls the python dog toward us and hands me half. "Ready?"

I take a sip of lemonade to clear my palate. I close my eyes, but he tugs my hand. "Nope, that's cheating. Okay? One. Two. Three."

We both take a bite, our gazes locked, and his brows shoot up into his curls. Then he laughs. Hard. For a long while.

"Too chewy," I say, downing lemonade. Turns out python tastes pretty much like any old hot dog.

He devours the rest of it while I focus on the chili dog, digging in with a fork and knife. "Stop staring."

"Can. Not. You used a fork on a hot dog. You asked to be judged."

"Do you like Cow Camp?" I ask over a mouthful of samosa-spiced veggie dog. Not bad.

He shrugs. "Pretty much what I expected. Long days, lots of sweat, lots of drama."

"At the dorms?" I ask. "I kind of feel like I'm missing out."

"Trust me, it's not that interesting. Just everyone comparing net worths and early acceptances, and tracking who's hooking up with who. Like at home."

"So who's hooking up?"

He threatens to toss a cheesy fry at me.

I shrug. "I don't really hang with you guys—here or at home. No Punjabi school, no hookups, no antics. I only hear about it through my mom and the aunties. And Cherry. Who definitely tracks shit."

He laughs. "Yeah, they sure love to gup-shup. The girls here are like the junior set, aunties in training."

"Even Dolly?"

He rolls his eyes. "Especially Dolly."

I frown into my food.

"What?" he says, his eyes curious.

"Cherry doesn't like me—uh, hanging out with you. Because truckbois are trouble." I can't help but smile as I say it. "She even made a hashtag."

He raises his palms, perches a single brow. "How am I a truckboi?"

I shrug. "You have a bit of a rep."

He sighs. "People believe what they want. I've been with one girl for three years." Then he grins. "But my truck is pretty kick-ass."

I guess I'm quiet, because he peers at me again, like he's waiting for me to say something, to ask.

"You okay?"

"I feel like there's so much pressure—on this summer, on this to-do list, all these expectations." I grab another fry. "It's too much."

"And—"

"And not what I want."

He reaches for my hand, even though we're both a mess. "What do you want?"

I shrug. "Not to shovel shit and milk cows and pick garlic all my life."

He whistles low, the whoosh of air blowing his curls up. "I could tell." He grins. "The question is, what are you going to do about it?"

I frown into my plate. "What can I do about it?"

"You should do what you want." He takes another swig of lemonade. "Might be your only chance. All I can do is nudge you along, like you did for me with the music class."

I nod. "I don't think I'm quite that brave. But I do want to get back to the city again."

He grins. "I think that can be arranged."

By the time we're done, I feel like I need to be rolled all the way home in a wheelbarrow. I clean up with the wet wipes the waiter left on the table, wiping down my hands and my mouth, all prim.

Ranbir's looking at the menu again, even though he polished off most of the food once I gave up. "Sure you don't want dessert? Maybe to go? They have sticky toffee pudding."

I throw a napkin at him and rub my belly, which pokes lightly out of my jumpsuit.

He laughs and cleans himself up. Then he takes my hand. "Okay, let's walk it off," he says, offering me his signature cardamom pod as we head out the door.

The walk home is long, maybe a couple of miles. It's pretty dark out, but he doesn't let go of my hand—clammy, sweaty as it is—the whole time.

"You excited about your class?" I ask him as we get closer to campus.

He nods. "I still can't believe it. I got the textbooks yesterday. They're pretty intense. I need to learn how to read music better. I should have probably taken something more basic."

"My papa always says headfirst is the best way for something new. It's how he taught us all to swim—tossing us right into the deep end."

"Wow," Ranbir says. His thumb keeps rubbing mine, like he's trying to start a thumb war. It's kind of funny. And kind of sweet. "Glad you didn't drown."

"Nearly did. Once. But I can swim."

He laughs again. Before I know it, we're half a block from Roop's, the path lit by lamplight. My stomach flutters, this weird mix of excitement and dread. Or maybe chili dog. The night is almost over. It was so fun, and now we both have big-time onion breath. Well, tempered by cardamom. The disappointment hits me hard.

He pauses, tugging my arm as I keep moving. "Hey, you okay?"

I nod. "Why?"

"Your face, the way it keeps flashing with all these different expressions when you're lost in thought. It's like you can't hide anything."

I shrug. "I don't know. It's just—"

He steps closer again, the light like little sparks in his eyes as he looks down at me.

"I don't get what we're doing. You're clearly still into Dolly. But we keep hanging out. I like you, but I don't want to get attached if—"

He takes a deep breath. "I'm not into Dolly. It's complicated." He runs his hands through his curls. "She can't let go. I get why. But we're not a good fit."

I look down at my shoes, the cobalt velvet black in the dim light, sort of holding my breath. "Well then, you should be clear."

He sighs. "I'm trying. She's like family, you know? There are all these expectations. Hers, yeah. But her parents. My parents."

"Your parents like her?" Of course they do.

"What's not to like?" He reads my face, disappointed, and reaches for my hand again. "She's perfect on paper. Doesn't mean she's actually perfect."

I nod. "I know how it is. My mom's not that pushy. But she's always ushering me in the right direction, one way or the other."

Like with Guru. Or even in Ranbir's direction. Is he just another goal planted in my head? One more thing on Ma's to-do list. Or do I actually like him? His eyes crinkle again as he smiles, and the flutter in my stomach tells me that I do.

He takes a step closer. "Maya." He lifts my chin, making me look at him. "Listen."

"What?" I say, even though I know. This is it. Time to let it go.

Instead, he pulls me forward, into his arms, my head on his chest, his heart racing. Or maybe it's mine, pounding in my ears. His hands wind around my waist, and I'm on my tiptoes as he leans down, finally closing the gap. Stubble scrapes my skin, then his mouth is on mine, salt and cardamom, and that familiar pungency as he grins down at me, his lips still on mine, his eyes turning into one big telescope eye as our foreheads press together.

"You've got onion breath," I say, pulling away, and he laughs.

"So do you." Then he tugs me closer, kissing me again, his hands warm on my waist. We're there in the lamplight for what seems like forever, and I'm lightheaded, breathless.

"You okay?" he whispers into my hair.

I nod, still dazed. "I should go, though." My stomach flip-flops as I look toward Roop's building, trying to ground myself. "What time is it?"

"Almost eleven," he says, taking my hand again as we walk the rest of the way, getting there way too soon. "Maya—"

My heart pounds in my ears. "I should go," I say as he steps closer again. Like I've turned into a pumpkin. Or wait, was that the coach? I run up the steps and hit the buzzer. "Good night."

He's still standing there when I look back. Grinning. "'Night."

By the time I get to the fourth floor, trudging up the endless stairs, I'm breathless and dizzy. But I can't wipe the smile from my face.

"Guess it was a good night?" Shenaz's voice calls from the sofa, where she's curled up, her legs thrown casually over Roop's lap. They don't bother to move, even though they're lounging on my bed. Technically, I guess, they do pay the rent. And own the couch.

"I'm gonna make a call," I say—to no response—and take my phone to their bedroom, since they still haven't bothered to move.

I haven't been in the bedroom at all so far; it's like a boundary we haven't crossed, the final frontier. It's neater than I expected, with lilac-ish walls and a soft, white cotton bedspread covered with a thousand pretty velvet pillows in pastel tones. Near the door, another clothes rack sits crushed under the weight of Shenaz's couture. Against the far wall, under the window that looks into the nonexistent yard, there's a desk. Roop's, no doubt, with three shelves suspended next to it, medical books. A few framed pictures of Roop and Shenaz, including one from when they first met, so young. And, surprisingly, an old framed family photo of all of us from that summer after her dad died, when I was ten, arranged in the big wisteria tree in the farmhouse garden—Roop, her mom, my mom, and the Gera men.

My mother has the same one in the living room, and dusts it lovingly three times a week. As another wave of homesickness washes over me, I perch on the chair and hit the video chat button.

Cherry answers immediately. She's in pj's—my pink bunny ones—and lounging on my bed, an avocado face mask turning her green, cucumber slices covering her eyes.

"You'll never believe what happened," I say, and the mask cracks as she grins, making her look like a merry Elphaba from *Wicked*. One of our favorite Broadway soundtracks. Maybe I'll manage to see a show this summer.

"He kiss you, finally?" she drops, casual as can be.

"You take the fun out of everything." But I'm smiling, my hands touching my lips again.

She removes a cucumber slice, popping it into her mouth. "So yes."

I nod, suddenly shy.

"Maya," she says, a warning in her voice.

"What?"

"Dude, you're, like, courting trouble." She's aimed the camera so I can see the stern line of her mouth, the hard eyes. Eye, singular. A cucumber slice on the other. And her face is still green, which makes me laugh.

She laughs, too. "Look, I'm not trying to be an asshole about

69

this. But you're like a little chick. And he's like head rooster, ready to devour you or whatever."

I frown. "That's a really gross analogy. I don't think roosters eat chicks, anyway?"

"You know what I'm talking about." She nibbles the other cucumber slice, focusing on my face.

"It's not like that." But what if she's right?

"Maya," she says again in her best mom tone, way stiffer than Ma's. "They were together for like four years. They'll be back together in a minute. Their families have known each other forever. They are a fucking 'strategic alliance.'" She takes a deep breath, trying to soften the harsh. "You're too good for a random fling. Especially when—"

"I have no idea what I'm doing."

She stares at the ceiling, away from the phone. "Yeah."

"Well, let me learn the hard way, okay?" I say. "Just this one time."

She nods, sighing. "You got it, kid."

The door opens, and it's Roop. "Hey, we're gonna turn in." She looks at me, perched on the chair, the phone in my hand. "Is that Buaji? Can I talk to her?"

That's, like, more words than she's said to me the entire time I've been here.

"Hey, Roop," Cherry calls out.

"Hey, Cher." Familiar. Not like it's been ages. Roop takes the phone from me. "How goes the fruit stand?"

Cherry shrugs. "Same ole tourists. How's your boss? Still an ass?"

Roop laughs. It's a strange, exciting sound. One I haven't heard in ages. "Yeah, but I got moved to pediatric ICU, so not his jurisdiction anymore. Exhausting, though."

I stand, not bothering to hide my annoyance. Not like they notice. "I'm gonna go to bed."

Roop nods, focused on the phone.

70

I head to the bathroom, change into pajamas, wash my face, and brush my teeth, admittedly with some violence. WTAF was that? All casual and connected, like I wasn't even in the room. Like they have this whole other existence without me. The one where the cousin I've always idolized plays doting big sister to my BFF, and I have no clue.

Shenaz knocks. "You done, Maya?"

I unlock the door, drying my face with a towel. "It's been a really long day."

She nods, and hands me my phone as she pushes past me. "I made your bed." She turns back. "You okay?"

Why does everyone keep asking me that? I head toward the sofa. I sigh, throwing myself down on it, trying to get comfortable, to recapture the excitement I felt earlier tonight. My first kiss, the way Ranbir made my insides mushy. But all I see when I close my eyes is orange-rage sun.

"Sweet dreams, Maya Memsahib," Shenaz calls as she heads into the bedroom.

No chance of that tonight.

7

Sunday, bright and early, Shenaz and I are on the train. This morning, as she puttered around, I ever-so-casually asked her if I could come help at *Fierce* again. "I thought that was a done deal," she said, grinning. "I'm definitely the boss of you, Maya Memsahib."

But I proudly dressed myself today, wearing a custom, black-and-white-striped dress Cherry made for me. My hair is in two low pigtails, my makeup light and dewy, kajal, lip gloss, and blush, with a compact of sheer powder tucked away in my little blue leather bag for shine reduction, per Cherry's strict instructions. Fancy golden, strappy sandals. And luckily, Shenaz brought me a black jewel-buttoned cardigan, because I totally forgot about the blasting AC on the train. I could pass for *Fierce* fashion, maybe. Gotta keep the confidence up.

Shenaz stares at her laptop, headphones on, making a to-do list of tasks—prepping a shoot and unpacking and logging items for spring seasonal. She called it a snoozefest, but I'm thrilled. I can't believe I'll get to breathe that Times Square air, to walk those hallowed halls again.

"What are you grinning about, dollface?" Shenaz says, tugging at her earbuds. "Ranbir? You should ask him to meet you in the city. We'll be done around three."

"I'm so excited to be back at *Fierce*. Truly, this is beyond my wildest dreams."

"Glad to be of service," she says. "I remember how elated I was when I started. I wish I still felt like that about it. But I know too much now."

We detour to grab coffee and a bagel. I pause to pose in my Suite Cherry Bombe frock in front of the giant needle and button for Cherry. Then we double-time to the office, clocking in around ten.

I'm glad Shenaz green-lit my look, though, because there are definitely more people around today than there were the first time. As soon as we get off the elevator on thirty-two, we run into Shenaz's boss, the notorious LuLu Chang, whom I recognize instantly from the magazine's fashion pages. She's long and lean, with pale skin and dark hair flowing in long waves, wrapped in a hot-pink dress that emphasizes flawless proportions. What Shenaz means when she says "sample size," I'd guess. She's pursing her lips, pondering a shipment at reception.

"Hey, LuLu," Shenaz says, startling her. "Let me get that. By the way, this is my girlfriend's niece, Maya."

LuLu looks confused but composes herself. "Thanks, Shaz," she says, waving toward the stuff. "Hello, little one." She flashes teeth, then is all business again. "I need to pull looks for the shoot, but these need to be logged. Get settled and meet me in the conference room in fifteen, 'kay?" She bustles off without another word, a cloud of silk floating behind her.

"LuLu Chang. Intense," I say, still breathing in the orchid scent she's left in her wake. "I can't believe she actually exists. And that she's your boss." I look down at my clothes, feeling frumpy despite my fab frock. "Didn't realize she'd be here today."

Shenaz seems distracted, tapping her lip again as we head toward the closet. "We've got a shoot this week, so there's a lot to do." She stops, turns toward the boxes at reception, then back to me. "I need to pull picks for the shoot. Do me a favor? Take these boxes and log them—the way you did with the boots last time. Remember the return forms you filled out? There's another one for intake. We need one on each item, pulling details from the packing slips. Do you think you can manage that?"

I nod, even though I'm nervous. She scrawls her log-in information on a Post-it, hands me her ID, then rushes off toward the closet, leaving me to deal with the boxes. There are four, and they're large, which makes me wonder what might be inside. I shake one of the boxes. Shoes, maybe?

I'm dragging it slowly, painfully, in the direction of the closet when the elevator opens.

"Need help?" Xander. Thank god.

"Yes, please," I say, peering from behind the box.

"Oh, hey." He grins, and there's the dimple. Delicious. "Working the weekend, huh? Suck-up."

I tap my lovely gold sandal. "You should talk."

He takes the box, and I grab another one, following him toward the closet. "Guess you did a good job last time?"

"With your help." My face is hot. Weird.

He grins again. "Why don't you start logging, and I'll get the rest."

I tear into the two boxes we brought in and laugh. Bikinis. Hundreds of them. But not for this summer, which might as well be over. In magazine land, this is next spring's resort stuff. And it is gorgeous. I lift out a few items, holding them up against myself, picturing what my ideal vacation would look like if this was the life I lived. The Hamptons for sure, a home just off the beach, a big kidney-shaped pool in the backyard, like in a '70s Bollywood film, and those funny doughnut floaties. Cherry and I lounging, painted toenails in the water, oversized sunglasses perched on our heads, one of those awesome trays drifting by with piña coladas. I wonder if I like piña coladas. I like pineapple and coconut, so probably.

I hold up a bikini and snap a selfie for Cherry. It's rainbow striped, like the queer flag, and she'd totally love it. She sends back a thousand exclamation marks. I pose with another, this one bright blue and beaded, and hit send.

Xander clears his throat, having appeared in the door in stealth silence. I wish he'd stop doing that. He points upward. Cameras. Oh yeah.

"Those are embargoed. Till actual spring. Next year," he says, warning. But there's laughter underneath. "Tell your friend not to share, okay?"

"She would never," I say, all dramatic. I can't even look at him without getting overheated, the words from all the Mr. X posts on the *Fierce* site branded in my brain.

"What?" he says, taking one of the box cutters and pulling open another crate of swimwear. He turns to look right at me. "You've been reading?"

Uf, called out. "I have no idea what you're talking about."

"You're totally staring." He shrugs. "Not the first time."

I lift my jaw up off the floor and stand with indignation. "I'll have you know that—"

"Happens. How do you think I got this job?" He laughs when my jaw drops again. "You gotta work what you've got."

"You mean . . ."

"Nah. But, like, why do you think I landed at a women's mag?"

Oh. That makes sense. Sort of.

"Right. I filled a need." My cheeks burn again. And this time, he's staring at the floor, too. "I mean, they *needed* a male voice for the dating pages. Not like that."

I nod. "Sure." I start scanning bikinis, logging them quickly, trying not to stare. Or at least not to be obvious about it.

"Anyway, it's a good place to get some clips, if you want."

"What?" I'm so focused on logging, I kind of hear him wrong.

"You could pitch something."

"To who?"

"Whom," he says, and I grimace. "Me. I edit those pages."

"As an assistant?"

"At the moment. But there's an assistant editor gig open. I'm already doing the work."

Wait, but how does he manage that? "But you're—"

"So young. I know," he says, tagging another suit—Meera Khanna, madras plaid. Covetous. "But I'm the one to pitch."

A real-life editor. Sort of. "What would I write about?"

"You're supposed to tell me." There's that dent again. "You've read the section, right?"

He hands me another batch of bikinis to scan. "We're always looking for new voices."

I wonder if I should ask. Since he's the expert, or whatever. "Okay, give me your take first."

"On what?" He starts stacking the logged bikinis, categorizing them by some metric I can't quite figure out.

"I'm sort of seeing this guy."

"Sort of?"

"I've known him for a while. Casually. But we connected this spring. At a wedding."

"Connected?" He smirks.

"But he was with someone for a long time. Like three years."

He grins. "Forever." Is he laughing at me?

I frown. "Never mind."

"No." He steps closer. "I'm interested. Tell me more."

"They broke up. A few months ago. We've been hanging out. But it's—" I sigh. "I don't know. Intense. Too intense." I realize I'm smiling to myself, staring at the screen, and compose myself. "But she's always around." And it's infuriating.

"Is he still into her?"

"He says he's not." I can't look at him. "But she's definitely into him. Stalkerishly."

He lets out a big whoosh of air. "Those types are rough. She's going to do her best to make you miserable."

I nod. "Seems like it. The thing is, how do I know if it's even worth it?"

"Well, if it's just a sex thing, then probably not." He's grinning. "But I don't think it is with you."

What's that supposed to mean?

He's dimpling again. "I can tell. The way you talk about him." Then he frowns for a second. "But he's rebounding heavy. Be careful, Maya."

"Ugh." I can feel the pout coming on. "Why does everyone keep saying that?"

He laughs. "Guess you look like the type who needs a warning."

My phone buzzes, a good distraction. It's Ranbir. Asking about afternoon plans. I text back that I'm in the city.

Can I meet you there? NYU tour today.

Fierce and Ranbir and the city. All in one day. I don't think my brain can handle all the excitement.

"That's some smile," Xander says, and I nearly drop my phone.

"Yeah, it's, uh—" I stash my phone, staring at the computer.

"Your friend? Rebound Dude?" He grins. "That's what you should write about."

No thanks. "Do you know where Shenaz went?" I still have her ID.

"She's with LuLu in the studio, nailing down the shoot." He combs through another box, pulling out the last of the bikinis. "Is fashion your thing?"

I shake my head. "Definitely more editorial. Though I'll take what I can get."

"Smart. So pitch me."

Maybe I will.

He logs the last one and saves the sheet, putting the batch into one of the intake bins. "Wanna grab a bite? We can wrap these after lunch."

"Actually, I'm gonna go meet Rebound Dude." He smirks.

"Stop it."

"Heed my words."

I grab my bag as my phone buzzes again and speed toward the door. "See ya next time."

* * *

Stepping out into the city streets solo is surreal—exhilarating and anxiety inducing all at once. The bustle moves around me like a wave, the energy pulsing and shifting, threatening to wash me away with it like the winter tide on a Monterey beach. I let the flow of the crowd carry me for a moment, ending up in the thick of Times Square. The sun is blazing and the humidity oppressive, but the buildings are lit up in cheerful neon anyway, like they're awaiting the evening crowds. Tourists mill and pose and point, lured by street vendors and Elmo and Cookie Monster. I pause, taking it in, and send Cherry a quick pic.

I'm supposed to meet Ranbir in about an hour, so I decide to take the subway, which Shenaz says is way cheaper than a cab. "Best bet is the A-C-E or the B-D-F-M," she said, then laughed when I frowned. "Blue or orange, mostly. Look at the giant map and check to make sure they hit close to Washington Square."

I buy a MetroCard for twenty dollars, swipe through, and manage to jump on a C train right as the doors are closing. There are no seats open, so I stand near the door, watching New Yorkers in their natural element. Men all dappered up, women in all kinds of fabrics and patterns and prints. No wonder fashion lives here; there's inspiration everywhere you look. A bunch of teens chat on the far side of the car, erupting into laughter as one of them nearly topples. They're wearing matching leotards and tutus, dressed for a performance, but each has a distinct vibe in the way they accessorize. One has a chunky stone choker looped around her neck; another rocks cut-off leggings and painted high-tops; a third has tightly woven, endless braids streaked with purple. They're about my age, but they feel older, more worldly, like I could never keep up. Nearby, an old Desi and auntie and uncle sit close, a metal cart full of bags in front of them, whispering in Punjabi. I catch their eye, and they grin at me.

There's a pregnant mom with a three-year-old grasping her leg who stands near me, frowning as she stares down strangers who apparently can't be bothered to offer a seat.

There's a young musician with locs carrying what looks like a massive violin. "Viola," he explains when he catches me staring. "I go to Juilliard."

"Fifty-Ninth Street, Fifty-Ninth!" the announcer grumbles over the loudspeaker as the doors open.

Wait, that doesn't sound right. "I thought the next stop was Thirty-Fourth?" I say, panicked.

"You need downtown," the mom says, and Juilliard tugs me off the train, lightning quick, right before the doors close.

He points to a track on the other side. "It can be confusing at first, but you'll get it. Downtown, where you going?"

"Washington Square."

He points across the way. "Take the A or E to Fourth Street. Those are express." He disappears into the crowd.

Forty minutes later, I finally find Washington Square. I'm sweaty and slightly scarred from my adventures, but I take a quick second to refresh with gloss and powder, then wander toward the Italian restaurant where I'm supposed to meet Ranbir. There are tables set outside, and a long line of people waiting. Ranbir stands among them, T-shirt, shorts, flip-flops, his curls loose and wild—decidedly California right here in New York. He's looking at his phone, frowning, but insta-grins when he spies me.

I'm slightly late, fully disheveled, and so happy to see him I pretty much run into his arms. He leans down and kisses me, taking in my Cherry Bombe dress, the sandals. "Wow, fancy," he says, wolf whistling. "This is how Maya got fierce, huh?" He kisses me again, whispering into my hair, "Swipe anything from the closet for me?"

"Women's accessories today," I say, showing off a set of thin pewter bangles Shenaz handed me when I was leaving. He reaches to touch them, then takes my hand and we start walking. "But I was chatting with this guy, Xander. He's pretty much living my dream life."

"That's fun. How'd he get it?"

I shrug. "Started writing for the magazine first, I guess, then worked his way in because they liked his stuff." I take a deep breath. "He's trying to land an AE gig. And he just started college."

"What's an AE?" He's holding my hand, strolling all casual, like we live here and have done this a million times before. Maybe we have, in some other timeline.

"Assistant editor. Right now he's an EA. Editorial assistant. The first rung on the ladder. He writes and edits stuff for the website and does grunt work for print. A step up from the internship, which is how he started." Then it hits me. "Maybe he needs an intern? Or Shenaz would, at least. She doesn't have one yet." I don't even quite know what I'm saying, but the thought solidifies in my mind as the words come out. "*I* could be an intern."

Ranbir grins and grabs my hand, leading the way. "That could be cool."

I shrug. "Maybe I'll ask."

"That's a great idea." Ranbir looks down at me, the sun sparkling in his eyes, haloing them with gold like it always does. "You could do that. Fetch coffee. Sort accessories. Write things."

"Maybe. He told me to pitch him. Xander."

"You definitely should. He sounds awesome."

He wouldn't say that if he knew Xander had dubbed him Rebound Dude.

We're near the big arch from the picture Ranbir sent me. There are groups of people gathered—college kids, families with blankets spread across a few grassy patches, kids jumping in the fountain. The air is so thick and humid, the water looks miraculous.

Next thing I know, Ranbir's scooped me up, throwing me right over his shoulder, and we're in the fountain, too, drenched and laughing. "Too hot," he says, pulling me close for a kiss as my clothes cling. "Sorry if I ruined your Prada sandals."

"They're Anita Dongre. Gladiators. But Cherry's gonna have your head about the dress."

He kisses me again, and we pull apart to a small audience. "Mama," a little girl says, tugging at her mother's shorts. "Did they get married?"

Ranbir laughs and helps me climb out of the fountain. "She's like a tiny auntie in training, straight out of a Bollywood drama."

She is, except her face is delighted, not horrified and judgy, her eyes on us, smitten, even as her mama leads her away.

I shiver, shaking water out of my hair. "I think the restaurant's out."

"We've got options." He takes my hand, and we find a row of food carts. Ma would cringe if she saw me ordering from one, but everything smells delicious. Roasted meats, a falafel truck, a cupcake cart, and—

"Dosa?" Ranbir says. "The orientation guide mentioned this guy." He orders a spicy Mysore for himself and a crispy rava with onion for me. We crunch on the potato-stuffed crepes, folded neatly into paper cones, as we walk through the winding streets of the Village, baking in the sun and taking in the bustle. It's all narrow gullies filled with small shops and restaurants, some fancy, some mom-and-pop. We turn down another little lane and discover a record shop. "Oh," Ranbir says, super excited as he pulls me forward. "I've heard this place has a stash of Hindi vinyls."

As we browse through the dusty and disordered stacks, he pulls me closer again, a story on his lips. "My mom still has this old Victrola that she's had since she was little," he says, looking through the Hindi section, only three bins deep. "It was her papa's, and he had all these ancient records from back in the day—old Bollywood tunes, a few Jagjit Singh collections, a Mirza Ghalib recording. But there was one she would play all the time. I can still hear it in my head, though it went missing one day, when we moved from the smaller house to the bigger one. I always thought it was 'Champakali.' Even asked when we were in India."

"'Champabati,'" I say, filling it in as he turns to look at me, incredulous. "It's one of my dadoo's favorites. Really old school. It's a great song."

"I've been trying to find it ever since."

I help him comb through the stacks, but there's nothing that old. I find a familiar Jagjit Singh vinyl. "Ah, my dad's favorite. I'm going to get it for Roop. She's got a record player in the apartment, stashed in a corner." Then I lift up a copy of *Dilwale Dulhania Le Jayenge*. "This brings back memories."

Ranbir grins. "Classic. I haven't watched that one in ages."

"Due for a rewatch."

"Let's buy it." He grabs it and the Jagjit vinyl from me, paying the cashier.

We start strolling again. The sky is purple, the sun dipping slowly. Not quite California, but a strong effort. "We should head back," I say. "The trains are mostly hourly on the weekend."

He grins, excitement in his eyes. "One more stop?"

A breeze picks up as the sun settles, the streetscapes changing from brownstones to skyscrapers, the numbers climbing as we walk and walk and walk, Ranbir checking his phone every so often.

"My feet are going to pay for today," I tell him as he leads the way, like he's done this a million times before, like he knows every inch of the city. "Do you know where we're going?"

"Most of Manhattan is a grid, numbered, easy," he says, as if he made the map himself. "Streets from top to bottom, avenues left to right. Hard to get lost. Except in the West Village, where you can be on the corner of Tenth Street and Tenth Street somehow. Learned that the hard way. But we're headed in the right direction. Toward Penn Station."

We walk a few more blocks, then pause in front of another Indian restaurant. All people do in this city is eat.

"More food?" I groan.

"Gimme one minute." He pops in and steps back out moments later, hands full. I can't believe my eyes. It's kulfi, sweet and melting and tall, on a tilla, shaped just like the Washington Monument.

"Tille-wali?" I shout, because I can't help it. "I didn't know they did that here."

"They have everything here." He grins down at me, holding both sticks out. "Rose? Or mango?"

"Both," I say, taking them and walking away with a grin. But he grabs me, kissing me again as I lick the rose first, then the mango. There's ice cream all over both of us.

"Okay, then," he says, laughing, as it dribbles on our hands, on our clothes, in our hair. "Guess we'll just have to share."

8

IT'S THE DRUDGERY FOR ME. AN ENDLESS CYCLE OF MILKING cows and shucking corn and lectures that make me want to nap. (Guilty. And I'm hardly the only one.) But the other part of it is the whispers, which waft like garlic fumes, thick and heady, overwhelming. Dolly and Jiya and even Guru stalk every move Ranbir makes, which means I live in the fishbowl by default, too.

"Let's move it, ladies!" Thursday morning, the sun's barely up, and I'm already over it. The humidity is oppressive, the sun unrelenting, the weather report promising rain that never comes. But Dean Maxwell's got the bullhorn out, determined, directing people to their tasks. "You three"—he points to me, Marcus, and Ranbir—"cows. And you girls, Guru, to the greenhouse for picking and sorting. We've got a lot to do this morning."

And New York beckons, inviting and seductive, but Shenaz has been frantic, focusing on closing the September issue and gearing up for October, so I haven't been able to run my pitches by her. And I don't know if she'll want me to tag along again. Maybe I can convince Ranbir to take me this weekend.

I hear the words in my head and want to squash them. I don't need him or anyone else to take me, I remind myself. I came all the way cross-country to Cow Camp solo. Well, I mean, it would have been solo, except Ranbir showed up on the plane in the next seat or whatever. I scoot away, putting space between us. It's only been a few weeks, and I'm already acting like that creeper. Like, missing him since his class started or whatever. I vow to make my own plans this weekend. Maybe even take myself into the city. Maybe.

The earthy scents of manure and hay waft around us, shaking the sleepy-headed among us out of our morning stupors. I still hate 6 A.M. call times, but Dolly and Jiya are all bright eyes and high ponytails, their makeup impeccable and their clothes actually ironed. I'm in shorts and a Sassy Sherni T-shirt Cherry made, bubble gum pink with a rhinestoned lion about to roar. I'm pretty much through my entire wardrobe now, though, and desperately need to do laundry. There's none in our building, and I haven't caught Roop or Shenaz long enough to ask about it.

"Hey, does Easton have a washing machine?" I ask Ranbir. He turns to look at me like he forgot I was there. Awesome.

"What?"

"Laundry."

"Oh yeah, in the basement. Why?"

"Do you think I could, like, come wash my stuff?"

"You want to come over?" His voice is low, his grin sly. I worry for a second that he's going to kiss me again, right then and there on the bus, but he reads my expression and pulls back.

"The girls don't have a machine."

"Sure. Sunday? It's a date," he says, too loud, as the bus rolls to a stop. There's dead silence. Everyone heard. But no one says a word. As I shuffle ahead, I feel his hand clasp mine, warm, firm, all-encompassing, little patakhas of energy shooting right up my arm and down to my toes.

Then the daggers in my back, as usual. "Can you believe that bitch?" The words ring loud and clear, and when I turn around despite myself, Jiya's smug. Though the glare Ranbir shoots her shuts her up fast. But Dolly looks slightly stricken, and I can feel Ranbir tense up.

I try not to be annoyed, but I can't help it. "You should go talk to her," I say, and step away from him again. He needs to figure this out. I need to give him space to do it, as much as it sucks. I should focus on making the most of my summer. I'll work on coming up with the perfect pitch.

Marcus laces his arm through mine and tugs me full speed ahead. "Come on, gorgeous. We got work to do."

The morning is cow-milking duty—and Berta and Martha are not nearly as grinny as the horses, given the circumstances. Then we herd all the sheep into the pastures for their morning feed. There are a few little lambs among the group of twenty, and they are the most adorable things I've ever seen, fluffy and stumbling and mewling. Ranbir and Marcus usher them along via the sheepdogs, while I pick up one of the lambs and nuzzle it as we walk, posting a few selfies with the hashtag #lamblove. Cherry instantly comments with a thumbs-up and a tag for #cherrybombe and #sassysherni, which I totally forgot.

Our last task before lunch break is picking corn in the fields. Marcus is on the tractor—a little too excited—plowing through. So Ranbir and I take a few baskets and wander toward the far side, plucking the ears that look ripe and ready.

"The cornfields always remind me of my family's farm just outside Tarn Taran," he says as we round the next row. I can't stop watching his forearms, the strength in the way they stretch and flex as he plucks each ear of corn. "I haven't been back in years. But it would be fun to go."

"I was like seven when we went last," I say. "We never really get a break from the farm." Even now, Ma barely has a moment to chat. I miss her. "Especially during the summer harvest."

I can almost smell the waft of garlic, the scent of it curling around my ankles and nestling into my hair, making itself permanent. But I shake it off. I'm here, all the way across the country, as far from it as I could be. New York is just across the river, beckoning. I can't help but be jealous of Ranbir. I wish I was going, too.

"Do you love it?" I ask him. He pauses as he reaches up, about to pluck another ear of corn. "The class?"

"The material is intense. But it's amazing—my teacher has an MFA from Juilliard. Juilliard! Even if this is it, the one chance I get, it'll be enough."

Or it'll leave you wanting more. At least that's what it was like for me. At *Fierce*. "I'm really glad you decided to take the chance. Opportunities like this are rare."

He nods, looking deep into the thicket of cornfields, like he can see some shiny future beyond them. Or maybe that's just my wistful thinking. "It'll do. It'll have to." He waves one of his long arms around, the pale green corn husk glistening with dew and sun. "Because honestly, I have a lot to go back to, a lot waiting for me."

Me too. But at least he'll have tried. Me, I'll just keep following orders, marching down the path set for me. I should take my own advice, take a chance, pitch that story. Ask Shenaz about interning. Worst they could do is say no. Then I'd still be standing right here, in the fields, picking corn. Or garlic.

Today, though, I can't complain that much. The fields here are emerald and endless. They make me miss the winding roads of the Pacheco Pass, up the road from Gilroy, the fields of green and gold against those stunning blue-and-pink skies. When the orange rage of the fires dies down, at least. Cherry and I usually spend hours at the fruit stands each summer, selling tourists too-cheap baskets of strawberries and ripe avocados and, of course, garlic. Makes me want to dig my hands into the soil, to absorb the energy of the earth like we do in planting season. But here it's cornfields as far as the eye can see, ripe for plucking.

"Golden," I whisper to the stalks, which are taller than me. "Thank you for your service."

I giggle to myself, start filling up a basket quickly, chatting with them like I would with Cherry. I spill it all—the drama, my *Fierce* adventures, how Cow Camp makes me think I'm not quite cut out for #farmlife4ever. How those little pitches I've been crafting don't add up to much, but maybe I need to shoot my shot. "Do you think I should just hit send? I mean, probably as good as it's going to get, right?"

"Did you say something?" Ranbir says. I didn't realize he was still here. But when I look up, he's barely a foot away.

"Talking to the plants," I say, heat crawling up my throat.

"My mom does that sometimes." Like sunshine, that smile, bright and dazzling. "She heard it—"

"Helps them grow, yup." I pull a couple of cobs off the last one, whispering warm wishes into the thicket. "That's what my mom says, too. She's definitely got a green thumb."

"What did you say to it?" He inches in slowly.

"None of your business," I say, trying to step around him. He has me cornered, towering over me as I'm caught between him and the endless rows of corn, absorbing heat and cardamom.

"Is it me, or is it hot?" I say, ducking away and reaching for my water bottle.

"Definitely you," he says, grinning at me as I sip, water dribbling down.

It's sweltering, and I'm sticky slick, my T-shirt clinging like honey on a hive. I find myself wishing for rain again, the way my mama always does. The heat here is different, and it makes me dizzy. Or maybe that's just Ranbir. I catch him staring as I take another swig of water, his eyes lingering appreciatively even though I am a literal mess. I splash him with water, and he ducks and laughs, catching me by the waist and swinging me around, cornfields circling as far as the eye can see, straight out of a Bollywood film.

"More like a Punjabi movie," Ranbir says, reading my mind. "Except I don't have dark roots and blond spikes."

"And I don't have a fancy sports car that you just crashed into with your tractor." I laugh as he pulls me closer. "But maybe I should call my papa and his thugs to take you down anyway."

"You could try." There's a gleam in his eyes, and the sun makes a little halo around the edges, like copper edging into gold. "But they'll never find us here."

"Kheton mein," I say, and laugh, and he smiles down at me before leaning to brush his lips to mine, soft and salty, stubble scratching my skin. There's that familiar, flowery hint of cardamom, sweet and sharp all at once. No onion this time. Nervous, I gulp for air and start giggling, and he starts laughing, too.

"We do have the whole field to ourselves." His voice is low and rough in my ear, different from before. It makes my stomach flip and my heart race.

"Ah, but the auntie network has eyes and ears everywhere," I say, pulling away a little. I'm not even joking. If my instincts are right, Dolly can't be far away. Can't say I blame her. He's all sweaty and, yes, slightly stinky, but he looks good, his curls all tousled and pulled back, his skin bronzed from too much time in the sun.

"Then let them talk," he says, kissing me. My knees go weak, and I guess his do, too, because next thing I know we're rolling in the tall grass, and he wins, the weight of him pinning me down. *This is going to stain*, I think to myself, then he kisses me again, soft and sweet, and it's like my brain finally stops overthinking every single thing for a minute. We don't come up for air until we hear voices in the distance—Marcus, but others, too. I scramble away, but there's nowhere to go. Ranbir's still in his kissing stupor, reaching for me, delirious. I pull myself together the best I can, ready for Marcus to catch us in the act. Well, not *the* act. But, like, kissing or whatever.

The voices get closer, louder. One voice anyway. That wakes Ranbir up a bit. I'm on my feet now, pretending to focus on my basket, but Ranbir's still on the ground, cornsilk in his hair, the shine from my lip gloss on his face. Oops. I give him a hand, and he grins up at me, sheepish, then scrambles to his feet. I rub lip gloss off his mouth, and he grabs my hand, still amorous, but I

89

snatch it away just as Marcus, Dolly, and Jiya appear. Guru's right behind them, carrying a full bushel of Jersey tomatoes, grumping as usual.

"Guys!" Marcus says too loudly, announcing their arrival. Smart kid. "You ready for lunch? Because I'm starving."

"Yeah, we're just about done here," I say, taking another big gulp of water from my bottle. Ranbir's watching me again, still not totally together, and it's a bit adorable and a little infuriating. Does he want to get caught?

"You guys only did two baskets?" Jiya says, perpetually annoyed. "Maxwell isn't going to be happy."

"Maxwell's never happy," I say. "And it's like ninety-five degrees out. So I don't think we did too bad."

"You look like you fell in shit or something," Dolly says, her voice acidic. "You could really use a bath." Then her eyes land on Ranbir. "Both of you."

Dolly's furious, I can tell, but Marcus shrugs and starts talking about weighing and parceling corn. "Two whole baskets are way more than I would have managed in an hour." He high-fives Ranbir, who's still grinning. "Way to go."

"I don't think you should be out here in the cornfields alone," Jiya announces, channeling the nosiest of aunties. "It isn't proper. I might talk to Maxwell about that. What would your parents—"

"How would they ever know?" Ranbir says, cold, silencing her instantly. "Unless someone here took it upon herself to tell them?" He looks pointedly at Dolly, who's still seething but leans in closer and pulls a strand of cornsilk from his hair.

"Well, I did promise Rami Auntie I'd keep an eye on Maya," Dolly says, her voice dripping sugar now. "After all, Maya's here all by her lonesome. And Auntie and I have been connecting a lot lately."

Wait, what? I must look confused, because she's got this thrilled, vampiric grin going, like she's going to sink her teeth into me any second. "Haven't you heard? Your mom, my mom—they're going to be partners. Spice Goddess is in talks to license the infamous Gera Garlic chutney for our new line. The perfect pairing. So delicious, so unique." She bares her fangs again. "Wouldn't want anything to mess that up, right?"

The heat is making me dizzy. I must have heard wrong.

"What are you talking about?" I ask, taking another sip of my water. My mouth is suddenly so dry. "She's not licensing anything. She wants—"

Dolly laughs, and I swear the fangs get sharper.

"Ask Rana. Or Guru. They talked to the Pathaks, too. But Daddy made them a deal they couldn't refuse. Gotta save that precious farm, right? What is it now, Guru? Twenty whole acres—"

It's like the earth has spun right off its axis. My heart races, and sweat slicks my skin, which feels oddly clammy and cool. Like I'm going to be sick. Cherry said Papa was taking meetings, but this is ridiculous. It can't be true. But that glimmer in Dolly's eye as she stands there, basking in everyone's attention, reveling in the way my face fell, my jaw dropped, tells me she's not messing around.

"That's bullshit." Ranbir is one thing. My mom? That's too much.

"Ask her." Dolly bites her lip, all drama, pouting. "She's been complaining that you never call. That she's spoken to me more than she's talked to you. Maybe I should tell her you're too busy out in the cornfields."

I spoke to Ma two days ago. She didn't say a word. She didn't—

"Guess you're not the only one keeping secrets, Maya," Dolly says, laughing. "Don't worry, though. We told Auntie we'll keep you informed. And we'll keep her up-to-date, too, if you want."

Her eyes flash toward Ranbir again, the look she throws him meaningful.

He reaches for my hand, but I step away. "Do not call my mother again, do you understand?" I say, and the bite makes her close her mouth, finally. "I can take care of myself and make my own decisions." I start to walk away, Marcus following, trying to take the basket from me.

"Seems to run in the family," Jiya calls after me, and I freeze, turning around slowly. "That penchant for trouble. For drama."

Oh hell no. I turn around, my fury enough to help me take her down, even though she's like twice my height. Marcus tugs me back, holding me in place.

"Been hearing about your cousin," she says, her tone all scandalized. "And her roommate." She waves her hand like a fan, and in that moment, I could drop the corn and strangle her. "Does Rami Auntie even know? Would be a shame for her to find out this way."

"Shenaz is awesome. They're not hiding anything. They have no reason to," I say. "And she has nothing to do with any of this."

"Sure she does," Dolly says. "After all, she's supposed to be your guardian. And here you are, completely slutting—"

"Completely what?" Ranbir says, stepping between us, staring her down. I'm frozen in shock behind him. The word stings like she actually slapped me across the face.

But his intervention shuts her up. For a minute, at least.

Marcus takes the basket in one arm and grabs my hand, pulling me away. "Come, let's get you out of here. Before you deck her and really get in trouble."

I follow him back toward the greenhouses, rage simmering like acid in my stomach. "Did you—did you hear what she called me?"

"Man, Maya, don't listen to her bullshit." I still can't believe it. The chutney. The farm. My mother. That word. "The drama those two bring." He's pacing now, my stress contagious. "But maybe you and Ranbir should cool it a bit. Let him deal with her."

I try to shrug, but I can't move my shoulder. "I mean, all we did was kiss," I say, my face streaking, wet. Am I crying? This all got intense fast. Way too fast. Marcus pulls me into a hug, but he's sticky and sweaty, which makes me step back. "How does that—how am I—?"

Marcus starts unloading corn into the big bins, then pauses, looking at me, his face composed, his voice careful. "Maya, I know you like him, but is it worth it? You got lucky today. What if Maxwell catches you? Or Dolly says something to your mother? She's clearly a wreck." He smiles, but he's serious. "These rich kids—you know how it goes. What if what she said about this whole thing—this deal—is true? What if your parents actually need this to work?"

It can't be true. But he's right. If it is, I may have screwed everything up.

"I get it, I do," he says with a sigh. "Being the oldest, seeing how hard your parents have worked, knowing it's all going to land on you, it's a lot. I've been there. It's why I'm here. It's why you're here." He shrugs and takes a deep breath. "They get to spend the summer away, have their fun. But you're not like them. You're like me. You have real responsibilities. And from what Dolly said, your parents really need this. So don't mess it up. Seems like you've got a lot more to lose."

I shrug. "I shouldn't be surprised. But it just hurts that they're leaving me out of such a big decision. Especially when I'm here"—I wave vaguely toward the campus all around us—"because I'm supposedly the future of Gera Garlic. They can't have it both ways."

And I don't want this anyway.

That's when the sky erupts, finally, like a warning, a little too on the nose.

Marcus runs toward the tractor, but I let the rain drench me for a good minute, absorbing the scents of earth and water. Soaked, I pop into one of the greenhouses, thankful to be alone. And then it hits me. That familiar top note. Garlic. Of course.

It makes me sad that I can't be excited about this stuff the way Ranbir and the others are. Embracing their history, leading it into the future. I'm clearly not cut out for this. It must be

93

obvious. Why else would Ma hand our legacy over to Dolly and the Randhawas?

I dig my hands into the soil, the dirt rich and soft under my fingernails, the familiar garlicky scent curling around me like a beacon home. I'm over this. I miss my bed and my books and especially my mama's chai and paranthas. The sunrise at the fruit stand with Cherry, and essays for AP English, and telling my brothers to shut up while Ma and I watch *Mahi Way*. Dadoo's haldi doodh and bare feet on parched grass and the hug of oven heat at noon, dry and all-encompassing. Those rare breezes and fire-streaked sunsets and, yes, even that pungent garlic stench, working itself into my hair and blood.

Instead, I still have six weeks of humidity and humiliation to deal with. I'm glad the odd tear that trickles blends in with the rain and the mud streaking my face, my arms, my clothes. I couldn't bear the thought that Dolly might see me cry. Not today. Not ever.

I've made a decision. Now I just have to see if I have the strength to go through with it.

How to Score—and Defeat—a Nemesis in 7 Simple Steps

BY BECCA TAYLOR-KRAUSE

GotFierce.com

1. **It's all about the goals.** If you want what they want? If you have what they want? Time to throw down.
2. **Make it effortless.** The easier you make it look to steal that man/plan/van, the more rage you'll elicit.
3. **Raise the stakes.** You're winning beyond their wildest dreams. The challenge has been issued!
4. **Be loud and proud about your triumphs.** Bragging will definitely activate takedown tendencies.
5. **But stay sweet as sugar.** Celebrate successes with grace and kill 'em with kindness, so they never see you coming.
6. **Take the high road, even if it stings.** Making yourself look good will definitely make them look bad.
7. **Never let them see you sweat.** Keep your cool, because nothing makes them madder than knowing they can't ruffle you.

9

I CALL AS SOON AS I GET HOME. I NEED TO KNOW THE TRUTH. Once and for all. And my mother is not going to give it to me. But when Cherry answers, there's something soft on the edges, like she might cry. Or has been crying. I've hardly ever seen her cry. Not since her mom died. We were eight.

"I just miss you," she says with a shrug.

"I miss you, too." I want to tell her everything. About Dolly and slut-shaming and her threats and my conversation with Ma.

"I—" Her voice cracks, and it startles me. "Ava and I are done. Over. She's hooking up with that girl at UCLA. I knew it. I asked her, straight out. She didn't deny it. Said they—it just happened." She shrugs, trying to shake it off. "But how could something like that 'just happen?'"

I wonder if that's how Dolly feels about Ranbir and me. But he actually broke up with her first. "I don't know, Cherry pie," I say, working hard to pep up my voice. "But you know what? You're amazing. If she doesn't see that, she's definitely not worthy. And you have so many other options. All the options." It's true. People slide into her DMs nonstop, drooling, and she mostly ignores them. "Give yourself a minute to breathe. Figure yourself out."

It's good advice. I should take it myself.

She nods. "I'll work on some new designs. For fall. And help with the harvest. Or whatever."

I have to ask. "Dolly said something today. Did Ma—"

She nods again. "I told her to tell you. But she didn't want to say anything until it was a done deal. They're drafting paperwork, but the lawyer said it will take several weeks." I can see her scanning my face, looking for clues even from three thousand miles away. Unraveling my brain. "Maya. Don't do anything rash, okay?" She takes a deep breath. "I think they need this. Your parents. For the farm. For all of us."

I nod. But maybe there's something—

"I'm serious, Maya. Do not fuck this up."

I can't tell her I might have already done that. How fast it went from just a kiss to a lot more. How we almost got caught. How much they hate me. I should tell her. What if Dolly says something first? Posts something? I don't want Cherry to hear it from someone else. Or, like, go on a murderous rampage.

"This summer means a lot to your family," she says. "And to mine, too, you know? Don't do anything to ruin it." She takes a deep breath. "But try to have fun anyway. For both of us."

"Maybe I should come home." I can't stop thinking that's it. The easy answer. But I'm so close now, I can almost touch it.

"Don't you dare. You have a big opportunity here."

And not all of us get one.

She means the farm. But I can't stop thinking about *Fierce.* "You sure you'll be okay?"

"I'll survive. I'll be fine. You know how it is here, same, same. Nothing ever changes. Still no rain. Hundred-degree days. Fires burning on the hills."

"And orange Creamsicle skies."

"Those, too," she says, her eyes disappearing as she grins. "Okay, then. Have fun for the both of us. But not too much fun." She sticks out her tongue.

I nod. "I'll be careful," I say, before she adds it. Again. "Promise."

"And use some sunblock."

If I could throw something at her, I would. "You should talk."

"Love you," she says, then disappears. Like she was never there. As I shower, washing away the stresses of Cow Camp, I keep hearing that warning in my head, the one that seems to be coming to me from every corner of the universe. Good Indian Girls don't mess things up. Good Indian Girls follow the path. And keep their heads down. And don't cause trouble. Good Indian Girls don't chase their dreams, not when everyone is relying on them.

Never thought I'd hear it from Cherry.

But then again, she did say something else, too, before she evaporated. To take the chance while I have it. Like Roop and Shenaz did, pushing through, doing what they had to for themselves despite what it cost, despite the damage it may have left in their wake.

They couldn't not do it. I wish I had that in me.

And maybe I do. I have to take the chance while I have it. Right?

My stomach grumbles as I ponder my next move.

That's it. It must be done. I need to go get food. By myself. It'll be fine. I'm a big girl. I grab my keys, a couple of satchels, and head to the grocery store, about five blocks away.

It's much smaller than the ones in California, and the prices are ridiculous—$4.50 for half a gallon of milk, four bucks for bread, four bucks for eggs. But omelets are the perfect anytime food. And bagels are only a dollar each, so I pick up a stash of those, too.

Ranbir's sitting on the stoop with two bags of groceries when I get home. He smirks. "Great minds, or whatever."

"What's that?" I ask. His eyes take in my still-damp, Hinoki-scented hair and the summer dress I stole from Shenaz's rack.

He lifts up a bottle of proscato. "And a few things my uncle brought me when he swung by. We barely cook at the dorm, so I thought you could use them here." He grabs the bags I'm carrying and plants a kiss on the top of my head. I follow him upstairs as he takes them two at a time, clearly excited. But it feels weird, different. Like she ruined it. The word still stings.

"How was your class?" I fumble the keys a few times, suddenly nervous to be alone with him in the apartment.

"It was amazing." His eyes are doing that crinkle, lashes so long and dark I want to reach out and touch them. "There's only like ten of us in the class—and everyone else is older, obviously, college or grad students, and most of them have studied music profession-ally." He takes a breath. "But I think I hold my own." I finally get the door unlocked, and he follows me in, bringing the bags, slip-ping off his flip-flops and leaving them next to mine. "I brought adrak for chai, too. Thought maybe you could use some."

"Oh, that's perfect. I've been craving it," I say as he follows me toward the kitchen, and it makes me realize again how small the place is. No matter where he stands, there's barely two feet between us. "Do you know how to read music?"

"A bit. From a summer camp here and there. The gurdwara doesn't really use sheet music." His fingers tap the counter as I shuf-fle around, stashing milk and bread and the rest of it, more food than this place has seen in . . . probably ever. "I would love to take a few music theory classes, figure out the way things work."

"It's like another language, right? Or math." I put away the last few things and turn around. "A lot to learn."

He nods, staring down at me, like his eyes are memorizing every part of my face. "Thank you for convincing me to take that class," he says, stepping closer. "I wouldn't have done it, I don't think—"

"You would have. It's in you." His eyes are so bright, so curious, they're trying to read me like a book. It's too intense, the way he's looking at me. I want to step back, but the counter is behind me, and there's no place to go. I turn around, shuffling through the mess on the counter. I'm such a rude host; Ma would be appalled. "Oh, you want a drink? Or something?" I open the fridge, then close it. "We have . . . tap water. Milk. The wine. And that's about it."

"Sure," he says, and puts the wine in the fridge. "That's really it, huh?" He grabs some stuff from the bag he brought and pulls a saucepan out from a cabinet under the sink. "Chai, then?"

I nod, and watch him as he quickly throws together a pot—ginger, black tea, a couple of crushed cardamom pods—and he pops one in his mouth, as usual. He brings it to a rolling boil before he adds milk and lets it go again. I play with the jars of spices he brought as the tea brews—one has Dolly's face on it, along with the Spice Goddess moniker.

"She's got eyes everywhere," I say, trying to keep the bitter edge out of my voice, and he steps close again, taking the jar out of my hands.

"We had a big talk. I told her to back off." He sighs. "I'm sorry—I get it if you don't want to deal."

I try to smile, but it comes out awkward, pained. "I like you. I do. I just—" I take a deep breath. "It's a lot to handle."

"Maya," he says, his breath on my hair, my cheeks, and then there's that familiar sizzle.

The chai, about to boil over.

"Shit," he says, turning around and mopping up the spillover. "Salvaged, just in time."

He strains and pours the tea into mismatched mugs. I inhale the familiar spicy scent, gingery and delicious. Like home.

A few minutes later, we're settled on the couch with our chai and a few Nice Time biscuits. Thank god I cleaned up a bit.

"I talked to Cherry," I say, playing with the fringe on a pillow I've placed between us. "It's true. What Dolly said." I take a sip of too-hot chai. "But I can't imagine it out there without the Gera Garlic name."

His hand hovers near mine on the pillow, fingers tracing the fringe, the tips of my fingers. "It's a lot." He takes a deep breath. "I can't blame your mom, though, because it seems like a big process. Do you think you guys could do it yourself?"

I shrug. "We're already kind of drowning." I blow on the chai, scooping the skim of malai up and into my mouth. "I couldn't bring myself to ask about the farm, though—like, are they going to sell it? Might make sense. The whole town has felt different since the shooting, and for a long time before that really. But lately it feels even weirder, this heavy tension."

How can we call it home when we don't feel safe? Ma and the twins were at the festival that day, selling chutney. Papa and Dadoo and Uncle were at the farm, me and Cherry working the fruit stand. Ma and the boys managed to escape unhurt, but not unscathed. None of us did. It's left a scar. One that's still sore to the touch.

"And being here, it made me realize something," I say, so low I barely hear it myself. "It's not really what I want to do."

There. I said it.

Ranbir's eyes are intent on mine, even though I'm avoiding his gaze.

"But I can't not do it." I'm the oldest. And let's be honest, the smartest. "The twins couldn't handle things. There's no one else. I can't let them all down."

He nods. Looking straight ahead, avoiding my gaze. "That's the thing with Dolly. All the expectations, from her, and our families. She needs to move on, to focus on something—maybe someone—else. But we've been together so long, too long." He sighs, turning to look at me. "I made it clear that it's over. That she's not what I want."

He turns to look at me again, taking my hand, too close. His fingers trace something on my palm, a word I can't quite make out. I pull my hand away, taking my last sip of chai. "I don't know what's wrong with me. Like, my parents sent me here with such high hopes, and here I am, messing it all up. I wish I could just figure myself out."

"You already have." He shrugs. "I mean, you've known all along."

He leans in closer, his whole body tuned in to mine. A smirk tugging at his lips. Must. Not. Kiss. Him. "What?" I say. "What's so funny?"

"You act like it's some big pronouncement, this huge declaration of truth. But you've already decided. So do it already. It's your real reason for being here. Because it definitely wasn't Cow Camp."

I turn to look at him, confused. I shake my head, loosening the thought. "You mean *Fierce*?"

"You said it yourself. You need to take this chance, Maya. You needed an in," he says, logical. "You have an in. It's right there. It's so clearly yours. Reach for it already." Then he leans forward, grabs a tissue, and hands it to me. I don't know when I started crying. "Stop sniffling, drink your chai, and get it together."

I should. I stand up, firm, collecting cups, and head toward the sink. He looks disappointed, still sitting there on the couch. "My mom gave me a recipe to try," I say, taking out the giant jar. "Using the chutney. Garlic chicken and rice."

"Perfect," he says, standing. "I'll follow your lead."

He's good at taking orders. He preps the chicken—mixing the garlic chutney with yogurt for a marinade—while I chop onions and tomatoes, making a quick and easy masala base spiked with ginger, cumin, coriander, and turmeric, plus whole spices. Then he cooks the rice while I sauté the chicken the way my mom told me to, the marinade becoming this thick, red, garlicky gravy in just a few minutes. It smells like Ma's kitchen, and the homesickness that's been pinching stabs now.

"Do you like staying here with Roop?" Ranbir says, closing the few inches of space between us as he reaches for the plates in the cabinet above. There's only paper. Of course.

I shrug. "She's been pretty aloof. She's been through a lot." I gather utensils. "I feel like I barely know her." But I have to do what I can to help. I hope Ranbir's talk with Dolly doesn't make things worse. "She's always doing rounds, so I hardly see her. Thank god for Shenaz."

"And *Fierce*." He's grinning.

"She's who I want to grow up to be." I look down at my hands. They look unfamiliar, raw from all the planting and farm work, browner from the unrelenting sun, and small. Too small. Like this is too big for little me. "It's like this whole other world, one I could never be a part of. One I never saw myself in. So maybe that's sort of it. I want to tell the stories of the kids who look like me. I want to write myself into the narrative."

He's grinning again, but turns away to add some ghee to the rice, casual, like he's done it a million times before. "That's what I like about you." He turns back, his hand reaching for a stray lock on my forehead. "Prada pack, yes. But there's more to the story. Always." He steps closer again, not an inch between us. "The way your eyes totally lit up when you said that. Like nothing I've ever seen."

I take a deep breath. "I'm going to do it. Apply for the internship. Pitch a story. Take my chance, shoot my shot, whatever."

He nods, staring down at me, his eyes dark and melty and serious, his lips curving a bit at the edges, the scent of lemon and cardamon drawing me in again. "I think that's awesome."

"But I have to quit camp. And I want to." The words are sharp and pungent, like raw garlic, untempered. "Probably a really selfish thing to do, right?"

He frowns for a moment, like he's not sure what the right answer is. Me neither.

"If my parents have already given up, why shouldn't I?"

I don't mean to cry again, but I can feel the tears gathering, ready to fall. He leans closer, his thumb stroking my cheek. My heart pounds like a hammer. "Sometimes you just have to do what's best for you." He hugs me, but it's different, the tension in his shoulders, like maybe he's thinking about Dolly, too.

I step away, grabbing the spoon, stirring the pot one more time. "The chicken's ready. Should we eat?"

He nods and murmurs something I can't quite make out. I focus on plating the rice and chicken, adding a medley of cucumbers, tomatoes, and onions along the side of each dish.

We sit on the floor in front of the sofa, and I turn on the TV.

"Movie?" I ask as I scroll through. "Akshay Kumar. Nope. Salman Khan. Definite nope. Shah Rukh. Maybe?"

"What's that?" he says, pointing the remote at the screen. "In the corner. I didn't take you for a Desi soap kind of girl."

He hits play and the credits roll, giving a brief rundown of the Desi drama and antics.

"*Mahi Way* is not like one of those old-school Desi soaps," I inform him, then take another bite. The chicken is tender, the sharpness of the garlic softened, a touch of sweetness from the tomato. Not bad at all. Almost like Ma's. "It's actually old, from when I was little. Kind of *Ugly Betty*–ish. It's about this misfit girl who works at a fashion magazine in Delhi. She's too big, too clumsy, too lost in her own head. But she does it anyway. It's part of the reason I got obsessed with magazines. She's a total fish out of water, with all these Bollywood flights of fancy, but she's determined to make her dreams come true. No matter what."

I try not to shovel my chicken to stop myself from talking, but I can feel his eyes on me again. Maybe I have rice in my hair now or something? "She's too focused on guys, like falling for the obviously wrong dude while the obviously right dude is right there in front of her the whole time, and he gets the real her, but she's so clueless—I—"

He's leaning closer, our knees touching, and I can't. Now I do have garlic breath. Garlic and onion breath, actually, so this is all wrong. But I guess it wouldn't be the first time.

"I can't stop thinking about the cornfields," he says, his hands reaching for me. His face is so close that all I can see are eyes, then his nose is pressed against mine before he tilts his head a little and we just fit, lips barely touching, his arms snaking around my waist, our plates probably spilling and making a colossal mess as he closes the space between us. This time his lips are salty, spicy, the garlic heady and mellow. His hands tangle in my hair, and our bodies keep inching closer, like we don't really control them at all.

He can still hear my thoughts going a thousand miles a minute, I think, or my heart, or something, because he pulls away to say, "Shhh, it's okay." His hands stroke my cheek and then my hair, then he pulls back again, grinning.

"Wait, I'm not done yet." I scramble forward, pulling him up to the couch, right on top of me, locking us together once more as the weight of him pushes me down, his tongue tangling with mine, confounding and delicious. Garlic and onion and cardamom and citrus and a million other things, all the flavors and scents mingling together for one breathless minute, all wrong, but so very right. Too much, too fast, too intense. "You okay?" he whispers, and I nod and kiss him again, pulling him closer.

Keys clink in the lock, and the door swings open. Shenaz stands there, frozen, bright and curious and confused but smiling as she says, "Oh, hello. I didn't know we were having company. Hello, Ranbir."

Ranbir scrambles to his feet, his hand running through his hair sheepishly, then offers me the other so I can get up, too.

"We made dinner" is all I can think to say, the master of the obvious. "Garlic chicken. Ranbir's a great cook."

"Yum," Shenaz says, shedding her shoes and removing her earrings, casual and relaxed, like she's used to walking in on her girlfriend's underaged niece hooking up in the living room on a random Friday night. "I'm gonna go change. Fix me a plate?"

She disappears into the bedroom. For a moment, at least.

"Should I go?" Ranbir says, all nerves again. "You're right, she does seem cool." But maybe not that cool, his worried voice suggests, ready to bolt.

"No, stay," I say, mostly because I want him to. "She won't mind." I hope.

He nods. "I'll make her a plate."

He busies himself in the kitchen while I clear up some of the mess we made.

"What are we watching?" Shenaz says, startling us both again as she settles onto the couch. Ranbir hands her the plate, and she takes a bite. "Actual food! This is amazing. Is that the garlic chutney?"

"My mom uses it as a marinade," I say, settling my plate onto my lap as I take a seat on the couch, too. Ranbir sits on the floor, a safe distance away. Smart boy. "With yogurt so it stays tender."

"Roop is going to love this," Shenaz says around another bite. "She always says she misses your mom's cooking." Then she adds, "Does she know about the boy? Your mom?"

Caught. Ranbir shrugs. But I'm the one she's asking. "She knows of him. Of his family." I pause, taking a deep breath. "I think she would approve." I can feel Ranbir grinning again, but I don't dare look his way. "But maybe she doesn't need to know just yet?"

"Uh-huh, well, it's not like I'm going to tattle. You're a big girl. But do let us know if you're going to have company."

I nod. "Of course."

"And we've got to do something about all these secrets," she adds, shutting us both right up.

We eat in silence for a few minutes before I dare to speak again. "I was thinking," I say. My voice is so tentative, I want to shoot myself. Instead, I focus on speaking it into existence.

I perch at the edge of the sofa. "Remember you mentioned that *Fierce* didn't have a fashion intern yet this summer? Right when I first got here?"

She nods. "The one we had got hired at *Cosmo*. But LuLu's making final decisions this week. We need the help."

My face falls. "I'm too late?"

She taps her lower lip, the way she always does, thinking. "Maybe," she says. "Maybe not. Do you have a résumé?"

I shake my head. "I'll make one?"

She looks at the calendar on her phone, slightly frantic. I lean in and watch as she slots me into LuLu's calendar in the only empty spot. Monday morning, 10:30 A.M. "LuLu gets final say." Then she turns to look at me, her face falling. "But Maya Memsahib, the internships are full-time. You can't—"

"I can. I will." I've decided. One way or the other. "This is what I want."

"What about camp—"

"I'm not going back," I say definitively. "There's no salvaging it. I mean, they're talking about selling the farm. To Dolly and her family, of all people. So why am I torturing myself? When I have this once-in-a-lifetime chance—"

She nods sagely. "You have to do it."

I take a deep breath. "You think there's a shot?" I think about what Xander said about getting in the door. Some people do a thousand internships and never really make it.

"Worth a try," Shenaz says. "We'll figure it out. And you've been helping me already." Shenaz pauses, her spoon lifted halfway to her mouth. She waves it a little in my direction. "We'll work on your look, dollface. Now shush so I can finish my chicken." Then she hits play, silencing us all as we bask in the glow of the TV. "Oh, *Mahi Way*. Love that show."

This will work. It has to.

I'm about to make all my fiercest dreams come true.

10

MONDAY MORNING DAWNS DREARY AND DISASTROUS.

"I'll be okay," Shenaz says, but the way her lip and eye have puffed up, all swollen like a softball hit them (I know from experience), I find that hard to believe. She can barely blink. "Maybe there were nuts in it." She sighs. "Sometimes they add them. It'll wear off. Eventually. But I can't show my face like this." She leans in toward the bathroom mirror again, shrugs. "So you better get a move on if you want to catch the eight thirty."

"There's no way." The panic makes my voice squeak. "Reschedule. I can't do this alone."

She grabs my shoulders, steadying me, then grins, which makes her look like a lopsided jack-o'-lantern. Unfortunate. "You can and you will. This is a big-girl job, so you have to be a big girl. And LuLu doesn't reschedule. So if you want this—"

"You know I do."

"Then get it together." She ponders my wardrobe, combing through her couture rack. "Get in the shower. Now."

Once I'm scrubbed clean, Shenaz dresses me in a few strategic pieces that pull together an NYC vibe. "The blazer is a layering piece," she says, posing with it over her shoulder like one of Cherry's fave '70s Bollywood stars. "It pairs nicely with this print skirt and a silk shell. A little staid, maybe." She taps a finger on her lip, thinking. "Oh, I have just the thing." She runs back to the clothing rack and rifles, returning with two items. "The teal of the butterfly scarf will really stand out against your skin. And these sandals are to die. Let me see your toes."

Not good. Shenaz grimaces. "Guess Cow Camp was hard on the feet. We'll fix that. But no sandals today." She heads back to the rack, combing through a box of shoes. "The Lisa Lees it is." She hands me the velvet slip-ons.

She turns away, sneezes, and grabs another tissue. "Oh god, here it comes again."

"Bless you." I really do mean it. She's like Oprah, doling out miracles. "For real."

She smiles, still swollen. I want to hug her, but she looks wary. "Go get dressed. Now."

She passes me a small vegan leather Valentino backpack, my phone—loaded with a map app—and the blazer. "Take the train in like we always do; tell Tony to send you up. It'll be like a five-minute chat—who you are, why you want to work at *Fierce*, why fashion. She's great; you'll do fine. Done deal. She'll love you. Promise."

My stomach churns—definitely need a bagel—but it's the thought of going solo that's got the bile going. "I'll get lost. I'll say something silly. Are you sure we can't reschedule? Maybe this is a bad sign."

"This is a hundred percent a sign. That you need to decide. Listen, I hauled my ass across an ocean for this gig. You'll be okay taking a train solo. But make up your mind: Do you want this? Or no? Now or never, right? So what will it be? If you can't even take the train by yourself, then—"

"You're right." I swallow hard. "I want this. More than anything. I better move."

I barely make the train, and it's too crowded to find a seat. But a little more than an hour later, I'm finally in Manhattan. And alive.

I race forward, my body half carried, half shoved along the path to the stairs by an endless wave of commuters. Do they do this every day? It seems quite soul sucking. No wonder grown-ups stay mad. Here they are in the greatest city in the United States, some might even say on the whole of Planet Earth, and they can barely muster even the tiniest spark of excitement.

I follow the crowd up the escalator. Where do I go from here? I look at my phone and the instructions Shenaz texted. Exit on Eighth Avenue and Thirty-Third, then walk up nine blocks to Forty-Second Street. Straight shot. No detours. Fifteen minutes tops. And don't talk to strangers.

"It's just a grid," I say to no one and myself, letting the bustle carry me, making sure the numbers on the street signs are going up, not down.

The Empire State Building is to my right, about two avenues away. Stay on this block and walk away from it. But away from it where? There are three other possible directions, and to be honest, none of them look particularly appealing. "Times Square?" I shout at the people passing by, who mostly ignore me. But one points and keeps on moving. Do I follow? Could this be right? I peer at my phone, the *Fierce* address locked on Google Maps. It tells me it's a straight shot up Eighth Avenue, just like Shenaz said.

I walk, taking bold strides, looking straight ahead (with occasional peeks at the map on my phone). Shockingly, the little dot is getting closer. Slowly but surely. By the time I get to the building, I'm pretty sure my makeup is melted, but I'll try to find a bathroom before I meet LuLu. Looking around to get my bearings, I realize I'm standing right in front of the McIntyre-Scott Tower: 682 Eighth Avenue. I'm here. And in one piece.

I follow the bustle through the lobby. It feels enormous, all chrome and glass and shiny, pretty people. I get to the desk, and there's Tony. He waves me up. Thank god.

I can't believe I've managed to pull it off—so far. But it's only a matter of time. I try my mom's slow breathing trick to calm myself down, closing my eyes and counting backward from ten to one. When I open them, there's someone standing next to me, smiling. Xander.

"You beat me here," he says. "Just barely."

"Huh?" So very articulate.

"Working in the closet today?"

I shake my head, hitting the button for thirty-two. "Interview. Ten thirty." I look at my phone. "Shit." It's ten thirty now.

"Cool." He calls after me as I bolt, just as the elevator doors open. "Break a leg."

With my luck, I will.

Ten minutes later, I finally find the "fashion pod," as the snarky receptionist calls it. There's no one there. Not a soul. Just endless cubicles. I pause at the one with pictures of Shenaz and Roop pinned up. It's sheer chaos and endless racks of clothes, no doubt headed to the closet. No actual people. And definitely not LuLu.

I can't even be upset. I'm the one who's late. I wouldn't hire me either. I've ruined everything. Again.

I stand around for ten minutes, then twenty, trying to figure out what to do and where to go. I text Shenaz.

> **SHENAZ:** Sit tight. LuLu will be back, sooner or later, and definitely when she wants her half-caf triple soy matcha latte and Cobb salad, oil and vinegar on the side. Which you should get for her if she asks.

I'm fidgety, so I snoop, peering at the fall fashion spreads pinned to the giant hot-pink corkboard—for the October issue already, judging from all the Halloweenie-ness—then combing through the pictures and accessories on Shenaz's desk.

Then there's LuLu. Oh god. She looks cranky but beautiful. Simple black shift dress, hair pulled back, strappy sandals.

"H-Hi," I stammer. "I'm Maya—your ten thirty." It's nearly eleven fifteen now, I realize, looking at my phone. "Shenaz—"

LuLu sucks her teeth and looks me up and down, taking in the ensemble Shenaz carefully pulled together for me like she's checking off boxes. I'm doing okay, I think. Then she gets to my feet. Last season's shoes.

"Nope. Not fashion," she says, and disappears. Gone. Just like that.

"Wait," I say to no one. "Was that it?"

I'm not sure what to do, so I text Shenaz again. No response. Do I go home? Wait for LuLu to come back? Sit down and bawl? I wonder if this mascara is waterproof.

After what feels like forever, I decide to take a seat in Shenaz's chair. It's turquoise-blue velvet—all the chairs here are jewel-toned silk or velvet with gold accents, and I kind of want to eat them— and I adjust it to rise and then fall.

I can't resist. I must spin. Fast. And furious. I haven't done this in ages—years, even—and it's a true delight, the way all the poppy colors of the *Fierce* office mix and mingle and form a mishmashed rainbow in my head.

A woman walking down the hall pauses to ponder my splendor, smiling as she passes the pod. She's tall and Black, with braids hanging down to her shoulder and a really familiar face. Oh, I know why. She's only slightly my idol, and I've seen her do TV a gazillion times. Even when the Gilroy shooting happened. Ericka Turner. Features editor. The woman who assigns all those cool stories I love reading. She interviewed Beyoncé in last month's issue, and it was epic.

"Are you my delivery?"

I stop spinning short, but the world's moving on without me. Whoa. Maybe I am in a dream. "I'm sorry?"

"Thai food?" she asks, looking slightly concerned as she steps closer. "They keep sending people to the wrong floor."

I grin. I should say something. Anything.

She scans my face. "Oh wait, you're obviously not delivering. Are you my eleven thirty? Maybe *I'm* late. I thought I asked Becca to cancel—"

"I'm here for an interview." But not with you, I should clarify.
"What'd you order?"

"Green curry with beef and a side of curry puffs. PURE makes
the best ones, crispy but not greasy."

My stomach rumbles. I never did get that bagel. "Have you
had Cambodian food? Where I'm from, there's this big community, and it's sort of close to Thai, but also crosses over with Lao-
tian. And the flavors are amazing. Lemongrass, a muted chili, the
brightness of lime, a sour punch of tamarind."

"Are you a writer, doll?"

Oh my god. I don't know how to answer that question. I never
really had to say it out loud before. "It's Maya. And I hope to be.
I mean, I'm trying."

Ericka throws her head back and laughs. "Aren't we all?" The
delivery guy ambles through, bag in hand. Just when things
were starting to get good. "There you are. Thank you." She
tips him and turns back to me. "Wanna try some of these curry
puffs?"

The way my eyes light up—and the drool probably hits the
floor—she knows she doesn't have to ask me twice. I follow her
up two flights of stairs, then down the hall toward her office. It's
bright and airy, with a pocket door and a wall of windows. She-Ra
and other girl-powered collectibles sit ready for a fight on the win-
dowsill, books by authors like Morrison and Coates line the shelf,
and an old record player claims one corner of the desk, a stack
of vinyl bearing names like Nirvana and Dylan. But the view is
what captures my attention. It looks right into the heart of Times
Square. Peering a thousand miles down like that might make me
dizzy. But I can't stop looking.

"It's pretty fucking cool," Ericka says, unpacking her lunch
onto the desk. "I still can't believe this is my office now. So, writer
girl, tell me, where are you from?"

"Gilroy. Northern California. The Garlic Capital of the World."

She passes me the box of curry puffs, pushing forward the dipping sauce. "Home of the garlic festival—the one that . . ."

"Yup." I sigh. "It's definitely left a scar. But the community seems to be stronger than ever." A little lie, a little hope.

I take a small bite of the curry puff. She's right. Airy, crisp, tender but crunchy, with a flavorful mix of veggies inside. Not greasy. "This is amazing. I've never had one this light before."

"Try the chili sauce."

"How could I not?" I dip, and take another bite. I'm sitting here, eating lunch with my idol. Amazing.

"What interested you in *Fierce*?" she asks, and it hits me that this is actually an interview. In features instead of fashion. The best possible mistake. And finally, a question I know the answer to.

"I've been reading it ever since my cousin gave it to me when I was ten," I say, confident and confessional, the way Shenaz suggested. *What's your why?* I can hear her say in my head. "Forever ago. It's a window into all these different, amazing worlds, lives I could never live. I can try them on for size, walk in someone else's usually super-fancy couture shoes for a day. I love the feel of the paper, the clean lines, the way the colors pop on the page. I read the website all the time, but there's something about ink and paper that feels sacred."

"For someone so young, you feel like an old soul."

"I mean, I'm on my phone all day, pretty much. But looking at the actual magazine, it's like a literal escape. No distractions. Just headfirst into stories."

She smiles again, scooping a small portion of green curry and rice into a bowl and passing it over. "What would you say could use improvement here?"

A trick question, one I knew was coming, thanks to Shenaz's weekend prep. But I've always known my answer. "It's the same critique I've had since I was ten. There's a real lack of diversity in both the staff and the coverage. You're here, and Dulcie St. Claire just took the reins. I'm really excited about what that means. But it's not enough. I want all of us to feel seen, and while I love the magazine, I don't think it's there yet. Maybe I can help with that."

"Well said. So you *are* a writer." She scoops up the last of her curry.

"More like a dreamer. And you're living my actual dream." Then it occurs to me. "Do you want my résumé, by the way?" I reach for my bag. Shenaz helped me pull it together. "I have a hard copy."

She shakes her head. "I don't do résumés." She pushes the bowl away and grabs a notepad. "I think they are a tool of the systemic problems in publishing—used to weed out talent that doesn't 'fit the culture.' Talent that this business badly needs." Then she laughs. "Ask me how I know. Thankfully, I'm not the only one who believes that, or the first. It's how I got in the door here with Legend Scott a few years ago and how Dulcie ended up as editor in chief." She takes a deep breath. "I'd rather learn about the way you think, the person you are, the ideas you bring to the table."

"That's amazing." I'm floored, not quite sure what to say.

"So tell me, Maya. What's your favorite recent thing you read in *Fierce*?"

"I loved that article last month on how to manage anxiety as a marginalized person—dealing with microaggressions on top of everything else."

"And systemic racism, too," she says with a sigh. "I'll be honest, that was a tough one to get through the top of the masthead."

I lean forward, intrigued. "Really? It was brilliant."

"I agree. But before Dulcie got here—and it's only been a month—everything went through the old editor, and you've heard that story. And"—she lowers her voice—"Jude always had final say. Still does, sort of. But the new mandate should temper that."

"Is that why they brought Dulcie—I mean, Ms. St. Claire—in?" I spent the weekend reading all about it, but I want to hear Ericka's take.

"There have been countless controversies lately about the very whiteness of publishing. A lot of necessary upheaval. But women's magazines were relatively unscathed. Until now. Legend was all about it—especially with all the nonsense the previous editor, Lilly McIntyre, put everyone through for thirty years. But it was Jude's family, so of course he protected her." She takes a deep breath. "Then there were some lawsuits, which I'm not at liberty to discuss." She grins. "But Dulcie is like this little tornado, clearing all the nonsense right out of here. And I think the numbers are what finally started to sway the board. About forty percent of our readership is women of color. It's a battle to serve them well, even with Dulcie taking the helm. Because—and this is so off the record—like eighty percent of the staff is 'nice white ladies.' And they just don't get it."

Should I say it? "About that," I say, then reconsider. Maybe this will kill my chance. But looking at Ericka's face, open and interested, I think I have to. "I've actually been published in *Fierce* before. A letter to the editor. Back when it was Lilly."

Ericka raises a perfectly groomed brow, intrigued. "Oh yeah?"

"About that Indian Stunner spread."

Ericka drops her head to the desk. "That one. Hall of shame, totally." She sighs. "So appropriative. I'd like to think that would never happen on my watch. But sometimes I'm overruled."

We sit in silence for a minute because I don't know quite what she means, and I'm a little scared to ask.

Her phone buzzes, my chance to ask lost. "I'm sure you fight every day," I say. The words sound hollow.

"The numbers need to shift, on staff, in edit, in sales, in marketing, across the board. Bottom line. Maybe you can help with that." She sighs and shuffles some papers. "Remind me of your full name, Maya—"

"Maya Malhotra." It just comes out. The byline I always imagined. My name and my mom's, fused. Right there, in ink, on the masthead. On all those *Fierce* stories.

"Maya Malhotra. I like it. I'm going to decide on this in the next few days because I need the help. You could be a contender." She finds the file she was looking for and pushes it my way. "Why don't you send me some updated clips and this edit test? By Friday, latest. Then we can catch up and figure this out."

I take the papers and shove them quickly into my bag. Edit tests. For interns. Ouch. But worth it, either way, just to see what it's like. To live the dream, even for a minute. "That sounds great. It was awesome meeting you, and thank you so much for everything you've done. You're one of the highlights of the magazine for me each month."

Ericka smiles and stands, papers in her hand, as she starts to walk me out. "I look forward to reading your work. Friday?"

"Definitely," I say, racing to keep up the pace. I need to pinch myself. But I don't want to wake up and see the dream disappear. "Either way, thank you so much for sitting down with me. It's truly an honor to walk these halls."

Ericka stops short, smiling down at me near the lobby door. "That's lovely to hear," she says. "It's how I used to feel about this place, too, once upon a time. It would be nice to have someone who's actually excited about working in magazines, about working here. I feel like you're a dying breed."

"Here I am, alive and enthusiastic." I wince.

She grins. "Bye, Maya Malhotra."

She closes the door and disappears, like a figment, and then I do really pinch myself. It hurts so good. This is real. An internship at *Fierce* might be mine. I could actually have the opportunity to live my dream.

I'm not about to blow this chance.

As I'm walking out of the building, still floating, I get a text from Ranbir:

How'd it go? Missed you today. Then he adds: Told Maxwell you're sick.

I text him back: Tell him I'm sick all week. Maybe we'll celebrate this weekend. By doing laundry?

He sends back a smiley face emoji. Oh yeah, that.

I've got to figure this out, and fast. But that should buy me some time, at least.

I retrace my steps from this morning to get back to the train, pausing here and there to take pictures. The city feels less intimidating now that I can meander and take it all in. It's a faded version of what I imagined, all neon and glowing, but the crowds still have this energy, a collective pulse that throbs just under the surface. It latched on to my heartbeat, digging in, holding on. Like I'll never be able to readjust to the slow and steady of the winding roads and hills of Northern California.

I pick a few photos to post—one of Times Square, another of a sad mime, then a selfie with the Empire State Building in the background. The perfect caption:

Still dreaming and wide awake.

Then I send one to Ma—me in front of a kati roll shop on Thirty-Ninth Street. I take my mango lassi and lamb bhuna roll to go, walking and eating and relishing my actual, current reality. I still can't believe it.

On the train, I text Shenaz that I'll grab her some more allergy meds and tell her all about my day once I'm home, in person. I pull out the test Ericka gave me and look it over. It's like four pages long, including a call for story pitches, a two-page story to edit, a grammar and usage quiz, and a short personal statement. Days' worth of work. For an internship! They sure take this stuff seriously at *Fierce*. But I know I can hack it.

I watch the world go by as New York turns into New Jersey, and ponder the graffiti out the window. There's the girl and her lion again. *Fierce*, I think, then laugh. That's how I feel right now, in this moment. Fierce. It's delicious.

When I get home, Shenaz is slumped on the couch, dozing and watching *Mahi Way*.

"How'd it go?" she asks, immediately perky. "Not a peep from LuLu."

I sit down, tentative, and break the news. "I saw her. For like a minute." I sigh. "She looked at me, said, 'Nope, not fashion,' then disappeared. Never came back."

She shoots straight up, wide awake now. "What?" Her brows are perched, ready for takeoff. It's really cute. "Shit, Maya. That's not good."

"I waited in the fashion pod for like an hour, but no one was around."

She flops back onto the couch, defeated. "That's it, then, no internship." She looks slightly devastated. "I can't green-light you without the okay from LuLu."

I lean back, too, trying not to beam. "Actually, I think I might have gotten an internship anyway. In editorial."

Shenaz leans forward and peers at me. "What? How?"

I give her the rundown—Ericka, Thai food, the chat we had.

"Ericka Turner wants to hire you?" She's up and pacing now. "I'm truly gobsmacked. She's major. Major."

"She's only, like, my idol."

"And she gave you a test?" The pacing is making me a bit dizzy. "For an internship?"

"Yes. It's a lot. But I think I can do it. Will you look it over for me?" I pull it out of my backpack and show her, so she finally sits again.

"That's intense. But doable. I'll totally help. First: food?"

Oh yeah! "I brought you a kati roll. Chicken tikka. No nuts. I asked."

She leaps up again. "Maya Memsahib, you are my hero!"

11

I SHOULD BE AT CAMP. BUT NOW THAT I'VE DECIDED TO QUIT, I can't say I miss it. I spend the rest of the week working on my edit test, researching a gazillion pitches, reading and refining the story I'm supposed to work over, and crafting my personal statement. I start it and delete it a hundred times, until it finally hits me, what I want to say about the magazine and what it means to me. How it shifted my world and my view. How it forced me to claim my own story.

> "I grew up on a garlic farm in Gilroy, California,
> selling produce street-side to tourists, helping
> my mom with the cooking and cleaning, living
> for adventures and opportunities I'd never have.
> The only reason I knew they even existed was
> because I read about them in *Fierce*—a magazine
> I've subscribed to since I was ten years old. In it,
> I followed the stories of girls just like me, except
> they got to do big things, like discover new ways to
> purify water, or direct their first movie at seventeen,
> or even train for a mission to Mars.
>   In the pages of *Fierce*, I learned that it was okay
> to dream big, to turn dreams into goals, to embrace
> my inner fierceness and claim my space in the world.
> Even if it was only at a fruit stand in the thick of
> garlic fields.
>   Reading the magazine forever also solidified my

love of storytelling in all its forms, from the Found Fashion on the streets of New York and across the globe, to the personal essays that revealed big, bold insights about the world through tiny, specific details. And most especially, in the profiles that shared what made my biggest heroes tick.

One thing that always stood out, though, is how rarely I saw girls who looked like me on those pages. In fact, that's what led to my very first *Fierce* byline, if it counts—and I hope it does.

In the magazine's thirtieth anniversary issue, about five years ago, I was thrilled to see a fashion spread called Indian Stunner. It featured heavy gold-worked lehengas and bright, poppy saris that reflected my own Punjabi heritage. Truth be told, it was the first time I'd witnessed my own culture represented in major media that wasn't a Bollywood movie.

But even there, I couldn't really see myself. Every model in that spread was white. I didn't quite understand what cultural appropriation meant at the time, but it sure did pinch when I saw it. Because I was still missing from the narrative. From my very own story.

Things are starting to shift now, with the addition of strong voices of color, like Legend Scott, Dulcie St. Claire, and you, Ericka Turner. But I hold fast to that memory, that moment, because it serves as a real reminder. Seeing that story in the pages of *Fierce* helped me unravel something critical.

Sometimes, you have to claim your Fierce, take the reins, rewrite the narrative. That's what I've decided to do now by applying to *Fierce*. I'm writing myself into the story. And I can't wait to share it with the world, so other girls who look and feel like me can see themselves reflected, too."

By Friday, I've refined my statement a thousand times. I think it works. I know it works. But I live in a bubble, and I need another human's opinion. I make Cherry read it, and she assures me it's great. But she has to. She loves me. Or she will until she finds out what actually happened.

"When will you find time?" she asks again on video chat, her eyes scanning my face, curious, skeptical.

"I told you, it's a weekend thing," I lie. "An internship, writing for the website. I'll take whatever I can get."

She shrugs. "Don't overwhelm yourself, Maya."

I can hear the rest of it in my head: *Our future—the fate of the farm—rests in your little hands.*

Maybe I should just tell Cherry the truth. But I couldn't bear to see the disappointment on her face. So I just live in my head and focus on *Fierce* and making my test the best it can be.

I haven't been to camp in a week. Ranbir told Maxwell I've got a summer flu. And Shenaz fudged it when he called to check on me. But they're going to get suspicious soon. I have to send this thing in today.

I take a deep breath and hand the edit test over to Shenaz for her take. She clicks here and there, tapping away furiously for a few minutes. She stares at the screen for an endless, infinite moment. My heart falls into my stomach watching her. Maybe it's not as good as I thought it was. Maybe it's awful, terrible. Shit. Maybe I'm not cut out for this at all. Maybe I should pack my bags and go home. That's truly the logical thing to do. Back to Cow Camp. Back to the farm and garlic and cozy chai and TV nights with Ma. Heaven and hell all in one.

I can't give up so fast. I have to make this work.

Shenaz finally turns away from the laptop screen, peering at me curiously. She doesn't say anything for a minute, then two, then three, just stares.

"You're driving me mad," I say, hovering. "If you hate it, just tell me, rip it off like a Band-Aid. I can take it." I have to.

"Maya Memsahib, I'm astounded. A lot of people want to work in magazines. It's not an easy world to break into—especially as a brown person." That's it. I'm not cut out for this. Fact. A person who actually would know just laid it bare. "You have to be good." She pauses, all dramatic. "And, Maya, you're good."

I haven't quite managed to pick my jaw up off the floor, so she just rambles on. "You nailed it," she says. "Like the quiz could go to print as is, it's that clean." She's beaming. "Send it. Right now."

She stands, super pleased with herself and the world. "And for the record, dollface, garlic or no garlic, you're definitely an NYC girl."

She waltzes off, shuffling through the couture rack, and I stare at my laptop screen. It's now or never. I compose an email, as professional as can be, thanking Ericka for her time and our chat, and attach my document. Then I hit send. I've done my best. It's make-or-break time now. The fate of my summer, and maybe my whole life, sits in her hands.

The rest of the day is endless, but I try not to check my email. She probably had a million applicants, who all sent their tests today. "At least a week," Shenaz keeps reminding me. "And it's Friday night. Go do something fun."

"Oh yeah, I am," I say, grinning. "Laundry."

* * *

The basement's empty when we get there, a veritable heaven of washing machines. But painful to get to. Ranbir helped me drag two whole bags' worth of clothes down three flights of stairs, then across the street to Easton. I brought everything I have with me to wash, so I'm wearing shorts and a T-shirt today, even though Shenaz frowned mightily about that. I grabbed her and Roop's stuff, too, as a surprise. It's an odd mix of scrubs and haute couture, so now I'm sorting, checking each label carefully, into two separate loads, one hygiene clean, one delicates, exhausted by my efforts.

But Ranbir's got mine pretty much sorted and started, measuring a dash of detergent and a splash of softener and slashing a credit card to run the machine. "Hey," I say as it kicks into gear. The heat settles into my cheeks, permanent now, as I snatch away underwear, dropping it into the machine like a bomb. "Let me do that stuff."

"I'm not looking, just sorting, I swear." He leans down for a kiss. It's sweet and sharp—no garlic, no onions, just lemon and mint and always cardamom. "Want to go up to the dorm? This stuff will take about an hour." I nod and follow as he leads the way.

Suite 605 is quiet. "They're at the pool," Ranbir says, looking at the clock as we kick off our shoes. "You hungry?" I shake my head. We head toward the sofa but discover Guru sprawled across it, passed out, the flat-screen flashing a soccer game on mute. There are a bunch of beer cans and empty bags of chips on the coffee table in front of him, but he seems good and zonked.

Ranbir frowns, grabbing the stuff and tossing it all in the trash. "Sorry it's such a mess. Four guys, you know how it goes."

I follow him into his room. It's pretty bare, and very much what I imagine a dorm room to look like: sun streaming in through two wide windows, two desks, two beds, a shelf of agriculture books. But there's sheet music pinned to the bulletin board over his desk, and a stack of folders from NYU.

He shuts the door, then scrolls through his phone, putting on some music and syncing it with the speaker. "Look what I found."

It's "Champabati," the song we talked about at the record shop. It sounds tinny, far away, but it always did. I can't believe it. "They do actually have the vinyl at this place in San Fran, so maybe we can go find it when we're back," he says, running a hand through his curls.

"That would be awesome. My dad would be thrilled." We're both grinning, frozen in place, him at his desk, me standing in the middle of the room, awkward. The moment seems endless.

I finally decide to take charge, sitting on his bed—the one that's made, so I think it's his, anyway—and leaning back against the wall. It's surprisingly soft for a dorm bed, not that I've experienced many dorm beds. The sheets are cool against my skin. God, I miss actual beds.

He plops down next to me, our arms and legs touching. My heart races. I should have read more of those Mr. X stories. I should have read all of them. Then maybe I'd know what to do now, how to navigate this. But I guess Ranbir knows, because he takes my hand, tracing along the lines in that same familiar pattern, the one he's done before.

"What are you writing?" I ask, watching as he does it again.

"Your name, silly." He grins. "In Gurmukhi."

"You know how to read it?"

He nods. "You don't? We learned in Punjabi school, all of us. Mandatory. Every Sunday at the gurdwara."

"We never went," I say. Maybe it's because my dad is Sikh, my mom is Hindu. Or maybe it's because it was too much on top of everything else. "Kind of wish we did, though. I can't read Hindi. I can't read Punjabi. My parents just wanted us to be really good at English, to be able to figure out all the things they couldn't when they first got here."

"All the translating." He's still tracing, and it tickles. "It can be a lot."

I turn to face him, my leg slightly over his, which is all sun toasted and really hairy. "Where'd you learn to do laundry like that?" I ask. "And to cook? Like, that rice came out flawless, with

126

the little scoop of ghee. The grains all separated. I can never get it quite right."

He shrugs. "My nanima taught me. She's lived with us a long time. I can do laundry, I can make rice and chicken, I can make aloo ke paranthe. I can pay bills and balance a checkbook." I must look confused, because he takes a deep breath, then starts again, looking straight ahead. Still holding my hand, though the tracing has stopped. "It's a long story. One I don't talk about a lot. My mom has breast cancer. She's had it on and off for, like, forever. Since I was little. For a while it went away. But it came back, pretty hard-core, about four years ago. Before me and Dolly got together, sort of. Her family is one of the few that knows about the cancer, and they're like—family." He sighs. "So when we started hanging out, everyone got really excited. Because it was like a part of the puzzle was solved. Like it was meant to be." He's looking at me, trying to figure out what I'm thinking, but my face is stone. "It was the one thing that was easy. But the pieces don't quite fit. And now it's hard to untangle it."

"Your metaphor doesn't work," I say. I'm not trying to be an asshole. It just happens sometimes. "But I'm really sorry. About your mom."

"She's really sick now," he says, his voice cracking. "My mom. So it's bad timing, messing all this up. But I can't let Dolly think we're forever when I know it's not true."

I sigh, resting my head on his shoulder for a minute, holding his hand. It's a lot to absorb. I don't know what to say.

"My mom isn't thrilled about it. The breakup. The uncertainty. That's part of the reason I'm here. I mean, aside from the whole First Big Step thing. She thought maybe this would fix it, help me figure it out, being away from her and the cancer and the drama. Being away from everyone's eyes on us all the time. And it did help me figure it out. Just not the way she wanted."

"Oh man, do I know what you mean," I say. "That's what my

parents wanted, too. But now it's all messed up, with this chutney deal, and the farm."

"And me." He's tracing again. "I really like you, Maya. The way I can see every thought in your head right on your face. Yes, even now. The way you're strutting one minute and stumbling the next. The way you have all these big dreams in your head, and you're not afraid to chase them."

I literally laugh out loud. "Not afraid?" My heart is pounding again, like it might just burst right through my chest, like it might explode right here on this bed, all over both of us, a giant mess. "I'm like the biggest scaredy-cat that ever lived."

He shakes his head. "No you're not. You're here. You keep pushing people, shoving them out of their safety net, making them chase the things they want. Like Cherry. Your mom, with the chutney. And me. And you finally started taking your own advice."

I turn to look at him. "What if I don't get it?"

He leans toward me, his eyes soft, melty. He grins. "You will. I know you."

Then we're kissing. This time I started it, sweet and slow, pulling him closer. I'm on his lap, and his arms tighten around me, and the blood's rushing in my ears as the kiss deepens, my hands in his hair. His tongue pushes its way into my mouth, familiar, soft at first, but then more aggressive as his hands slip under my T-shirt, searching for skin. He finds my bra strap and pauses, pulling back to look at me. "Is this okay?" he asks, and I nod. He unhooks it in one fluid motion, sliding straps down my shoulders, pulling it right through my sleeve. Too easy, too practiced. "Pink," he says, tossing my bra on the floor, and something flickers in his eyes.

That's when the spiral starts. One minute we're sitting, and then he's on top of me, his mouth hot on my neck, his hands roaming. I guess he hears it in the way my breath goes fast, feels it in the way my body tenses. Because he pulls away again, sitting up, and helping me up, too. "Too much, too soon, maybe," he says, and I nod, even though my whole body burns, the heat expanding to every inch of me, head to toe. "It's okay, Maya," he says into my hair. "We don't have to do anything."

"But I like kissing you."

He grins. "I like kissing you, too. But we can go as slow as you want."

I nod again and pull him back down toward me, so we're both lying on our sides, facing each other, the way Cherry and I do when she sleeps over. Close enough to talk in whispers.

"Will you tell me a story?" I ask. "About when you were little."

He kisses me lightly on the nose. "Okay." He thinks for a minute, then grins, his eyes crinkling in that familiar way. "When I was about seven, my nanima first came to live with us. She was very strict and stern, and Simi—she was three at the time—was definitely her favorite. Even though Nanima was the one who started calling me Rana." *King.* His voice is soothing, a melody, and I close my eyes to listen. "Sim was sweet and easy, and Nanima didn't have to chase her around the whole day like she did with me. I was always stealing underripe peaches from her tree—I like them better when they're crunchy, still a little tart, and it made her mad. 'Bhagatha retha hai,' she'd always complain to my mom. One day, though, she came up with a solution. And honestly, it was a stroke of genius. She bought me this little motorized vehicle—you know the kind kids have. But this one was special, customized just for me, big and blue, with a two-seater up front and a truck bed that could hold a whole bushel of peaches, maybe even two. That's right, Maya, when I was seven, I got my very first truck. So you can, in fact, blame Nanima for my truckboi status."

I think he's still talking, somewhere in my head, but when I open my eyes again, the room is dark, the sun gone. I'm alone on the bed, covered with a soft blanket. I sit up, looking around, trying not to let panic settle. But Ranbir's right there, on the chair at his desk, in the glow of a desk lamp, humming something with his headphones on, fingers tapping a specific rhythm with a pencil. Next to him are the laundry bags, everything washed and folded, my pink lace bra sitting right on top.

"Hey," I call, and he smiles.

"Guess you were tired," he says, standing, flipping the lights on. "Snoring away."

"I don't snore." Do I? "What time is it?"

He shrugs. "Like eleven." Then it strikes him. "We should probably get you home. But the boys got pizza. You want?"

It occurs to me then that I am, in fact, starving. "Yeah."

"Just so you know, they can be a lot," he says as I stand, ready to follow him out the door. He turns back, the grin hitting his eyes. "You should probably put that on first," he says, waving toward the basket. Oh yeah.

Five minutes later, I come into the living room, and he's right, it's chaos. There are six dudes gathered, and four pies scattered in various fractions all over the table, like one of those horrible math problems. I look for Ranbir, but he's MIA.

"Hey, Lachi," Marcus says, stuffing his face with pepperoni. "You look like you're feeling better." He laughs. "Sit. Eat." He scoots a little, making a tiny space for me on the couch, which is covered in crumbs.

"Uh, I'll stand." I grab a slice of something with vegetables and frown, shaking off sleepiness. "Wait, what did you just call me?"

"Lachi." He shrugs. "You know, like Ranbir—"

"What do you mean, Lachi?"

He looks stressed, like he messed something up. "I don't know. It's what Ranbir always says when he's talking about you. Lachi. He said it's sharp. Sweet. A little unexpected. I thought it was cute." He looks a bit abashed. "Why, is it like a family name or something? My bad, Maya."

I almost swoon, it's so sweet. *He calls me Lachi.* Secretly.

Marcus is still confused. "You okay?"

"It's elaichi," Guru says, uncharmed, as he picks at the pepperoni on his slice. "Cardamom." Then he thinks about it. "Fits, I guess. Though it can turn bitter quickly."

Ouch, what'd I ever do to him? I guess he's always been Team Dolly. I thought it was because he was, like, into Dolly. I'm sure he'll report back to her on my disappearing into their room for like eight hours on a Friday evening. Oh.

Ranbir comes out of the bathroom, yawning. "We should probably go, Maya. Shenaz keeps texting me."

Oops. "I made the mistake of giving her your number."

He frowns, then grins. "No big deal." He grabs both sacks of laundry, and I wave to the guys as I follow him out the door, slice still in hand.

"You okay?" he asks as he lugs the bags up the stairs, trying his best to make it look effortless. I keep offering to help, but he waves me off.

"Yeah. Thanks for the laundry. And the pizza. And the kissing."

He drops the bags in front of the door on the fourth floor, his breath ragged. "Anytime," he says, turning to go.

"I'll let you know when I hear." I take a deep breath. "Hopefully soon. I know I have to talk to Maxwell."

He nods. "It'll be a yes." He looks at his watch, stress ridging his forehead. "I should go. But let me know, okay?" He plants a kiss on the top of my head and disappears.

12

THE EMAIL HITS MY IN-BOX BRIGHT AND EARLY ON SATURDAY morning, which means an instant rejection, right?

But it's not. Just a single line:

> I'd love to offer you the role. Can you come in
> Monday at 10?
> —Ericka

I rub my eyes for a moment, staring at the screen, trying to absorb what it says. It can't be real. But it's right there, in black and white, all lit up.

You meaning *me*. She wants *me* to work for her. As an intern. In editorial. For *Fierce*.

I sit in stunned silence for a minute, knocked out of it only by the tremors that rock my body, the salt of my tears. The first step toward my literal dream job. The first step into the rest of my life.

I look one more time, to be absolutely sure. But I can't trust myself. I have to be dreaming. So I respond immediately, without thinking or discussing or overanalyzing.

> I'll be there. And thank you!—Maya

And *then* I panic. "Shenaz." My voice sounds far away, floaty, like I'm actually in a dream. "I need you to look at something."

She looks at my tear-stained face and pulls me into a hug. "It's okay, Maya," she says. "It was a long shot. But you're so young. You can still work for me in the closet. And you can try again."

I shake my head and hand her my phone, watching as she scans the screen. Her eyes light up, a huge grin taking over her small face. "I knew it! I knew it!" She jumps up, nearly dropping my phone, and spins me in a half hug, half dance. "It's going to be perfect. I'll be your manic pixie fashionista godmum, we'll give you a makeover, we'll grab lunch, I can't wait!" She spins some more, and I try not to jump up and down with glee. "But Monday's looming. We've got a lot of work to do."

"We do?"

"You need to set up a bank account and make sure you have your paperwork in order—ID, you can use this address, of course, and maybe working papers, since you're under eighteen," she says, tapping her lip. "They'll go over that stuff once you get there. And you can still do weekends in the closet. Which reminds me: Most importantly, we need to figure out what you're going to wear."

I follow her into the living room, watching as she combs through the rack for options. "Nope, nope, nope, maybe, hmm . . ." She ponders, turns to look at me, appraising, then turns back to the rack. "I wonder . . . no. Or maybe—" She glances back at me again, then tugs at my hair, braided but frizzing. "A deep condition, yes. Maybe a mud mask, too?"

Another email pops up, and we both freeze for a second when we see Ericka's name. Maybe she's realized her mistake and is emailing to take back the offer. That must be it. I click it open, wincing:

> Great! I'll be on a shoot. Look for Becca, who'll get you settled. And yay!
> —Ericka

I sit on the bed, the weight of what just happened crushing me for a second. I don't know whether to panic or dance or curl up into a ball and go to sleep. Never in my wildest dreams did I imagine that I'd actually get to work at *Fierce*. That I'd be worthy of walking those hallowed halls. That I'd be able to work with Ericka Turner, who's one of the biggest names in publishing. It has to be a mistake. I'm just a kid, and a pretty clueless one at that. What if I can't hack it?

I must have said that part aloud, because Shenaz squishes in close, wrapping an arm around me, and says in that sharp Brit accent, "Of course you can hack it. You're seventeen and you just got your dream gig, Maya Memsahib. Because you rocked that edit test. You have a voice—and something to say. Some people don't figure that out their whole lives, whether they're seventeen or seventy. That's what Ericka saw in you."

"You think?" I stare at the email again, snapping a picture, in case it disappears.

"Your essay made me weepy—and you know I don't even bother with waterproof mascara. You got this, Maya. You earned it." Shenaz stands. "I'm going to go take a shower, and then we'll get to work. Now make me some chai so we can properly celebrate."

I spend the rest of the day plotting with Shenaz, who decides on three different outfits for me before scrapping them all and starting from scratch. It gets old fast, so I text Ranbir and ask him to meet me for a walk.

"I brought you something," he says, holding up a manila envelope. I make a grab for it, intrigued, and he laughs. "Don't get too excited. It's just the withdrawal paperwork. For Cow Camp."

"But I didn't even tell you yet."

He shrugs, tugging me close for a kiss. "They'd be stupid not to pick you."

"I start on Monday. Shenaz has been making me try on potential first-day outfits all weekend. It's as exhausting as it sounds."

He laughs, but something's off. He's still hungover from the shenanigans, I can tell. He keeps rubbing his eyes and yawning, even though it's almost dinnertime. We grab a couple of iced coffees and head toward the waterfront, the sun glinting off the Raritan River like stonework on a blue velvet lehenga. I snap a picture for Cherry.

"Remind me never to drink with Marcus again," Ranbir says, taking a long sip of coffee. "I may be the Punjabi one, but that kid can throw down."

I raise a well-groomed brow—another of Shenaz's weekend projects. "Seemed like he'd already had quite a bit when I left."

Ranbir rubs the back of his neck, sheepish. "You missed all the antics." He grins. "Sobbing, yelling, gossip, drama." He grimaces on that last word. "There's been some tension between Dolly and Guru. Did you know they're hooking up?"

I stop short, his hand tugging me forward. "What?"

He shrugs. "Yeah, caught most of us off guard. Even Jiya didn't know."

"I can imagine." I don't mention Guru's jab the other night, though it pinched. "Must be weird for you."

He shrugs. "Not really. She can do what she wants." He steps closer. "I've clearly moved on."

"But he's your roommate."

"That was the point, I think," he says. "She wanted to get my attention. But I usually make myself scarce when she shows up. They've been hanging when I have class." He leans in, whispering, even though there's no one really around. "By the way, she still thinks I'm with you on Monday and Thursday nights. They all do. Except Marcus. And I guess Guru." He sighs. "Sheet music and stuff." His breath is warm in my ears, his arms slipping around my waist. "Hope that's okay."

He leans down for a long kiss, not waiting for an answer. It's sweet and sharp, like cardamom, and his hands are all tangled in my hair, wavy now that it's unbraided. I pull away, trying to catch my breath, looking around for spies. Or aunties in training. But it's mostly college kids, a few medical residents.

"I'll keep your secret if you keep mine," I say, and tug him forward again.

His eyes crinkle, catching sun and glitter, and it's breathtaking. "I can't wait to see the words you write. Your name in print."

Oh yeah, that. My words, my name. For the world to see. Something I'll need to figure out for sure. Because the world is one thing. But my parents? Totally another.

"I have to figure out what to tell them. My parents." I take a deep breath. "It's going to break their hearts, I think. Maybe I shouldn't say anything at all. Ride it out."

"Or you could just tell them." He's looking down at me, the little line between his eyebrows working, that tension right on the surface again. "Maybe they'd be happy for you."

I shrug. "They don't tell me anything. So maybe I'll return the favor."

But part of me wishes I could share. The good news. My words and my stories. Let them see their own name, their legacy right there on the page.

Sometimes I feel like I'm not the right version of Maya, the one they were expecting, the one they hoped for. I always do exactly the wrong thing. "I can't tell them. Not yet. That's why I need a pen name."

Ranbir nods, staring out at the Raritan River, murky as the sun starts to set. He steps back a minute, something flashing on his face again. Pain, maybe worry. "Ever imagine what it would be like?" he asks, his head resting atop mine, his voice so soft I have to snuggle closer to hear. "If we could just do what we want, chase our dreams? I can almost see us here next year, college and the chaos of it, the freedom. You working there at *Fierce*, taking journalism and writing classes, me studying music, taking you to concerts. All the things we'd do, the places we'd go."

I grin. "I kind of felt that the day we were in the city, eating kulfi. Like that was the right timeline."

"I know I can't have it, though," he says, and there's that stabbing again. He winces. "She's getting worse. My mom. They're not saying it. But I can feel it. And she keeps pushing me toward it anyway. Telling me to do what I want, to be what I want. Insistent. But what will be left of us, of my family, when she's gone?" He says it like it's inevitable. "What will happen to Papaji, to Simi, to me? I have to be there. To pick up the pieces. But sometimes I wish I could just be free."

I nod. I get it. I do. Always stuck, trapped. But it's not the same for me. Not as hard to let it go. There's not as much at stake. Or maybe there is. And I just won't let myself see it. Feel it.

"Then it's like you said," I say, pulling him closer again. "We just have to make the most of the time we do get."

He nods and leans down to kiss me, soft.

The apartment is empty and sticky when I finally make it up the last flight of stairs, huffing and puffing. Farm life's got nothing on a four-story walk-up. No one is home, as usual. Roop's on call, and Shenaz has a shoot. I'm a mess, sweaty and gross, and the quiet should be soothing. Instead, it's lonely. I keep thinking about Ranbir and his mom, and before I know it, I'm calling my own.

I hit video chat, and Ma's face pops up on my screen, mostly forehead, the graying baby hairs a little crown on her head, a slick of summer sweat streaking her cheeks. She's sipping chai, watching Desi soaps while she's got some peace and quiet in the house before dinner. The boys are probably holed up now, unshowered and playing video games, and Papa and Dadoo are no doubt still supervising the first haul in the barn as the sun starts to set. I haven't talked to them in days, but it's always like this during the harvest.

"Hi, beta," she says, teeth flashing on-screen as she grins. She pulls the camera away a bit, and I can see her, finally. Don't cry, don't cry, don't cry. "Ki gal si?" Her face is instantly worried. "Homesick? Tummy trouble? What's wrong?"

137

I shrug, sniffling. "I just miss you," I say, realizing how true it is as soon as the words fall out of my mouth. "It's too much. The people are terrible, the days are endless, it's so hot and sticky and—"

I can't tell her about Ranbir and his mother. I can't tell her about *Fierce*. I can't tell her about the incident with Dolly. I can't— But the tears are falling again, whether I want them to or not.

"Dolly says you're going to license the chutney?" I try to keep the judgment out of my voice, but there it is, underneath, like dry rot trying to dig its way through. "To Spice Goddess. I thought you wanted to do it yourself?"

Mom sighs. "It's too much work." The defeat on her face flattens me. "Papa has no interest, and it would cost so much, and I don't know anything about business. If you were older, then we could do it. You'll learn so much in this program, and maybe it would be different. But—"

"Ma, that recipe's been in the family for ages," I say, sounding like a whiny child, even to myself. "You can't just give it away—"

"I'm not giving anything away," she snaps, and I can see her teacup shaking. "There is a way to meet in the middle, beta. A way to embrace and celebrate your past while building your future. Don't fault me for trying to find that way. For all of us. Papa made a good deal, after a lot of thinking, a lot of talking. They will pay for it, and pay well. And it's better to be able to share it, nah, rather than just have cupboards full to hoard for ourselves. Then my mother's legacy can live on. Otherwise it might just die with me."

Ouch. But she's right. I've never actually bothered to learn how to make it. Or much else. Just the few things I've helped her on, here and there, everyday stuff like thari chicken and dal. "Maybe you can show me?"

I can hear what she doesn't say: too little too late. That I've never had any interest before, as hard as she tried to teach me, to get me excited, to get me invested. In the chutney, the farm, all of it. It's always been a chore. How can I guarantee her my interest in the future when I've barely been present? *And you don't actually want to*, the voice in my head reminds me helpfully. But I can't just let it all go, can I?

"Mama, please." I have to try. "I'll help, I swear. I can figure it out, if you just give me time."

"Maya, bachi, there is no time." There's this finality in her voice, resignation. It kills me a little. And makes me wonder what she's leaving out of the story. What I still don't know. She takes a wobbly sip of tea. "How is Roop? And her roommate? Are you eating okay?"

I shrug and wave the phone toward the kitchen. "They've been working a lot." I need to soften it before she freaks out. "But maybe—" I need to do something, anything, to fix it. To make her at least feel like I'll be okay. Even if I don't feel okay. "Maybe I'll make them something tonight." I sigh. "I should go." It's already getting late.

"So quickly?" The pout settles, familiar, and I realize she's where I got it. "I thought we could watch *Mahi Way*. I've been waiting."

I look at the clock. It's nearly seven thirty. "Okay, Mama, I think I can do one." I find the remote, click on the flat-screen, and find the episode where Mahi pitches her own column to the editor in chief, one about women's issues. But then one of her colleagues takes an idea she suggested and scores the gig instead.

"Oh, this one is my favorite," Ma says, clapping her hands gleefully.

"Ma, you wouldn't believe what the *Fierce* offices were like," I say, even though she's already absorbed in the show. I wish I could unravel it somehow, find a way to tell her without shattering everything. "Way more glam than Mahi's office. And right in the middle of Times Square. I can't wait to go again."

That gets her attention. "Beta, I don't think you should go to Manhattan by yourself."

"I'm never by myself. Shenaz—"

"Shenaz is a stranger. And Sukhi Mamiji—I don't want trouble."

"Okay, Ma," I say, quiet. There's no point arguing once she gets something in her head. And she doesn't have to know. If they can keep me in the dark, then I can play that game, too.

"Go see your mamiji, beta," she says, her eyes on the screen. "It's been weeks. Roop should, too."

"I'll talk to her about it." I can't concentrate on the show anymore, between the rumbles in my stomach and the noise in my head. "Ma, it's really late."

I need to figure out food and Ranbir and the farm and *Fierce* and my whole life.

"Theek hai phir," she says, even though I can see the disappointment. "Maybe this weekend?" I nod, and she blows a kiss. "July fourth, time for patakhas and parties. Send me pictures. I keep imagining where you are, but it's like Punjab in my head."

I laugh. New Brunswick is definitely not Punjab. "I'll take some tomorrow. 'Night, Ma."

"Love you."

I stare at the phone for a few minutes after it goes blank, homesickness settling like the thick, sticky air.

I must have drifted off because the sun has set already when I hear keys rattling in the door.

"Hey," a voice says, flipping on the lights. Roop, not Shenaz, which surprises me. She's been on call the whole week. She's still in scrubs, her curls a wild halo around her head, the exhaustion sitting on her hunched shoulders like a weight.

"You're home?" She's carrying a bag of food, and it smells amazing. "Yeah." She sounds surprised—annoyed?—too. I open my mouth to say Ranbir has a class, but then it occurs to me that she probably doesn't care. "Did you eat?"

I can almost hear my stomach grumble in response. "No."

"I brought food. Give me five minutes to shower." She disappears into the bathroom.

I check my phone, and there are messages from Ranbir. Baby pictures, and a recent shot of him and his mom. She has the same mouth, the same eyes—the same crinkle when she laughs. I hope I get to meet her.

The bathroom door opens, and Roop shuffles out, wearing a clean set of scrubs, her favorite pajamas. Her curls are pulled into a high ponytail on her head, spilling down in dark, wet ringlets. Her face is pink from the heat of the shower, and she's trying not to scowl, which I appreciate. She grabs the bag from the counter, along with some paper plates, and sets them all in front of me on the coffee table. "Kati rolls," she says. "Chicken or lamb?"

"I'm good with either," I say, even though I'd really prefer lamb.

She hands me one, along with a paper plate, and as I unwrap it, I grin to myself. I think about the little lamb I took pictures with at the camp and suddenly feel guilty. But now I'm committed. I take a bite and can't help but savor the tender, spicy meat, the crunch of red onion, the sharp spike of mint and cilantro from the chutney. "This is delicious," I say, mouth full.

"I know it's your favorite," she says over a bite of kati roll. "It's not like I forgot."

I ponder that, trying to bite my tongue, but I have to say it. "Sometimes it feels like it."

Shock registers. "Guess I deserve that. Cherry said you were pretty upset," she says, her face flashing with stress, confusion, more stress. "I know I disappeared on you. On everyone. But the past few years have been a lot. Medical school, residency, all the stuff with my mom . . ."

"You could have told me."

"It's not like I was hiding anything. My mom's the one who—" She shrugs. "I don't know. I had to figure shit out for myself."

"But Cherry knew."

141

Something flickers in her eyes, familiar. Maybe rage. "Cherry needed to know."

"I needed you, too." It comes out so quiet, I wonder if I said it at all. But it's not the same. That much, I get.

"Ma didn't tell Buaji," she says with a sigh. "Or anyone really. She wouldn't let me either. We don't talk a lot."

I take a deep breath. "I think my mom knows. Something. But you could tell her. I mean, she knows all about Cherry, and it's not— Maybe it would help. With the tension between you and Mamiji. She keeps telling me to make sure I visit, to bring you with me."

"That's not going to happen." She picks at her kati roll, but seems to have lost her appetite. "The last time Shenaz and I saw her, it was pretty bad."

She clearly doesn't want to say more, so I don't ask. She starts wrapping up her food and stands, about to disappear again.

"How did you and Shenaz meet?" I ask. They seem so different. She grins, sitting again. "It's a really funny story," she says, turning toward me. "I was working a shift in emergency—this was before I settled on pediatrics. She showed up with a fractured ankle because she'd been wearing these sky-high heels—Louboutins, I think—and broke one in a grate. She was sobbing, and I tried to calm her down. I thought it was because she was hurt, but she was crying about—" She starts laughing and can't stop.

"About the shoes," I say. "I can understand why."

"She had just started at *Fierce* and 'borrowed' them from the closet."

I sigh. "Wow, talk about opposites attract."

"I managed to calm her down and took her to have falafel on College Avenue after my shift." She's grinning to herself now. "Then I tried to blow her off for weeks, but she just kept showing up."

Sounds like Shenaz. I tap Roop's hand, resting on the sofa, with my fingers. "I think she's pretty awesome. You guys make a good pair."

"I think so, too," she says, but pulls her hand away. "I'm glad she's been there for you the past few weeks. I know it must be an adjustment."

I sigh. "Thank you. I know it's not ideal, and three's a crowd. But I do appreciate it."

"It's family," she says, staring down at her plate. "It's not even a thing."

"And the internship—it's . . . So much more than I could have ever imagined."

She grins, briefly. "I'm glad that worked out. That you get to do it. If only for now."

She rises again, looking down at me like she used to when she was a full head taller. Considering I stopped growing at twelve, she's still pretty much a full head taller. "You deserve it, Maya," she says, and I think she might hug me. But then she checks her watch dramatically. "I've got a five A.M. call, so off to bed." She waves toward the bag. "Will you let Shenaz know there's food when she gets home?"

She disappears before I can answer.

13

MONDAY BARRELS IN OUT OF NOWHERE, A DAY OF GREAT expectations and potential calamity.

My stomach boils with anxiety, like a pot of chai about to erupt. And my fashionista fairy god mum is so not helping. Shenaz, dressed and ready, is once again considering my first-day look.

Correction: She's been pondering it for about forty-five minutes now. I'm dressed in the fourth outfit she picked before I threatened to go naked—a sleeveless pale pink silk tank and cashmere sweater (for the AC, she reminds me), a plum corduroy skirt, and silver strappy sandals, now that my toes are "appropriately done." (Nixed the neutral for *Fierce* haute pink, and she insisted on doing them herself.) My hair is down, big, loose curls, the makeup minimal, even though I think it makes me look too young. "Fresh-faced, Maya Memsahib. First impressions are everything," she keeps saying.

"I already met her."

"But you're going to meet *everyone*." She readjusts my hair, a pair of jeweled hairpins in her mouth. "Trust. I know what I'm talking about." She places another pin, pulling some curls to the side, then examines her handiwork. "Maybe a headband?" She pulls out a thin, purple sequined number.

"Too nineties." I take a step back.

But she crowns me, satisfied. "Oh, dollface, so young, so oblivious. It's seventies, way back. Like, do you even know who Zeenat Aman is?"

I turn to look, and it's actually really cute. "Yeah, Cherry is obsessed with her." But Shenaz ponders again, reaching for the headband, and I lightly thwack her hands away. "Nope. Done deal. We gotta bolt or we'll miss the train. That's definitely not the first impression I want to make. So come on, Fashionista God Mum. This time, I'm leading the way."

Miraculously, the train pulls up about two minutes after we huff and puff to the station, and we actually score a seat. The sweater is very necessary, because even the train is freezing, and I weave expertly through the foot traffic on our walk to Times Square. Then we're there, the Mac-Scott Tower looming large ahead of us.

I pause and take a deep breath. "Will you pinch me?" I ask Shenaz, and she laughs that bubbling, tinkling laugh.

"Oh, dollface, this is going to be amazing." She squeezes one of my cheeks like an annoying auntie. "Imagine the stories you'll tell when you're old."

It will make an awesome story someday. If I can pull it off.

My phone pings with a good luck message from Marcus. But nothing from Ranbir, which is weird. Whatever. Today will be perfect.

Shenaz scans me through the front turnstiles and ushers me into the elevator bank, hitting the button for the thirty-fourth floor. There are endless elegant media types milling through the lobby, the kind of people you only see in magazines or TV shows, in classic-cut business suits, designer dresses, or haute leather pants right off the runway. I can't help but stare, and Shenaz laughs again, gesturing for me to pick my jaw up off the floor. I hear the sharp clack of heels behind me and turn despite her warnings, caught.

It's her. Dulcie St. Claire. The newly minted queen of *Fierce*. One of the only Black women to be named editor in chief of a major global publication, and the only Black woman to claim such a leadership role at McIntyre-Scott in its sixty-year history.

"Hey, Shenaz," she says, stepping up all casual, like she doesn't run the world. She's in what looks like a vintage dress, short, flirty, and flowing, and dark locs tumble down her back, a new look that has all the beauty vloggers talking. Some say it's unprofessional. Others call those "beauty gurus" out on their blatant racism. As they should. "I loved your peacoat picks. Do you think, though, that we could throw a few more pops of color into that spread?"

Shenaz laughs. "I already pulled some. LuLu nixed them, but I have them stashed still because I knew you would say that."

"I'm glad you and I are on the same page about things," Dulcie says with a grin. "But let it come from me, to keep things smooth. I'll ping, and you respond with the selects. That way LuLu doesn't think you're going over her head."

Shenaz nods, then turns toward me. "By the way, Dulcie, I want to introduce you to *Fierce*'s newest team member, Maya. Ericka just brought her on."

"Oh, Maya," Dulcie says, sticking her hand out for me to shake, "so lovely to meet you. Rick mentioned your test. She was super impressed. In fact, I think Becca already has your quiz slated for the website."

Oh. My. God. Dulcie St. Claire said my name. And she's talking to me. Like, in real life.

"Awesome, you're not even in the door and you already have your first *Fierce* clip!" Shenaz says, nudging me as I stand there in awestruck silence. "Isn't that cool?" She pokes me again, harder this time.

"Cool, yes, of course, so nice to meet you, Dulcie, you're kind of like my idol, I still can't quite believe I'm here. SorryamItalkingtoofast?"

"Girl, breathe," Dulcie says, pulling me into a hug. "You're going to do great. Ericka has a good eye. And if you've got Shenaz on your team, you're all set." The elevator tings, and it's a special one, higher floors only. "Well, I've got a meeting at the top. Feels so weird to say that, still. Break a leg today, Maya. I look forward to hearing your voice."

Then she's gone, though I might still be hyperventilating.

Shenaz is still laughing when we get to thirty-four, and as she abandons me to reception in the *Fierce* lobby. To fend for myself. On my very first day. "You hardly need a babysitter, Maya Memsahib," she says as she flits off in a haze of email emergencies.

The sign looms large, those haute neon-pink letters against a pale wall. I stand there for a minute or ten, dazed, thrilled. I pinch my arm again, literally, to make sure I'm not dreaming. It hurts. And this is real. I'm standing here, in the *Fierce* lobby. Because I work here.

I breathe in the perfumed air and take a minute to appreciate it, posing for a selfie, of course. How could I not? I send it off to Cherry, who responds with immediate exclamations. Then I send it to Ranbir, too, expecting similar excitement. But he doesn't text back. Probably at camp, I remind myself. Which is where I would be, too. Except this is my new actual reality.

The thirty-fourth floor floats sky high above Times Square. Windows line one wall of the lobby, with plump, pink leather and velvet sofas set against it, so you can take in the stunning, glittering view below in comfort—even though it doesn't seem quite so sparkling at 10 A.M. Another wall is a mural of images from the magazine's history: nearly three decades of young women being fierce and feminist and strong AF. Some of the images are older than me, but they're timeless, striking and specific, as they reach out from history, demanding to be remembered.

My eyes find the ones I've seen before, their stories imprinted in my brain. There's the thirteen-year-old Syrian girl who safely navigated a busload of children out of harm's way as shells dropped, obliterating her small village. There's the youngest female chess protégé in history, one of the first girls to take the championship in a game dominated by men. There's the seventeen-year-old from Los Banos—just down the street from me, actually—who discovered a cell-splitting methodology that helped make modern-day stem transplants possible. They're all brilliant, world-changing geniuses in their own way, and reading about them from the time I was ten made me feel like I could do anything or be anyone, too.

Now here I am. The temp at reception has me sit for a minute, then ten, as she pings Becca to come get me. "No response," she says, sighing and shrugging. She hands me a bottle of water, and a copy of the July issue, which I've already read twice. Around ten thirty, she frowns. "You sure she was expecting you?"

I nod and flash the email. Ericka won't be here until noon, earliest. My first day has started out with a . . . whimper.

I fake-read for another five minutes, then reach over to the candy dish that's on the white lacquered coffee table, accidentally knocking it over. A thousand little individually wrapped candies crash to the floor. The receptionist frowns my way, busy rolling calls, so I scoot down, frantic, gathering them all back up. Do I put them back in the dish? Toss them? Offer to pay? There must be like forty dollars' worth of candy.

I'm on my knees, scooping them back up when a shadow falls upon me. All I see are the shiny, patent leather, red-bottomed loafers that almost stomp my fingers.

I follow the slim-line leather pants up to where they meet the long, lean torso of a *Fierce* icon. Jude McIntyre. The third. As in, third in line to the entire Mac Media empire. He's the scion of Jude the second, grandchild of Jude the first, who founded the company nearly sixty years ago when New York City was still thick with coal fumes and Irishmen. That's what it says on the website, anyway. He's taller than I expected, but has that familiar lanky frame, highlighted by couture leather and a Guns N' Roses T-shirt, vintage I'm sure. He's got a streak of cobalt lining ocean-colored eyes, and has definitely had work done on that plump pout.

All in all, very iconic.

Jude could be the editor of *Fierce* or any of the Mac magazines. I mean, technically, as the company's heir, he gets final say on everything. That reportedly ruffles Legend Scott, the music and media mogul who bought 49 percent of the company to revitalize it four years ago, when it nearly shut down amid major publishing shutterings. Legend brought in a slew of new titles, focusing on men's upstarts, like *CozyBoy* and *TechBro*—things that center subcultures. They've been dueling ever since. But Jude found his footing and reclaimed his spot in the news by running several of the magazines' gossip sections, chock-full of juicy blind items fed to him by famous friends. He obviously rocks at it.

"Are you lost?" he asks, uninterested. "You definitely look lost."

Ah, that signature snark. Also iconic.

I gently place the bowl, refilled with candy, back on the table and scramble up to stand. He towers over me by at least a foot.

"Jude McIntyre, so lovely to meet you." I stick out my hand, trying to be professional, but I may have already lost that battle. "I'm Maya."

"I'm about to get this ridiculous assistant fired." He looks at his watch. "Breakfast run, my ass."

"I'm supposed—I'm supposed to meet Ericka Turner. Features. Starting today."

He rubs his chin with his thumb, clearly unimpressed. "One of Dulcie's new imports. Should've known." He looks me up and down again and sighs. "Guess you can come with me in the meantime. Or do you need to do HR stuff?"

"I'm supposed to find Becca first. In editorial."

He scowls, clearly ready to make me not-his-problem. He slashes his ID, and I grab my bag, running to follow. "Come on."

Then a voice. Familiar. "Hey," Xander says. "Having a rough morning?" He looks at Jude, at me, at Jude. "I got her," he says.

Jude waves me away. "Take her, then." He disappears before Xander can even answer.

"Wow," Xander says, suppressing a laugh. "Seems you made an impression."

I guess I did, for better or worse.

"Glad you got your first Jude run-in out of the way," he says as I follow. "I have to say, I didn't realize it was you."

I'm confused. "What?"

"Maya Malhotra."

Oh. That. "It is—Gera, I—" Don't want my mom to find out? I can't say that.

"Pen name. I forgot. I'm supposed to show you around." The dimple appears briefly. I realize I've missed it. "Come on, I'll introduce you to Becca."

Then he leans toward me, whispering under his breath: "You're in for a wild ride."

14

WE WALK THROUGH AN ENDLESS HALL—THERE ARE CUBES AS far as the eye can see, and at each sits a real *Fierce* employee. I scan the room for familiar faces—and, let's be honest, anyone brown, besides me and Xander—but they're hard to find. Mostly white, but each is rocking a different, carefully cultivated vibe, from biker chic to runway runaway, all bright colors, bold cuts, bodies in different shapes and sizes.

I swallow hard. Shenaz told me the office is a regular fashion show, but this is a lot. Xander keeps stealing glances, amused, enjoying my newbie excitement.

I stand up straighter, doing my best to fake confidence. The energy here feels like a little revolution, like the power and passion in this room could change the way future generations look, feel, and think. It thrums through my veins like too much caffeine, and I can't wait to be a part of it all.

I grin at strangers, hoping they'll soon be friends. I've never been good at making friends, really. Besides Cherry, and she's sort of stuck with me. But so far, the folks here don't seem to notice me—or anything beyond their own cubes—all that much.

We stop at a batch of desks outside a set of glass-fronted offices. Ericka's is beckoning, familiar, filled to the brim with her bright personality and knickknacks.

I press my hands to the glass, hoping one day I'll have an office as awesome as hers.

When I look up, Xander is halfway down a bank of cubes, waving me over. Grinning.

I scramble after him, nearly dropping my bag, and pause to regain my balance.

Xander stifles a snicker. Whatever. I will compose myself now. I must.

"Hey, Becca." He waits for her to respond, but she's got headphones on, so he steps into the cube. "Becca?"

She jumps. "You scared me. I told you—" Then she sees me, and fixes her face.

Do I curtsy? Say hello? My body vibrates with electricity. I am standing in the presence of greatness. Becca Taylor-Krause. And that's not even her married name. She comes from a two-dad household, and they decided to join their names as a family. I know because she wrote an essay about it when I was in seventh grade. *I have two dads*, it concluded. *And I wouldn't have it any other way.*

She's got skin the color of fresh cream, cheeks blooming like the roses in my dadoo's front garden. Her eyes are a salty sea green, and her hair cascades the way you'd suspect a princess's would, long and lovely crimson waves that crash down her back. She's wearing an oversized men's tank belted into a dress, and jeweled sandals that look decidedly Desi, like the ones Shenaz put on my feet today. Guess Anita Dongre is really trying to make her mark stateside.

Becca writes a lot of the magazine's reported essays, like how to handle people being rude and nasty about her dads, or the reclaimed, feminist history of rompers and stompers. (A rhyming reference to Doc Martens.) If you read *Fierce*, you know she started a movement to reclaim the word *spinster*. And she's got the crochet needles to prove it. Now she's working on a book about the subject.

"Who is this?" She doesn't sound super pleased to meet me.

"Maya Malhotra. Ericka emailed about her. We need to get her set up. Today."

"Thanks so much, X." Becca does not seem impressed.

"My complete and total pleasure," he says, his tone cold and firm, and I can tell he means every word. "You two have fun. And let me know if you need anything." He's gone before I can blink.

"Okay," Becca says, standing, put out. "Ericka mentioned something about training you today. What'd you say your name was?"

"Maya. Malhotra."

"Isn't that a mouthful?" she says, and my lifelong love turns instantly to hate.

So she's one of those. Woke, but only when performing. I sigh.

I mean, my name's not much harder than Becca Taylor-Krause. Did I say that out loud?

No, thank god. But I kind of wish I had. I can see Xander smirking from his cube.

"Easy enough to learn. If you actually want to." Oops, I *did* just say that.

"A big if," she says, deadpan, and I hear Xander snort. Rude. "Although Mal—" She shrugs, unbothered.

"Ericka told me to get settled and that I'd be helping you on some pitches this morning," I say, determined to get past this. "She said she was wrapping up a shoot and would be late. And that she'd set me up with HR once she's back."

"That's just lovely," Becca says, the faux smile too bright, too fake. "Xander's working on some research now, so let's get you set up, too."

I can't let her see me flinch. Not when I've gotten this far. Not when I'm actually through the door.

Becca shuffles over, sucking her teeth. "I know Rick wanted you set up across from me," she says, walking across the aisle to an empty cube. "All yours."

It's absolutely bare. A fake wood desk, a blank computer screen, an empty bookshelf across the top. Waiting for me to stake my claim. Waiting for me to make my mark. I should be floating. But I swallow hard, holding back tears. Here I am, walking right into my dream. So why do I feel like shit?

The name on the fancy name card ID'ing the cube's resident reads:

Maya Malhotra, Assistant Features Editor.

Wait. What?

It's scrawled in handwriting, loopy and fancy, so I peer a little closer, because that can't be right. I blink and read again. But the words are still there.

Maya Malhotra, Assistant Features Editor.

There has to be some mistake.

Becca hovers. "Did Rick misspell your name?" she asks. "People do that shit to me all the time. There's no *Re* in *Becca*. The printed one will come from HR."

I take a deep breath. "It's just weird, right there on the cube, you know?"

Something is definitely not right here. Should I tell her? I can't.

She stares at me like I'm an annoying child she's being forced to babysit, so clearly she doesn't know. "Is this your first job?"

"Of—of course not," I stammer as Xander shuffles around in the next cube. I've got to stop acting like a total freshman. Or intern, I guess. Because that's not what it says I am. "This is just my first job in, uh, New York City."

Becca raises a brow. It's bushy. On trend right now. But it doesn't match the cherry hair. "Really?" she says, too curious. "Where were you before this?"

"In California. LA." Not Gilroy. Think fast. Think fast. "At a magazine called *The Stinking Rose.*" That's what Shenaz added to my résumé. She didn't clarify that it's the Gilroy Community Center newsletter.

Becca's mouth quirks in amusement, and she nibbles at her cuticles.

I've got to talk to Ericka.

"How'd you end up here?" Becca says. "Bet that's a story."

"Is it ever!" I put my bag down in the empty cube. "Guess

I should get settled. Should I plow through this stuff?" I wave toward a crate of packages that sits unopened, expectant.

Becca smirks again. "No, that's an intern task. Xander and the kids will handle it. I have bigger stuff for you to start on," she says, her face lighting up with something she clearly thinks is a brilliant idea. She walks over to the computer, hits a few keys, logging in. She scrawls the password on a Post-it, then pulls up the browser. "I'm working on a piece on the future of females in STEM. The whole piece was through copy, ready to go. But things have shifted because, you know, new management and all. I have to add two profiles, with a very specific mandate. Dulcie and Rick want something fresh, someone who"—she makes air quotes—"'doesn't fit the profile.'"

I'm trying to listen, but my heart is hammering. I need to do something, to fix this. To tell someone. But Ericka's not here, Becca's a crank, and Xander . . . I feel his eyes on me, amused.

Becca leans close, whispering. "That means they want someone ethnic, but not necessarily brown like you. An overcoming-the-odds thing, not an affirmative action thing. So get on that." She turns to walk away, then turns back for a second. "Oh, and they've got to be attractive. We don't want to perpetuate the stereotype that smart girls can't be beautiful."

A zing of heat climbs up my spine. Xander catches my eye, so I know he heard it, too.

Every time I hear Dulcie St. Claire talk about the magazine on TV, she makes it seem like the most progressive place on the planet. Like *Fierce* is so completely feminist. But Becca's take feels like it's more "white feminist" than anything else. Like she doesn't even realize that the rest of us exist. And she's given me what she thinks is mission impossible.

The gnawing pit in my stomach—the one I thought was just me starving because of missing breakfast—is an all-out riot of bile, swishing and swooshing. This is a test, a hazing ritual, I tell myself, the kind Shenaz warned me about. Like Dolly and her minions at camp. Just because I'm not a rich white New Yorker born into this world doesn't mean I can't cut it here. I can. I will. And once I find Ericka, I can explain everything, fix the confusion. Make it right. Because someone got it very, very wrong.

But in the meantime, I can do this. Becca wants me to find what she thinks is a unicorn: cute, rags to riches, and Black or brown to boot. But I know those kids. I went to coding camp with some of them sophomore year at CSU Fresno. And they know other kids. Lots of them.

I turn to the computer and open the browser. Time to get to work.

Of course my *Fierce* email isn't set up yet, so I use the one I created for Maya Malhotra. Close enough that my friends will get it. Far enough that it won't obviously track back to me. Which is better, because it leaves less of a paper trail. I don't want my parents to find out I bailed on camp from someone else. It has to come from me.

When I open the in-box, there's an email from McIntyre-Scott HR, with Ericka cc'd. They know. Thank god. It's probably taken care of already. I breathe out, relieved, and click open the email.

SUBJECT: Offer Letter and Documents

Dear Maya,

We're so pleased to welcome you to McIntyre-Scott Media and *Fierce* magazine. I understand that you're in the office starting today, so time is of the essence in processing paperwork. Ericka suggested email for efficiency. I'll need your social security number and government-issued ID, along with proof of address and banking information so that we can get you paid.

Speaking of which: I'm pleased to present your offer below, per discussion with Ericka Turner. Your title will be assistant features editor, and, as outlined by the pending union minimums, I'm authorized to offer you a starting salary of twenty dollars per hour for your first three months with us, after which you'll receive an annual salary of forty-two thousand dollars, as well as benefits and overtime for anything over forty hours a week, per the Mac-Scott standard agreement.

I know the process has been expedited here, so please do reach out if you have questions or concerns regarding this offer, so we can get things streamlined and moving ASAP.

I look forward to meeting you, and welcome to the *Fierce* team! You'll love it here.

Warm regards,
Marley Davidson, HR Associate

Oh my god, oh my god, oh my god. They really, truly do think I'm supposed to be assistant features editor? At twenty dollars an hour. That's more money than I've ever dreamed of. This can't be right. Maybe this was supposed to be Xander's offer? But it seems like he's still an EA. Which means . . .

I forward the email to Shenaz. She'll know how to fix this.

She texts back instantly:

> **SHENAZ:** Assistant features editor? $20? Get it, girl! Told you you were good. But I thought you applied for an internship.

MAYA: I did.

SHENAZ: This says assistant editor. Which is pretty kick-ass.

What she doesn't say is that's her title now, assistant fashion editor. And it took her four years on staff to get there.

MAYA: Which explains the endless edit test. I can't be assistant editor. I can barely be an intern.

SHENAZ: Apparently Ericka doesn't think so. You know what this means, Maya? This is a big fucking deal.

MAYA: WHAT DO I DO?

SHENAZ: Breathe, kid. Play along for now. Do what they ask you to. You trust me, right?

I nod, then realize she can't see me. But Xander can, and he's watching, curious dark brown eyes peering at me over the cube partition.

MAYA: Definitely.

SHENAZ: Get through today. Show 'em your chops. Kick ass. We'll deal with the fallout after we talk to Rick. We'll fix it. Promise.

I take a deep breath. She's right. Clearly, I'm here because Ericka thought I could hack it. Maya Malhotra. Assistant features editor. That's me. Or maybe one day it will be, if I can get through today. I need to show them what I've got.

I get to work. I send an email to the head geek camp counselor first. She'll know the standouts from the past three years—and she'll know exactly where to find them, too. Then I send an email with the same request—that I'm helping "a friend" at *Fierce*—to every other science-y kid I know. I send one to Roop, too, for good measure. I mean, she's a doctor.

My phone starts buzzing a few seconds later. It's Shenaz, checking in on text again. I can feel Becca scowling at me from across the way. Oh yeah. I should be working. I turn back to the desktop and activate the Messages app on the computer. There.

Shenaz texts again: Don't let her bug you. Rick loved you. Now remind her why!

She's right. I know I can do this, the actual work at least. I work for another hour, googling and emailing leads, trying to figure out just the right fit for *Fierce*. I check my in-box every so often. There are a few replies, some not so hot, but a couple of contenders. One of Cherry's pals from jujitsu sent a lead on a Ghanaian teen boxing champ from Allston, Massachusetts, who created a new holistic muscle ointment when she had an allergic reaction to the supertoxic extra-strength stuff.

Roop sent a lead about a teen girl genius from Princeton from her med school class—the youngest doctor in America—who helped a fellow teen (now her boyfriend!) find a marrow match.

My tech camp counselor sent a lead on a Mexican-Punjabi kid from Stockton, California, who worked with her mom to develop a soy-paneer Oaxaca cheese, a vegan version that can work in dishes from both cultures.

In less than two hours, I'm twirling in my blue velvet desk chair—and I don't even care that Becca's glaring. She can be a bore if she wants to. I may only get today, and I'm going to make this fun. Xander spies me and spins his chair, too, just twice, in solidarity. I can only see his eyes over the partition, but they're smiling for sure, and I kind of miss the dimple.

I have about ten viable candidates already. I hit print on my list happily and bring it over to Becca. "Who knew teen girls were doing so much to change the world?" I say with glee as she unpacks her lunch, a giant salad that looks delicious. I realize I'm starving. I should do something about that.

"We did. It's our job. We're *Fierce*, remember?" Oh yeah.

"These look good," she says between bites. "I'll let you know." She turns back to her screen, dismissing me.

"So where's the café?" I ask.

"Third." She waves me off. "Make sure you take your ID so you can get back in."

"I don't have an ID yet."

"Security didn't give you one this morning?"

I hold up the paper one. It has a barcode on it. Oh.

"Scan it at the door." I nod. "And get me a rose tea? Iced, but not too much ice."

"I'll take her," Xander says, appearing by my side, patient and waiting. "I'm going anyway."

I grab my ID and my wallet and follow him to the elevator bank.

"Didn't know you were applying for the assistant editor role." His voice disrupts my panic spiral, then sets off a whole new one.

"Neither did I." Shit. He knows. Definitely. He has to know.

He whistles, low. "Well, lucky you. Must have done something right. Because there were a lot of real contenders. Like me." Ouch. "Looks like I'll be working right under you."

The blush climbing my neck matches the one that instantly claims his face. But his eyes twinkle. "I meant— You know what I mean."

"Yeah."

Thankfully, the elevator doors open.

"After you."

I step on, and he follows. He keeps sneaking looks at me. "It's weird, because when we first met, I thought you were way younger. Like my age, maybe. Where were you before this?"

Wait, what? "Before this?" Like Penn Station? Or California?

"Did you work in the city? Here at Mac Media?" He's trying to do the math. Because assistant editor is a big leap from fashion closet freelancer. But he smiles, and there's that dent again. "I know you were freelancing. But other than that?"

"Not here. In California." Dammit. What did I tell Becca? "*The Stinking Rose*. It's a trade magazine." I read about that when looking up pitches—magazines that cover businesses or industries. Not nearly as sexy. "Garlic. In California." I take a deep breath, trying not to hyperventilate. "I learned a lot."

"I remember now. From garlic to *Fierce*." There's that dent again. "Quite a trip."

"You don't know the half of it." I laugh, and when I look up he's still staring, intrigued.

"You?" I take a deep breath. "Aside from Mr. X, of course."

"I grew up in Queens. Pitched a few things to *Teen Vogue*, then did an internship at *Dashing*, with Ramon Nieves, then interned here before I got the EA gig."

Shit, that's a lot of internships. He knows how to lay on the guilt. The doors open on the third floor, and I follow him as the silence stretches, awkward. The way his brain is calculating, he's going to have me unraveled in about 4.3 minutes. I need to escape. But at the same time, something in me wants to hold on to him for dear life.

The whole building is full of beautiful people, all so confident and adult-y, like they were born knowing how to navigate this confusing world. The women here travel in lovely, matching little groups of three, like they're preassigned by the teacher, and there's no room for anyone new. They're all exactly twenty-six, flawless, and eat only fancy salads in the East Village—or the Mac Café, it turns out. Where all the tables have three chairs. Because of course they do.

"What are you going to get?" Xander says, and I shrug. "Is it your first time? This cafeteria is legendary. The people here don't just change the narrative, they own the narrative."

I grin. "And one day, that'll be us."

"It is us," he says, waving his arms to embrace all of it. "We're right here. Right now."

But when we step farther into the café, all metal and glass and two stories high, his bluster deflates a little. Because it's big, and we're very, very small.

He turns to me and grins. "Meet you back here in twenty?"

I nod and take a deep breath as he disappears. I miss him instantly—he already feels like a safety net, in a way, although I can feel him poking holes in my story. The pressure is a lot to manage. I wander slowly through the café, taking it all in.

It feels like the first day of freshman year all over again—strangers who couldn't care less that I exist. At least I had Cherry back then. But this time, there's a magical out: I can take my lunch back to my desk. And eat alone. With Becca staring at me from across the aisle. That's still better than trying to figure out the cliques in this café. I head straight for the emptiest station—burgers and chicken fingers.

"Can I get a burger well done, with Pepper Jack, pickles, and onions?" I ask.

"Aren't you a bold one?" a fashion type says, giggling with her clone—I mean, friend. "All those carbs in that bun. And onions, too? Wow." Then she turns to the grill guy, who only glares. At everyone. "Turkey burger, patty only, please. No bread. No cheese. No fries."

The grill guy shoves a paper basket my way. "Well done," he grumbles. "Fries?"

Might as well. I nod, and he adds a batch. I grab ketchup, and a rose iced tea for Becca, then one for myself.

I head to the cashier, who smiles and rings me up. "Twenty-six seventy-five," she says, and I know I've misheard her.

"What?"

"Twenty-six seventy-five."

I frown into my wallet. I've only got a twenty on me. And two singles. And I thought I'd be spending maybe half of that. I swallow hard. "Can you break it down for me?"

The burger's twelve bucks, the fries are four, and the drinks are five. Each. Plus tax. Ouch. Guess I'll have water. From the faucet. I hand her back the iced tea, and then give her the twenty. I would say keep the change, but that would be rude because there isn't any.

"Got everything?" Xander says, catching up to me at our meeting spot. "This place is a bit steep, huh?"

He's got a sandwich, no fries, no drink. Smart.

"I'm going to have to hit the bank," I say. Too bad there's no actual cash in my account.

We take our lunches and head back upstairs to our cubes. I follow Xander, and he navigates us easily back to the editorial pod, pausing to grab a free iced tea and some chips from the kitchen. "Always check in here to see what's set out, or you'll blow your whole budget fast," he says. "Learned that the hard way. And the coffee's passable."

Back at the cubes, I head toward Becca's desk to hand her the rose tea and ask for my five bucks. Otherwise, I'll be headed home without a dime on me.

But when I look up, Ericka's standing there. Now's my chance. I'll explain the misunderstanding, offer to sign on as an intern, fix things. No big deal.

"I'd say the boxer for sure," Ericka says to Becca, beaming. "But there are so many good candidates!"

She likes my list. Loves it!

"There she is. So glad you're here! Welcome, Maya." Seeing her, I finally feel like I'm at the *Fierce* I imagined. The one where Black women like Dulcie St. Claire and Ericka Turner rule the masthead—and I get to learn from them. The one where I've always belonged. "Becca told me you've been so helpful this morning. I knew you'd be a great fit!"

"Thanks!" I say, and hand Becca the rose tea. Maybe it's tacky to ask her for the money now? "I'm so excited to be here. It's been a fun morning."

"Becca said you did a great job researching these candidates she found."

Wait, what?

Candidates *she* found?

She meaning Becca?

Because *she* is definitely not me.

"Maya's a great assistant," Becca says. Dropping the editor portion completely. Again.

"Assistant editor," I say, sweet as pie. Can't let that slide, even if it costs me later. "Still pinching myself."

"What a find, Rick. You know how to pick them." Becca smiles sweetly at both of us, then turns to her computer again. "Better get these assigned out. Thanks for the tea. I'll get you later."

Ericka walks toward her office, gesturing for me to follow. "We've got to set you up with Marley. You saw the email?"

I nod. Now's the time. Tell her. Fix it. "About that—" How do I start?

"Great, do you have what she needs? I want to get you up and running ASAP. We've got a big season ahead of us, and I think your voice will be an amazing addition."

"I didn't bring the social security card today, sorry," I say, my mind spiraling. "Tomorrow, for sure."

"Okay," Rick says, frustrated. "Is it the money? I can probably get them to go a bit higher. But we need paperwork complete this week so we can get you paid."

I nod. "I'll get it sorted this week for sure. But I—" I've got to tell her. But I might destroy everything. And I worked so hard to get here. And she really likes my pitches. And—

She nods. "Of course. Well, eat first, then come see me. I think a few of the pitches from your edit test could really work, so let's flesh them out and then we can have Becca assign them. And I want you to get comfortable with Xander, because you'll be managing him, okay?"

I nod and do my best to smile. "So which candidates do you think we're going with?" I ask Rick, even though I know I should leave it alone. I can't help it.

"She really killed it with this list. Glad you're around to help. The boxer, for one. And the doctor, for sure," Rick says. "So cool, and such a cute love story there."

I have to do it. Now or never. I can't just let Becca steal credit for my work. "Yeah, I found her through my cousin—they went to medical school together. The boyfriend's adorable, too. Apparently he's in the *Rock Star Boot Camp* finals now, and there's talk of a record deal."

Ericka looks confused for a moment, then her face clears with understanding. "Oh, *you* found the candidates. I see." Her mouth is a firm line as she looks toward Becca, in her cube, sipping my rose iced tea. "Thanks for letting me know. Do you want to do one of the features, then? On the doctor, maybe? The perfect way to kick off your new role."

"Yes, please."

I can't even believe it. Barely six hours, and I have an assignment. Definitely not something she'd give an intern. I should tell her. Now. But I can't. Not until I figure things out. Still, I have to know. I take a deep breath. Maybe it's unprofessional, but it's gnawing at me. "Can I ask—what made you pick me? I know you had some incredible candidates. Like Xander."

Ericka grins. "Oh, you kids and your 'praise me' vibes. Xander's awesome, but he's really young. He's also already very New York big media. And to be honest, it was your essay. I showed it to Dulcie." Ah, that's why she knew who I was. "And it was easy.

Dulcie wants to shake things up, reinvent what *Fierce* means, and you fit that energy—a fresh voice, someone who thinks outside of the standard East Coast–West Coast dichotomy. You've already proven, with your pitches today, that we made the right choice. Clearly, Becca could never—" She laughs. "Tread carefully here, because the politics are—a lot. Especially with Jude and the new regime. Although I guess you've already got that. So go ahead and set that profile up. And please bring your paperwork stuff tomorrow." The phone rings, and Ericka heads back toward her desk. "I better grab that. Oh, and tell Xander to train you on phones."

As I walk back to my cube, my stomach churns; my hands shake. I'm lying to everyone. But I keep hearing Xander's voice in my head, telling me these opportunities are rare. Then there's that pang again, because I pretty much stole his. I don't know what to do. There's been a major misunderstanding. But if I tell the truth, that's it, I'm done. I lose my chance. And if I've learned anything today, it's that I might actually really rock at this. Do I want to throw it all away? I can't. I'm here, in this place where so few people get to be. I have a chance to write myself into the narrative—the way I always wanted to. I have to shoot my shot. And I won't let anyone take it away from me.

As I pass Becca's cube, a newfound determination settles in my stomach. She clacks away on her keyboard, ignoring the heat of my glare.

Assistant features editor. My dream job. And clearly, I can hack it.

I can even handle Becca.

I won this round, and she doesn't even know it—yet.

And if that's how the game is played, well, no worries.

Because I'm a quick learner.

Now all I have to do is figure out a way to stay.

Just How Fierce Are You?

Unravel Your Fierceness Factor by Taking This Quick Quiz!

BY MAYA MALHOTRA

Comb through your closet. Your wardrobe is:
  a) Farm Girl Chic. Custom overalls and boots are totally your thing!
  b) Leather and metal. You're all about the industrial.
  c) Clean and classic. Schoolgirl skirts and button-downs.
  d) Thrift store fab. You're working a vintage vibe.

Truth or dare?
  a) Truth. Though you might need to bend it a little.
  b) Dare. Nothing scares you.
  c) Truth. You've got nothing to hide.
  d) Dare. The bolder the better!

Your secret dream:
  a) Growing fruit trees in your garden. A lot of work, but so worth it!
  b) Winning an Oscar for best screenplay.
  c) Running for president one day. Maybe not so secret.
  d) Working at your favorite magazine. And living in the fashion closet.

Your dream job?
   a) Park ranger. Working outdoors is definitely in your plans.
   b) Film school for sure. You're the next Ava.
   c) A doctor or a lawyer. Stable, sensible, and *ca-ching*!
   d) Media. You can see your byline splashed across the top right now!

The perfect date?
   a) Picnic in the park.
   b) An art show or movie premiere. See and be scene.
   c) Dinner and a movie. At home, and you'll cook.
   d) Exploring a new neighborhood in your favorite city.

If you could live anywhere, where would it be?
   a) California's rolling hills have always been your dream.
   b) Austin or Asheville, young, hip, and hungry.
   c) A small, charming suburb. Community and comfort is your vibe.
   d) New York. The city of dreams.

15

BY THE TIME THE TRAIN PULLS INTO NEW BRUNSWICK, I'VE given Shenaz the rundown. She can't stop laughing. Roaring. Long and hard and endless. At my pain.

"Oh my god, Maya Memsahib. Only you," she says, gasping for air as she gathers her stuff. "Only you." Then she takes a deep breath. "Twenty is a decent start. But there's a range. Always ask for more."

"I still don't get how it happened, though," I say as I race to follow her back to the apartment. "I applied for an internship—"

"That's the thing. I needed an intern. But Ericka was interviewing for an assistant editor, so that's what she thought you were applying for." Shenaz bustles around the kitchen, starting a pot of chai. I throw in some cardamom and ginger. I need it today.

"Okay. But HR should have seen the difference, right? I mean—"

Shenaz taps her lip. "It may be the wording on your résumé," she says, sheepish. "My vocabulary is a bit bombastic. I may have . . . embellished some things." I glare and she grins. "What? Everyone does it. Especially in fashion." She shrugs. "And you *did* write that newsletter."

"For the community center."

"And a bunch of articles." She pours milk into the pot as the chai bubbles.

"For my high school paper."

We both watch the pot, waiting for it to boil over. She sighs. "It is what it is. And writing is writing. Clearly, they liked your voice. As they should."

And then it hits me. "And Ericka doesn't 'believe in résumés.' Something about gatekeeping, racism, and the patriarchy. But now I'm—"

"Screwed, yup." She strains the chai into cups and hands one to me. "Just let your fashionista fairy god mum take a stab. I promise you, we'll fix it."

We sit on the sofa, and I pull open my laptop and pop up the HR email, staring at it like it's a puzzle.

"First things first," she says, turning to me. "Do you want to stay at *Fierce*?"

I nod. "Of course. If I confess, maybe I can just trade with Xander? Be the intern?" Like I thought I would be. I'm underqualified to be assistant features editor at my school paper, let alone at an award-winning national magazine that's been around way longer than I've been alive.

She shakes her head. "No, once you tell them, it's over," she says. "And you've already proven that you can do the work."

"I loved it," I admit. "It's what I always dreamed of. I mean, anxiety spirals and backstabbing aside. But they think I'm a full-on adult. Like twenty-six. With experience and ideas and some youthful enthusiasm. And once I hand HR my ID—"

"It's over." Shenaz sips her tea again, staring at the still blank screen. She sighs. "I'm sorry I got you into this mess, Maya. Maybe you should just fess up. It would be the honorable thing to do. And it was an honest mistake."

"Except for the résumé padding." Shenaz nods, guilty. I stare into my cup. "And I was good at it."

Shenaz sips her chai. "Clearly Ericka thought so, too. They posted your quiz on the site. And she assigned you an actual feature story already. That's huge."

She squishes in closer, taking the laptop, and types a bunch of things. *Legal trouble. Résumé. Working papers. Lying.* None of it is helping.

"Working papers would be an issue here, right?"

I nod. "I'm not legally allowed to work. I'm seventeen. I have to finish high school."

"And your parents definitely wouldn't let you quit to go work at a magazine in New York City?" She says it like it's a question, not a statement.

I crack a smile. "I don't think so, nope."

Then she leans in and starts clickety-clacking away, in some kind of flow state, like when she's writing one of her fashion treatises on the import of kitten heels or false lashes. "Voilà!"

Maya's Secret Dream Summer Action Plan
Step 1: Fake ID. Maya Malhotra, 26.
Step 2: Documents? This is a bit harder. Social security, bank account, the works.
Step 3: Lie. Lie to everyone.
Step 4: The actual work? Cake. You got this, Maya.

I stare at the list, gobsmacked, as Shenaz would say. Could it be that simple? And that horrifyingly complicated? "There's no way it will work."

"Come on. Didn't you ever watch that show *Younger*?" Shenaz says, like it ain't no thing. "If a forty-something white woman can turn herself twenty-six, then so can you, dollface."

"Dollface. That's part of the problem." I sigh.

Shenaz shrugs. "Everyone there looks eighteen—or aims to, anyway. Besides, you got through today. And you know I can help with that." She waves her arm toward the rack. It is solidly miraculous, true. "What you need to decide, Maya Memsahib, is, do you *want* to do this?"

After today? I can 100 percent, definitively say yes. "You know I do."

"No, dollface. You keep saying you do. But do you actually

want it? Are you willing to do what it takes?" I see it in her eyes: *Because it could cost a lot.*

I sit for a minute, doing the puzzle in my head. It's obvious. My forever dream. Right there for the plucking. But to do it, I'll have to lie to pretty much everyone. It's right there in black and white, number three on the list. And I'd only get to have it for, what, maybe six weeks. If no one found out. Then what? I bail? Back to high school and the farm. Give it all up after having lived it for the summer. Could that be enough? It might have to be.

"Think about it, Maya. You're already keeping a million secrets. And that's for nothing. A boy? This is your *dream.* One that seemed untouchable just a month ago. Will you claim it? Do you have the guts?" She grins, wicked. "I triple dog dare you."

She gets up and traipses toward the kitchen, straining more chai. "You sit. Ponder." She hands me another cup, heading off to her room. "I'm going to go change." She turns back for a second, dropping the mic: "And if you decide you can't risk it, guess we'll have to call your parents and let them know you quit Cow Camp. For nothing."

Four hours later, nearly midnight—nine in California—I still don't have anything figured out. I keep pacing through the apartment, tripping over shoes, makeup bags, all Shenaz's crap, trying to figure out my plan.

But no matter what I come up with, the pieces don't quite fit. Do I tell Ericka I'm seventeen and offer to intern? Shenaz keeps reminding me: no more slots, lots of paperwork to create new ones, no reason for them to make exceptions. Especially as the new Dulcie regime settles into place. Plus, they could just say, "Oh, you lied? Goodbye."

I don't think my heart could take that. Not when I'm so close. Not when I'm already in the door. There's no logical solution. But there is one very illogical one.

After listening to me babble all evening, Shenaz retreated about an hour ago, saying the drama was too much. But when the door rattles and Roop steps through, she's right there, with a kiss and some food, whispering in her ear.

"All night, she's been at it, deliberating, going back and forth, deciding and then undeciding," Shenaz says. She's clearly already downloaded the short version, but Roop's all unruffled and uninterested, as usual. "I can't take it anymore."

"She's seventeen," Roop says with a sigh. "Did you know what you wanted at seventeen?" Then she looks down at Shenaz fondly, kissing her on the nose. It makes me miss Ranbir. "Never mind. Don't answer that. I know you did."

"You did, too," Shenaz points out. "Now come to bed."

I feel like I'm intruding—in their space, in their tiny world. But I can't let this, or them, go. Not yet.

"What would you do?" I blurt, disrupting their moment. I need to know Roop's take. She is, after all, the all-knowing guardian.

Roop sighs, the exhaustion weighing her down like a dirty lab coat. "As much as it might seem like the opposite, no one can choose your path for you, Maya," she says. "I learned that the hard way. Do what you have to do to be who you need to be. I did. And yes, it cost me. A lot. But it would have cost me more not to. So I'd do it again in a heartbeat."

She turns back to Shenaz, bleary-eyed. "I'm going to get cleaned up and ready for bed. Don't be too late." Then she turns to me again. "And you. You know what your decision is, somewhere in that little head of yours. Accept it. Whatever you choose, we'll help you figure it out. Promise."

That surprises me. But she doesn't wait for a hug or thank-yous. Just disappears, shutting the door behind her.

She's right. No one can choose for me. I have to do it myself.

I weigh the pros and cons over and over. The math comes out differently each time. I mean, that's a definite thing with me. I suck at math. But words? Those I can work with. That's my dream. I hear Cherry's voice in my head, wise and omniscient (even though I've hidden everything from her this summer):

Goals are just dreams with an actual plan.

She put it on a T-shirt. In rainbow sequins, of course.

That's what she's done all our lives. Taught herself to sew, to design, to market. Built something out of nothing. That's what my grandfather did, and my dad, and Ma, too, even though she never gets credit. My dreams—goals, I remind myself—may look a little different, lopsided to some, maybe even upside down. But they're what I want. I know what I want.

I'm going to do it. I have to. This may be the only chance I get.

I grab my phone and pull up the email that HR sent this morning. I click reply, typing before I even know exactly what to say. And like Shenaz suggested, I ask for more.

It's a done deal. For as long as it lasts. Six days. Or six weeks. I'll make it work, living my dream come true.

No matter what happens after.

I can almost see the business cards in my hot little hands now:

MAYA MALHOTRA, ASSISTANT FEATURES EDITOR, FIERCE

16

My first week is a blur of pages and fury. And paperwork and lies.

But it seems like it's working: Roop got a lead on a fake ID, and the dude suggested I use Roop's name, since it came complete with credit history, address (where I'm actually living!), bank account, and social security card. And she's actually twenty-six, age appropriate. I thought that would be a hard sell, but she just handed it over with a shrug. Then he literally just swapped out the photo, and I sent a copy to HR yesterday with no word of hera pheri, though they did ask about the name. I said Maya Malhotra was my preferred pen name and email address, and that was it. Pushed right through. Too easy.

So fraud. Yes. But slightly less fraud than it could be, I keep telling myself. I pray that no one finds out.

And three days in, I feel like I'm starting to get the hang of it. I even managed to nab a bagel on my way in this morning, from this Desi uncle street vendor named Satbir, who insisted I try the jalapeño cream cheese, on him. I promised to bring him a jar of garlic chutney.

But the bagel's been sitting on my desk for forty minutes, because Becca attacked me with a bunch of "super-urgent" research tasks the minute I sat down. Now it's nearly noon, I have shit scheduled the rest of the day, and the bagel is cold and hard.

Tea. That's what I need. The chai here is cinnamon-vanilla, which makes me livid, so I've been dabbling in the herbal flavors in the kitchen—chamomile, Earl Grey, Moroccan Moon. I don't know what's in them, but they're mostly fruity and floral, not bad.

I set the bagel in the microwave for a minute and steep a cup, looking at my phone. Texts from Cherry—and I've been careful about sharing too much about *Fierce*, since she still thinks it's part-time—and a few from Ma. Marcus asking about a tour and whether I've met Ramon yet, of course. But still nothing from Ranbir. He's been MIA for days, and I just don't get it.

The crackle is what gets my attention. Like a little pop, then a sizzle, and then the smell. Like sulfur. Shit. I leap toward the microwave and see it, the little flame. I fling open the door and grab the bagel, tossing it, still alight, onto the ground and stomping on it with my Lisa Lees before it occurs to me to douse it. With my tea.

"What are you—" Xander, ever stealth, stands in the kitchen doorway, smirking. "You set the kitchen on fire?"

"It was the bagel. I didn't realize—"

He leans down and scoops up the smoldering mess. "They always wrap them in foil, then paper. To keep it warm. But not for like three hours." He's not laughing, but his eyes are. "There's no salvaging this, Maya. You could have taken down the whole building."

Shit. "I didn't—"

"Don't worry about it." He soaks a couple of napkins and cleans out the inside of the microwave. "I won't tell. But, dude, next time warn me before you deploy your evil plan to burn down Mac Media. I'd like to be a coconspirator." He reaches into the fridge, pulls out a couple of wraps, and offers me one. "Chicken fajita, courtesy of my mom." I shake my head, but he pushes it into my hand. "Eat. You've got tons of invoices to get through. You won't have time otherwise."

I nod. He's right. "Thanks. I appreciate it. And you won't—"

"Nope. Don't worry about it."

I take the wrap back to my desk and get set up. The difference between me and Xander has become crystal clear: I'm a kid, and he's, like, an actual grown-up. Even though he's not much older than me. (And his mom still makes his lunches.) I need to learn how to be an adult. But how do you do that, exactly?

Then it hits me. That could be a great pitch. Maybe even a column. I'm typing up some quick thoughts on it when Xander walks back to his desk, carrying two cups. "You forgot your tea," he says, handing me one as Becca looks over, ever suspicious. "Chamomile. Calming."

He snickers to himself, but I grin. "Thanks."

The rest of the week flies by, and my schedule is packed with tasks I love to check off my little to-do app with a satisfying ping. Almost (but not quite) like an adult.

I email the teen doctor—Saira Sehgal, MD—to set up an interview and pin down some times. I find candidates for another roundup, this one on female athletes with unexpected paths to success, to be banked for the January Olympics. I write a bunch of quizzes for the website, and I gather endless reams of research for Becca, who, it turns out, is an even bigger pain in the ass than it seemed at first. (I know.)

"There's a very specific hierarchy here," she says again, so loud the whole row of cubes can hear her. "So check with me before actually emailing any potential sources or subjects, okay? Pay your dues, put in the time, be willing to do the grunt work." She reminds me of Maxwell with his bullhorn. Except that hers would be rhinestone studded and personalized with BECCA NOT REBECCA. "That's how this business works. How it's always been done. You find a mentor and earn trust and show that you're worthy of climbing to the next rung on the ladder."

To prove her point, Becca has reworked every single thing I've pitched or written so far, spilling endless red on my docs, a bloodbath, even when I think it reads okay. In the end, it doesn't sound like me. It sounds like her. And I like her voice. I do. It's . . . just not mine. But she seems like the type who needs to leave her fingerprints on everything. To prove she did something at all.

"Got it," I say, sucking my teeth as she drones on, and hear Xander laugh in his cube. I roll my eyes, and Xander catches me, that perma-grin denting his cheeks again. He's always watching, studying, careful. Like he knows exactly what I'm up to. It's unnerving. But he's smart. Funny. Helpful. And, okay, pretty cute, smiling brown eyes forever peering over the edge of my cube. A pang of guilt punches its way up and out of my stomach. This gig could've been, would've been his. I stole it.

Nope. Didn't steal it. Earned it. Because I can do it, I remind myself. I'm holding my own. As painful as it is.

Becca's pretty much in charge of me, which is about as miserable as it sounds. She's all faux friendly and full of advice. Like:

- Don't talk to senior staffers unless they talk to you first.
- Study every issue of the magazine and pitch what's safe. Tried and true for a reason!
- Pick up all the tasks no one else wants. It'll prove your commitment.
- Don't question your editor's (read: her) changes. Red ink is a lesson earned.
- Get here super early, and be the last to leave. (But she *never* does that herself.)
- Always be overprepared. Never complain. And remember your place.

Whatever. Six weeks, I remind myself. Then the dream is over, and so is the nightmare of dealing with her. But as much as she sucks the joy out of every minute with her insistent commentary and mind-numbing busywork, she can't kill my groove here. I'm starting to develop a system—thanks in part to Ericka, who just skips right over Becca to assign me specific tasks. She and Dulcie are plotting something big—endless meetings with the team up top—and so a lot of the basics fall to me. I've researched and found new writers, made assignments, created lists of potential story subjects, and dug deep into what *Fierce's* competition looks like on the web, since the focus is shifting.

I do Ericka's tasks first, then get to Becca's nonsense when—and if—I can. She can stay mad.

Especially because today, I'm wrapping up my first interview for my first actual feature story. "Thanks so much, Saira," I say, checking again to make sure the call is still recording. I have it taping via the voice memo app on my phone, but also on a little device that plugs into my land line. Xander's suggestion, since you never know when something will go haywire. "It'll run in the October issue, tentatively. And you'll hear from photo. Tell Link good luck with the *Rock Star Boot Camp* finals. Or, uh, break a leg."

Xander peers over the banister between our cubes. I flash a thumbs-up, and he moseys—he always moseys, casual and relaxed—over, leaning close to peer at the phone. His scent makes my stomach rumble, sweet like cinnamon, spicy like black pepper. "Got it," he says, switching the recorder off. "Sounds like it went well."

"I think so," I say, grinning. "She said we could use some shots of them together, too."

I point to the screen, showing off the photos.

He smirks. "Swoonworthy."

I thwack his arm.

"Wanna grab lunch in five?" he asks.

"I should probably transcribe this," I say.

He's asked me every day. And I've avoided him every day.

"I'll assign it to one of the interns," he says, taking the recorder. "You've got other stuff to do."

That sounds lovely, not transcribing. But I'm running out of excuses. "Great."

We both freeze as Dulcie swings through, poking her head into Ericka's empty office.

"She's in a meeting with Jordan," I say, and she grins, walking toward me in my cube.

"So this is where you are. Settling in? I saw that pitch—the doctor. Love it. Great start."

"Just finished the interview, actually." I beam as Becca frowns from across the aisle. "They sound really adorable."

"I look forward to reading it," Dulcie says. "And I'll see you all at the monthly story meeting next Thursday, right? It's gonna be major."

"Wait, are we supposed to go to that?" Becca's voice squeaks. "The big one?"

Dulcie turns to look at her, confused. "Yeah, I want all of you to be there. Shaking things up. After all, this magazine's all about ideas. And they could come from anyone, anywhere. So have your pitches ready."

So much for lunch. Thank god.

An hour later, we're gathered for the Friday afternoon features meeting, our weekly brainstorming and pitch session. It's my first official one, and Xander grabs the seat right next to me, drumming his fingers on the table absentmindedly. My stomach drops for a second, and it hits me. Like Ranbir and his hand on his knee, casual, familiar. I haven't heard from him in days. I pull my phone onto my lap and send another text. My eighth this week, all unanswered. Just one word: Hey.

I feel Xander watching, so I stash my phone away.

Rick runs the show on this one, and she's like a conductor, managing sections and personalities, skimming the politics right off the top. "Becca, take the lead on the '20 Under 20 Girls Who'll Change the World.' Assign out the profiles as necessary—and please give the assistants and interns a chance at some."

Becca grimaces. "Okay, I'll comb through the pitches." Which means *I'll* comb through the pitches.

"Maya, I love the How to Be an Adult column idea. Work with art to see how we can break it down into something graphic driven—I'd love to see it as a spread with a hero image and breakout deep caps, bite-sized but chock-full. 'Save for Retirement' might be too staid, but I like 'Buy Health Insurance,' since so much of Gen Z is gig economy, and 'How to Adopt a Pet' and 'How to Move to a New City' are keepers, too, although 'Apply to College' skews a bit too teen."

Oh. Yeah. That.

Xander opens his mouth, then closes it again, but I nod in his direction, hopefully encouraging. "'Save for Retirement' might be smart, actually," he says, "since they say if you start stashing a hundred bucks a month when you're twenty, you'll have nearly two hundred thousand dollars by the time you're in your sixties. If you stash five hundred dollars a month, you could hit a million." He shrugs. "I know it's not easy for most folks, but we could do some tips on how to pile up some pennies, at least."

Ericka raises her brows. "I'm sold." She turns to me. "What do you think, Maya? It was your idea."

I grin. "I think Xander should do the 'Retirement' pitch, to be honest. He might need to school . . . us all . . . on that one." Wait, was that weird? Xander just taps his pen, scribbling notes on a pad.

"Great, collaborate and assign some to Xander. Moving on. Team," Ericka says, clasping her hands together in excitement. I can see the cheerleader in her when she does it. She wrote about being the only Black girl on the squad for the Stand Outs special issue last year. "We're going to start gearing up for the Next Best List, *Fierce*'s annual roundup of all things new and novel in January." So far away, because it's only July. "This is big-time forecasting. The point isn't to guess what *will* be big. The point is to *decide* what will be big. Remember: We're not covering culture, we're making it. We set the tone, we create the trends, and others follow. It's a huge responsibility, but I know you all can handle it." She turns and smiles at the new guy at the table—I mean, new to me, at least.

"Jordan, take it away."

The entertainment editor. Of course. "All right, team. Rick's pretty much said it all, but I think the easiest way to tackle this is to divide and conquer. I've got a directive from up on high: They want this issue to be bold, beautiful, and ballsy." We all groan.

"It's a women's mag, ass," Becca says. At least she puts it out there.

"I know, I know. But we're taking it back, co-opting it," Jordan says, catching my eye. "Right, Maya?" I didn't realize he knew my name. Xander's frowning, the drumming a bit more pointed. "So let's split it up. Becca, Xander, you guys take Play It by Ear—think music, podcasts, new radio, audiobooks, audiology tech, a mix of high-and lowbrow. Definitely diversify. But not for, you know, the sake of diversity. Get me the good stuff. Really dig in. Be bold." He laughs, but no one else does.

"I'm going to work on all things screen and streaming, and, Maya, I saw the Bollywood pitches you sent through, so you can work with me on that team—movies, TV, screens, streaming, 3D, whatever's new and hot. I'd love to break out some new-to-*Fierce* actors from other countries, people who are about to blow up the American scene. Pretty faces, yes, but something raw, indie, and amazing. Let's meet to chat about it on Monday, okay?"

I nod. I'll call Cherry. She's a Bollywood fanatic. She'll know exactly who to pitch, someone under the radar right now, here at least. "Maybe Shah Rukh Khan's kid." It feels weird to be able to just say it, to put my thoughts out there. A real voice, to contribute. They're all nodding and listening to me. Like I'm a grown-up. Like what I have to say matters. "He's decidedly swoonworthy." I can feel Xander smirking. "And actually, he has a sister who's super cute, too. And so does Janhvi Kapoor. There's a whole crop of rising Bollywood scions in their teens." I giggle at my own farm pun, but of course nobody else gets it. "And they're brown, bold, and beautiful." I scribble some notes. "And there are some on Disney and stuff now, too."

"Teens?" More groaning from Becca. "That'll skew way too young."

Oops. She's probably right. I turn to Xander. "If I give you a list, will you start working on pinning down press contacts for me?"

"You got it, boss," he says, flashing that dimple. "You want just Bollywood? Because global star kids could make this bigger and broader."

"Oh my god, yes, love that," Rick says. "You two take the lead, actually," she adds, and I see faces fall around the table. WTF. "It's perfect. Young, hot, vaguely familiar but on the edge. The Son Also Rises. Something punny, less gendered. Xander, follow Maya's lead. I think this could be amazing, maybe three spreads, breakout boxes, a centered running text to tie it together."

Jordan looks irritated, but nods. "Definitely different. We can talk more about it before we nail it down."

Xander's grinning, excited, but there's something weird underneath. It falters a bit, like he's trying to figure something— someone?—out. Me. Of course.

As we leave the conference room, Jordan catches my arm, and I startle for a second. "So, Monday. My office?" He's too close, towering over me. "Or lunch, maybe? I want to pin some of this stuff down." Xander's right behind us, and he looks weirded out, too.

"Sure," I say, gently tugging my arm back. "But let me pull some stuff together first. Let's do three P.M. Your office."

Xander pauses. "Okay if I join you?" he says. "I can take notes."

"Great," Jordan says, though he looks deflated. "See you then."

I race to catch up with Xander, who's speed-demoning through the hall like the New Yorker he truly is.

"Hey, thanks for doing that." I take a deep breath. "I dunno, felt weird."

He shrugs. "Was weird. We all felt it." He lowers his voice. "I've heard stuff about him. Be careful."

"Okay, Uncle."

"That's Tio to you," he says, and I laugh. "And thanks for letting me have that story, by the way. That was cool of you."

I shrug. "You'd do a much better job than me, clearly. I've barely got fifty bucks 'stashed' so far."

Back at the cubes, Becca's long gone, and the office is nearly empty, even though it's only like two o'clock. I must look confused, because Xander grins. "Summer Fridays. Take them while they last."

He starts gathering his stuff. "You wanna grab a bite?"

I do actually think about it for a minute. But then that little glimmer flashes in his eyes again, like he's trying to unravel me, figure me out, and I know I can't risk it. There's too much at stake. "I think I'm gonna stay, actually, work on this story and a few pitches."

"Kiss up." He grins. "See you Monday."

MA: FaceTime? *Mahi* marathon tonight?

MA: Call me, nah, baby. I miss you.

MA: Four weeks to go.

MAYA: Yeah, it's all going so fast. Tomorrow, Ma.

MA: Teek hai. Evening time, okay? Pukka?

MAYA: Pukka.

MA: Are you enjoying out there? Like the Cow Camp? Living with Roop?

MA: You never say.

MAYA: I love it out here, Ma. It's amazing. I wish you could visit.

MA: Me too.

17

WHEN I GET OFF THE TRAIN, RANBIR'S STANDING THERE, waiting. He looks like he's lost. But his eyes catch the setting sun when he sees me, all golden and lit again. It makes my breath catch.

It's been forever since I've seen him. Since the night of our walk at the waterfront, right before my whole life changed. Weeks since he even texted a *hey* back. So I decide to plow straight ahead, right past him, like I don't see him at all. But he grabs my arm.

"Maya, wait," he says, and there's something in his voice that makes me stop.

I look at him, and for a minute he just stares back, taking me in. "How is it?" he says, curiosity sparking. "The internship?"

"Now? After two weeks of silence?" I suck my teeth—a bad habit I picked up from Becca. But it helps with the rage. "You don't get to ask."

I start to walk away again, but then I turn around.

"I don't get it." I try to steady my voice, to keep the hurt out of it. "I texted you, I was excited, I wanted to celebrate. And clearly Marcus told you the news. But not a word." I take a deep breath. "And then Dolly—"

"I know. It's just—" He takes a deep breath and a step closer. "Maya, my mom's really sick again."

"What?" The shock, the pain of it, hits me hard.

"I went home. Just for a few days." I want to reach for him, to hug him, but I'm not sure if I'm allowed. "Anyway, I thought you should know. She's okay, at the moment. But they made me come back here. They think this is too important."

I nod. As much as it hurts, I get it. "So you're back."

He shrugs. "At least for now."

He looks sad, lost, in a different, deeper way. One that I don't quite know how to fix. But I'm glad he has Dolly, as much as it pinches. "Did she go with you?"

He shakes his head. "But she's been around. A little. A lot. I kind of need her right now."

"Because she gets it."

He nods again. "I know you do, too. But it's—"

She's family. He doesn't say it, but I know.

"I miss you, though." He sighs. "I kind of wish—"

I reach for him then, despite myself, my arms around his neck, my lips on his. He kisses me back with everything he's got—hunger, hurt, love, pain. He's crying when I let go.

"I'm sorry. About all of it."

We stand there for a long moment—just arms and hearts—my head resting on his chest, that familiar drumming in my ears. "It's not your fault."

Maybe one day we'll figure it out. Or maybe I'm not what he needs. Even though the thought kills me.

"Is it awesome?" he says. "Everything you dreamed?"

I smile into his chest. "Better. Faster. Fiercer."

"You must be amazing there." I can feel him grinning, his chin resting on the top of my head. "Like a little fireball. A patakha. They don't know what hit them."

"Yeah." I don't tell him about all the lies I told to get there, to stay there. I don't tell him about all the hard parts. "Maybe one day you'll see my name in print."

He leans back and kisses me on the nose. "I can't wait."

I sigh, and he pulls away a bit. "Don't. Just yet. Please?"

He shakes his head, taking a step back, about to disappear again. "I shouldn't have come. I shouldn't have—" He sighs. "I have to go."

I nod. "But you can call me, okay? Whenever you want. If you want to. It doesn't have to mean anything. Or you can not, if that's what you need. I'll be around."

He nods, and I watch him walk away.

I cry for hours, secretly, quietly, into couch cushions and pillows, the girls tiptoeing around me, afraid to ask. I'm sure they're completely sick of all my highs and lows. I'm like a bomb that went off in their living room, detonating and blowing their lives to smithereens. They still don't quite know what hit them.

"Did something happen at the magazine?" Roop asks Shenaz, careful as they putter around the kitchen bright and early Saturday morning. It's a rare day when we're all home together. Weird.

"She was fine when she left the office," Shenaz whispers, and I can see her shrug even with my face buried in the pillow. "Texted me that she was working late. Maybe with Xander?"

I can almost feel Roop's eyebrows rise, amused and confused. "Must be a boy thing, then," Roop says, the snark so thick I want to smack her. "I never understood it. So much drama."

Shenaz hands me a cup of chai—in a to-go cup. "Come on, Maya Memsahib. Shower and get dressed. We've got plans."

Roop looks surprised. "We do?"

Shenaz grins and sips. "Yup. And you're driving."

I dress in a daze—someone else's salwar kameez, a bit snug in the chest, but the chunni covers that up—and sniffle the whole way over.

Twenty minutes. Then there's that familiar golden dome. The gurdwara. Which just means a fresh round of tears.

"Saturdays are mattar paneer," Roop says, thrilled as she parks. We all grab chunnis, cover our heads, and step inside.

I sit, lost in thought, as the shabads swirl around me, familiar as lullabies, talking about finding your path and owning your mistakes and starting again if you have to.

I keep hoping Ranbir will magically appear, the rumble of his voice in my head as he sings the raag. Shenaz looks around, too, oddly furtive. "He's not here," I finally say, trying to keep my voice low.

"Not he, she."

What? Then I see her. Sukhi Mamiji, Roop's mom. Far corner, seated, her back leaning against the wall. So much older, so much frailer. Alone. "I called her," Shenaz says. Shit. Shenaz is asking for it. Roop hasn't seen her. Yet.

Shenaz notes the stress on my face and panics. Clearly, this was poorly plotted. Too late now.

I inhale the halwa they dole out as prasad, then rise. Maybe if we move fast enough, heading straight into the langar hall, they won't even see each other.

But as soon as Roop stands, scoping the room for the trash can, she spots her mother. And her mother sees her. I've seen Roop grumpy, disgruntled. But now she looks caught. And absolutely furious.

First, she glares at me. I shake my head, violently, to ensure I don't catch this wrath. "All her," I say, pointing frantically to Shenaz.

"She's your mother." Shenaz looks unfussed. "And your mamiji. Of course this is happening." She seems pleased with herself. Because only a fool would make a scene here, a busy Saturday at the gurdwara.

Mamiji makes her way over, leaning heavy on her cane. She's fully gray now, her hair thin and long in a braid, her frame much smaller than I remember. Shorter than me, if that's possible. But it doesn't seem right.

"Maya, baby," she says, reaching for me and locking me against her chest, which feels deflated, almost hollow, especially compared to Ma's. "Kitni badi ho gahi hai."

"Sat Sri Akaal, Mamiji," I say, trying to maintain my composure.

"You're a good girl." She pats my head. "Talk to your bhena."

She doesn't say a word to Roop. Or Shenaz. "I'll die without grand-children. I'll die without my daughter. This is what she wants? A girl? A Muslim. It can't work. It's not done. Make her understand."

I can feel the rage. It simmers, a spark about to blaze. "Nothing I need to understand," Roop says, practically spitting, as all eyes land on us. She doesn't care. "And I think Maya may be the only Malhotra who gets it."

She storms off, headed toward the parking lot.

"We better go," Shenaz says, snatching my hand and leading me away from my aunt, who looks shocked, like Roop's reaction might be what kills her. Like she didn't just try to destroy her own daughter. "She'll leave without us. Roop. I'm not joking."

As we race toward the car, which is already on, I turn back to look at the gurdwara. My mamiji is still standing there, watching us leave. Not making a move to stop us.

The ride back is a matchbox of tension. Roop stares straight ahead, focusing on the road, while Shenaz seems small in the pas-senger seat, chewing her cuticles. I've *never* seen her do that. But I keep my mouth shut. None of my business.

"You never learn." Roop is still seething.

"She's your mother."

"She's never going to accept who I am. Who you are. Who we are together. And I don't care. I'm not changing anything about us, about our life, for that woman. For anyone."

I feel what she says deep in my bones. Her mother looked right through her, talked right through her, like she wasn't even there. I can't even imagine what it must have been like to live like that all these years.

"I'm sorry," I say, and I realize too late that I'm crying. Because this isn't about me. Never was. This whole time, I was the one who wasn't there, all this time. I was the one who was MIA, who couldn't be bothered. Not Roop. "I didn't know. Mom didn't know. We would have been there, I promise you we would have."

I catch Roop's eye in the rearview mirror and see the tears staining her cheeks. "I know you would have," she says, in a voice that's almost too quiet. "That's kind of the hardest part."

We drive the rest of the way home in silence, Roop's words repeating in my head. I don't even know how to begin to fix this, but I have to. Roop might not have her mother—that much seems irreparable. But she will have her family, our family, if I have anything to say about it.

18

XANDER'S BEEN BRINGING ME BAGELS. I TRY NOT TO READ too much into it, but it's sweet, and they're always different kinds, from different shops.

"Someone's got to teach you how to be a New Yorker," he says in a fake Queens accent every time I thank him.

Turns out we work well together, like our brains just click, and he tackles one thing while I do the other. It's weird, and comfortable. And weird. Becca's definitely noticed. Which means other people probably have, too.

He's been helping me brainstorm ideas for the sections, manage freelancer emails and invoices, and flesh out story pitches. Like the column on adulting, which is coming together quickly.

"That graphic could be super cool," he says, leaning across the table as he chats with Marcie from art. She's pretty much adorable, round cheeks, red lips, short blond pigtails, big green eyes, a pop punk Bettie Page vibe, a little funky but high drama. And always rocking those hand-painted Mary Janes. "They're my thing," she said when I asked her about them. "The outlet, side hustle, or whatever. Painting relaxes me."

I told her she should be in Fashion, but she said Fashion doesn't do size fourteen, despite all the diversity talk. "Pleasantly plump is an eight to them," she told me with a shrug. So she does her own thing. She studied design at RISD in Rhode Island, and this is her first real job, which is why she exclaims "I love this column" every so often. "I'm going to learn so much."

She's created this amazing template for the layout using block art cutouts dipped in paint to design the spread so it looks textured, like it pops right off the page. Each version of the column will involve new blocks, but the vibe is worth it, in my humble opinion.

"That is kick-ass," I say, and she grins at me like a doting older sister, proud. "I think this is really going to get some attention. And help some people, too."

"I can't wait to work on the 'How to Adopt a Pet.' Can you imagine the cute little block cutout animals? So fucking adorable."

She leans on the table, pointing out a few other things on the current layout, and Xander steps close as they talk.

The first one I'm writing is on "How to Move to a New City," which has been eye opening to say the least. And what I'm learning is it takes a lot. Too much. I'm probably, definitely not ready to move anywhere solo, to be honest. But the thought of leaving this place in just about a month is slightly devastating, too.

"Wow, did you know that you can get an apartment in Columbus, Ohio, for under nine hundred dollars?" Marcie says, slapping the table. "Be right back, guys, I'm packing my bags."

I laugh, but then she walks out. We wait for a minute or two. I shrug. "Guess we're done with that."

"It's going to be awesome," Xander says, still staring at the layout. "Thanks again for letting me write one."

I frown. "Stop thanking me. You're good at this stuff. You should own it." I feel like I can hear Ranbir's voice in my head, telling me that. And now I'm here. *Better. Faster. Fiercer.* Just like I imagined. I can feel the waterworks coming on, so I decide to zoom in on something else.

"She's really cute, Marcie."

Xander shrugs. "I guess."

He looks down at the spread, then back up at me. "By the way, been meaning to ask. How's it going with Rebound Dude?"

I frown. "Don't call him that."

"That well, huh?"

I sigh. "It's complicated."

He grins. "Warned you."

I can't hack it. "Whatever. Let's just focus," I say, gathering all the spreads and heading out of the conference room. "We've got the scions roundup at three, okay? I'm going to grab a bite, and I'll meet you there."

Most of my time at *Fierce* is amazing. But there are moments when I kind of get why they call it work. Like when Jordan drones on and on about his favorite '90s movies, expecting me to know exactly what he's talking about, and to play the budding ingenue, ethnic edition, he's somehow turned me into in his head. "We could do a thing on all the nineties movie reboots, comparing the new ones to the originals."

I don't know where Xander is. I waited for him before I came to the meeting, but didn't want to be late. Now I'm stuck here on the sofa in Jordan's office—and I'm jealous he gets a sofa and an office, which: goals—and feeling decidedly uncomfortable, since he's sitting way too close. Like almost on top of me. I scoot again, making space, but he leans closer.

"If you tell me about the originals you want to include, I can check to see if there are already reboots in the works." My voice squeaks, up-speaking with nerves, and it makes me cringe. His hand is on my thigh now. How the fuck did that happen? "Jordan," I say, scooting again. "You're kind of—"

"Hey," Xander says, plowing right in. Jordan leaps away and scampers toward his desk, leaving a full two thirds of the sofa empty. Xander takes a seat toward the middle, pointed, deliberate. But I'm still squished. "Sorry I was late. Becca had me on a few tasks I needed to wrap up."

I take a deep breath. "Yeah, so Jordan wants to do a spread charting nineties reboots, comparing them to current updates and remakes. I haven't seen a lot of them, the old versions, I mean," I confess, and Jordan turns sort of red. "You know, because I was really young then." Or like, not even born. "But I can watch. For research."

"We can do a movie night at my place," he says. "I have a sixty-five inch."

Ew. Xander rolls his eyes.

"Or I can pull copies in the media room, if you'd prefer, Maya," Xander says, his tone light even though I can see him seething underneath. "I know you have a lot of commitments postwork this week. And we want to get moving."

Jordan frowns. "I have screening passes for—"

"Already called in the screeners for all the forthcoming titles, which should include these remakes," Xander says, his smile even and bright. "So Maya can download them and watch at home. But I'll double-check. Ericka told me to call everything in so we'd be ready to go for the January special."

Jordan looks like he's about to breathe fire now, and it makes me want to giggle. "Well, aren't you just hyperefficient," he says.

Xander grins, the dimple presenting itself. Then he looks at me, my cue.

"This should be pretty straightforward, once we have the titles gathered." I turn to Jordan. "You could probably put the rest of that information in an email. No need for more meetings, since everyone's so busy. Ericka likes us to use our time wisely."

Jordan nods. "Yeah, guess so."

"Anyway, for January, we've got celeb scions from India, Korea, Brazil, and Nigeria on board already," I say. "Xander's looking into China and Japan. What we need to decide is: Shoot? Or existing art? I can loop photo to see what's out there. We'd need to make it look cohesive visually. Because given the international scope of the story, it'll get expensive quick."

"We have to use existing," Jordan says, suddenly dismissive. "We just don't have the budget. And when we go digital-first, we're—"

"Wait, what?" I say. Digital-first? *Fierce.* "You mean . . ."

"Oh, oops, I think I spilled. Yeah, it was part of the deal for bringing Dulcie in at all, because, well, you know, something's gotta give. As of January, they're going to eliminate the monthly print. Makes sense. Circs are way down across the board, especially in the young women's category, and they're focusing on building all the websites into more robust spaces. It's just numbers. Business as usual." Then he smirks. "But you didn't hear it from me."

"You okay, Maya?" Xander's peering at me, concerned.

"It's just, the magazine's always been known for these stunning spreads, for the photography and the amazing visual storytelling and—"

Jordan shrugs. "It is what it is in magazines nowadays. Been happening for years, and inevitable. Relax. At least it's not a full video pivot."

"And they're not killing it all dead," Xander adds. "Like they've done to so many mags before *Fierce*."

Especially magazines that attempt to center marginalized voices, I think.

"That too. But sharpen those skills while you're still young," Jordan says, rising, as if we're dismissed. "Video and audio are it now. And you're cute. We've all got to adjust." He walks toward the door. "So full speed ahead on this, and, Maya, send me those other pitches. Once we nail down the others, we'll find a writer to pull it all together and get this all locked down."

That catches me off guard. We're doing all the research and reporting, Xander and I. "But Ericka said—I thought we'd write—"

"Nah, this is too big. We need someone who can synthesize it all, unify the whole thing but also bring their own presence and authority," he says, a hint of glee in his voice. "Sorry, kid, ain't you. Yet. You managed to get into the room. But you've got to prove you have the chops. Plus, you guys will have your hands full with February stuff already."

As we walk out of the office, my blood boils. "What an ass."

"You talking to me?" Xander says, swerving back with a smirk. Then he turns serious. "Sorry I left you alone with that guy. The stuff Ramon has told me—" He whistles. "It could fill a tell-all. Becca was holding me hostage again. I swear she—"

"Why doesn't anyone report him?" I ask, seething. "I should—"

"He's one of Jude's installs. Not going anywhere. You're literally just going to get yourself on the shit list."

"He totally got off on telling me I—we—pretty much get no credit for this."

Xander shrugs. "I mean, makes sense," he says. "Kind of how it works here. But yeah, he sure was thrilled to break the news."

The thing no one tells you about being an adult: It's meetings, meetings, meetings. When it could just be a text. Or, like, worst case, an email. These people need to learn how to stop talking so much and write shit down in concise, direct little lists. Things would move so much faster. I've been here nearly three weeks now—and my summer's almost over already—but if things keep up the way they've been, I'll only have one print piece to show for myself. It'll be a good one, but it kind of sucks. Especially if the *Fierce* I've always known and loved disappears altogether.

But I barely have time to write. I'm always doing research or gathering thoughts or "reaching out" or finding writers—other people to write stuff!—or pitching nonstop. Then combing through freelance ideas and sending rejections. Like the one I would have gotten.

Then there's this secondary to-do list Becca keeps for me of what I like to call Exceedingly Dull Tasks: tracking all the assignments, chasing writers and sources, tracking invoices, managing the assistant, aka Xander, and maybe, if I can squeeze in some actual editing, doing a first-pass edit on some of the short posts for the website.

Is this really my dream? Sometimes it feels more like a nightmare. "Tell me again why we wanted to do this?"

Xander laughs. But I'm still frowning. "It's been three weeks, dude. Chill with your Gen Z entitlement." Then he puts on this croaky old man voice. "Don't you know, kid, that you've got to pay them dues? Slog, slog, slog, start from the bottom, work your way up. Play your cards right. And preferably be white." He grins again. "Oh well, we both missed that boat. Too bad, so sad. Guess you'll just have to work a hundred times harder."

"Ericka says it's a thousand. At least."

"At least you've got her in your corner."

"Yeah, but she can't control everything. And she doesn't know half of the bullshit Becca pulls."

"Suck it up, Maya. You can't tattle, and you gotta deal. You need this. You want this. You told me so yourself. Do the work. Make it work."

I nod. "You're right. I have to get it together." But I want to write more. I know he does, too. The hope, it dangles. Just out of reach. "Jordan, though, could you believe him?"

He pretends to paw me like a bear, bulldozing my way, but I duck. "Guess he could tell that I wasn't interested," I say, "especially because, dude, you shut him down at every turn."

He shudders. "Smarmy. That's what you call guys like that. And so condescending. 'When I was your age . . .'" He smirks again. "And he actually thinks you're twenty-six."

My mouth hangs open, and I try to speak, but nothing quite comes out. Shit. I knew it was inevitable. I just didn't—

"You thought I didn't know?" His face is incredulous. "That I wouldn't figure it out? Or that I'd never call you on it?" He laughs. It's low and husky and maybe a little mean. "I looked you up." He shakes his head. "After that second day in the closet. Because I thought you were kind of cute."

He pushes silky strands off his face, annoyed. "But you didn't really exist. I mean, hundreds of Maya Malhotras. But not you. Then you showed up here, with some new name on your ID—the one Ericka made me take to HR. Something completely different, and if you do a little poking, hate to tell you, it's obvious. To anyone with rudimentary reporting skills. And mine are stellar, let's be honest."

He laughs again, like he's still astounded. I'm still astounded. "You look like a teenager, you have no impulse control, and there is no *Stinking Rose*. There's no RoopKiran Malhotra from Gilroy—only a resident on staff at Robert Wood Johnson in Jersey. Who's related to a Maya Gera. Rising senior at Gilroy West High School. On the school paper, complete with clips about garlic farming. Seventeen. Looks a lot like you." He sighs, taking in my panic. "It's so obvious. And yeah, I am kind of pissed. You don't just go from high school to assistant editor." He's moving again, and I'm hot on his heels, so I crash into him when he stops short. "How'd you manage it, anyway?"

I look around, walking toward my cube, making sure we don't have company. Almost everyone's gone already.

I take a deep breath. I guess I owe him the truth.

"I'm seventeen. They think I'm twenty-six. I was supposed to interview for a fashion internship, under Shenaz. But LuLu had to green-light it." It's a relief to let it all out.

"And you're so 'not fashion.'" He laughs when I scowl. "Come on."

I nod. "No go. Then I ran into Ericka. Who's like my literal hero. We started talking. She thought I was her eleven-thirty interview. I thought she was hiring an intern."

"Not assistant editor?"

I shrug. "I didn't know that job even existed—I saw the posting after she offered it to me. By then, all the internships were full, and Shenaz said the whole hiring thing was a mess because of all the changes, and—and, truth be told, I needed the money. And I did a good job on the test. I worked my ass off. So she offered me the role. She didn't realize—"

"And you didn't tell her." He starts aggressively packing up his stuff. "That's super shady, Maya."

"I didn't know until I got here. Until Becca started talking, and then HR emailed, and by then, it was too late. I'd had a taste." I sigh. "I couldn't just give it up. I should be in Rutgers right now. At Cow Camp." He looks up, cocking an eyebrow. "I'm a farm girl from Gilroy. My whole life is garlic. I live and breathe it. My hair used to smell like it." The words spill out like tears, unstoppable. "I've read and loved *Fierce* since I was ten. Yes, that's only seven years ago. But those are seven formative years. I hardly ever saw myself on the page. Until Shenaz. She's my cousin's girlfriend. And my cousin is the real RoopKiran Malhotra. It's her name. Her ID. Her address. Her birthdate. She's twenty-six. She did this. For me. Point is, Shenaz was the first brown person I saw in these pages, the first clue that maybe I could be someone different, do something different. And when I got here, there she was, this living breathing, beautiful human, chasing her dreams. When I quit Cow Camp—"

He laughs. "Wait, what's Cow Camp?"

"Long story. Too long. Someday. Not now." He's sitting in my chair, intrigued, that curious energy back full speed. And I know he notices our knees are touching when I sit on the filing cabinet across from him. Because I do, too. "I quit because I had to shoot my shot. It's like you said—you only get so many. And it was the chance of a lifetime when Shenaz said I could help her in the closet this summer. And then everything just—got mixed up. Now here I am."

He doesn't look as convinced anymore. But for some reason, I need him to understand.

"So maybe I skipped a few steps."

"A lot of steps."

"And told a few lies."

"A lot of lies."

"Too many lies," I say, suddenly exhausted. I'm tired of defending myself to everyone about everything. "But this is my dream. I got this one weird, rare shot at it. To live it. A total fluke. Are you telling me you would pass it up?"

He shakes his head. "I already told you I wouldn't. I didn't. You know how hard I worked to get here, to be here."

"I've wanted this. For as long as I can remember. I always wanted to share other people's stories. And maybe to share my own stories, too. It could all fall apart any second, but in the meantime, I'm here. I'm living the dream. But to get here, I've had to lie to almost everyone. My whole family, who still don't know. Not even about Cow Camp. To Ericka. Becca. Dulcie. HR. You."

"Was it worth it?" he says, his voice quiet.

"Hell yeah, it was." My conviction surprises me.

He doesn't flinch. "Okay, then."

I peer at his face, and it's peaceful now. Like maybe he understands. "Okay, then what?"

"I won't spill."

"So you get it?"

"Yeah." His fingers are drumming again, and I kind of want to reach for them. To make it stop or something. It's too familiar. It pinches. "Kind of. My parents weren't really into this either. They wanted me to be a lawyer or something, to help my community, my mom always says. They need me. She doesn't know the power we have here, the change we can effect. How we can shift the narrative."

The drumming starts again, and I can't help it, I reach for his hand. To make it stop. He looks up, surprised. "By writing ourselves into it," I say.

"Yeah." He grins. "That." He takes a deep breath. "You headed back to Jersey?"

I nod. "But I'm gonna go grab a bite first." I look up at him,

regretting the words already. This is going to be trouble, I can tell.
"You down?"

There's that dent again. "But not the cafeteria, okay?"

"Nope. Can't quite afford that. Not till payday at least." I grab
my bag. "But I know a place. Do you like kati rolls?"

19

Thursday's meeting is the big one. The monthly planning extravaganza with Dulcie. And it's clear something's up.

The memo she sent said all the "official staff" must be present. And I'm so excited because that includes me.

"Let me repeat, lest you forget, that while ideas are critical, there's a hierarchy in place for a reason. Listen and learn, see how it's done," Becca lectures as we race down the hall. "But remember: It's an honor just to be in the room where it happens. You've got to earn the privilege. Keep your head down, take notes, and listen. Otherwise you're overstepping. I literally didn't speak to the editor in chief for my first two years at the magazine."

"Well, that's rude," I say, and she rolls her eyes. What did I ever see in her?

Dulcie's already front and center, setting up the video chat by the door, and when I walk in, she waves. Becca, confused, looks behind her. At me.

"How's it going?" Dulcie says, pausing me as I walk past. "I love the green polka dots." I do my little twirl, showing off my new dress, and she wolf whistles. It makes me miss Ranbir. "A Shenaz selection?"

"Actually, my friend Cherry made it," I say. "But Shenaz featured me in one of Cherry's dresses in Found Fashion on the website once, and boom! Such an uptick in sales. And I'm having a blast. Thank you for letting me have a seat at the table."

Dulcie winks, and I swear, Becca nearly passes out on the spot.

As we're settling in—at the far end of the table, of course—I can feel her seething. "All my advice is totally wasted on you," she says.

"It is. But I'd like to think it's going pretty well," I reply, trying to keep the bite out of my voice. "She's, like, human or whatever."

Becca frowns. "You don't get it. There are rules. You need to learn them. Otherwise you're stepping out of line."

Nope, she doesn't get it. The hierarchy she's talking about, all the rules and ladders and systems, historically and to this day, were put in place to protect people who look like her. Not people who look like me. If that's about to topple, I couldn't be happier. Xander would appreciate that thought, I think, and peer around, looking for him. He's on the far end of the room, seated with the other team assistants on stools by the wall of windows. When he spies me spying, he nods. But it's all business.

"Okay," Dulcie says, clapping her hands as she steps to the front. "I'm excited to welcome you to the new *Fierce* team. We're going to do things differently from here on out. I know some of you have heard inklings—because the media press won't stop speculating. But the rumors are true. December will be the final print issue of *Fierce* magazine, almost exactly thirty-five years since it was born."

Murmurs float throughout the room. Jordan's heads-up was real. But it still feels like a punch to the gut. I'm here, finally, a dream come true. And now the dream is dying.

"Oh, your faces," Dulcie says, looking from person to person. "So sad. But you shouldn't be. Because this new version of *Fierce* that I've been brought on to reimagine—along with my mentor Legend Scott, Ericka Turner, and some of the core team from the previous regime—has big things planned. This new *Fierce* is truly going to take bigger, stronger, faster, fiercer to soaring new heights. And you will all be part of that."

There is some light applause, but my hands are too shaky to join in.

"We will live primarily on the web, and are in the thick of a redesign—with creative director Legend Scott helming, and final approval from Jude McIntyre, of course—that will make *Fierce* a leader in bringing the real and necessary voices of the twenty-first century to the readers who need them. Truly diverse voices for a truly diverse readership. The best way to reach those readers— the teens and twentysomethings of today and tomorrow? On their phones, tablets, computers, incorporating art, video, and audio to create a more 360 experience. The critical thing for you all to know and remember, though, is that reenvisioning *Fierce* as a web-forward publication means we can be even more ambitious and immediate in the scope of our reporting and analysis, and in delivering critical stories to our readership fast, fierce, and dirty."

That gets some laughs.

"With all that said," Dulcie says, "what we're discussing in today's meeting—the remaining three print issues of *Fierce*—will become its legacy on paper. Which means I need your best, brightest, boldest takes. Come on, now. Bring 'em."

The meeting gets underway, and each team starts pitching, some still mourning or caught off guard, some enthused and excited.

I don't know quite how to feel. Mournful, because it's the end of an era? Or honored, because I get to be part of it? Whatever we do now, we have to make it count.

I try to focus on what Becca suggested, since it's my first (and last) full staff meeting: I listen and take a lot of notes. I scribble down suggestions I can make to improve other people's pitches, and think about how we could twist something this way or that to make it fresher and fiercer. But Ericka will do the talking for our team, mostly, since she's the features editor, so she's right up front near Dulcie, and our shared Basecamp, which I'm managing for record keeping, will keep all our collective wisdom right at our fingertips.

"It's time for another look at teen pregnancy across the board," Ericka says. From reading the magazine the past seven years, I know this is one of their annual hot takes, something with a twist to bring the conversation forward.

"I'd almost skip it," Dulcie says. "Space in these three issues is premium. And we've done it like forty times. Hard to keep it fresh."

The room goes silent. Kill the whole thing? Just like that? "But it's a critical topic," Ericka says. "Seventy-five percent of teen pregnancies in the United States are unplanned."

Huh. What an odd number. What about that other 25 percent? Are there teenagers who actually *plan* pregnancies?

Dulcie frowns. "Not worth the real estate," she says. "It's dull. Repetitive. The numbers have barely changed. What's new about it?"

Not a peep from the rest of us.

But that 25 percent thing is stuck in my head. Then it hits me. I know some of those kids. I grew up with them. And I don't quite know if it's new, really. But I've never seen a story on anything like it.

"We could do something a bit more unexpected," I say, loud and clear, surprising myself. "I'm from rural California, and in some of the old-school communities there—Punjabi like mine, but also Mexican, and other traditional cultures—it's still pretty common for young women to actually be wed and have children in their teens. That other 25 percent, which never gets covered. The planned teen pregnancies. I have friends who graduated high school—I mean, like, I know of kids who graduated like this year, then got married, and pregnant, immediately. They're eighteen, nineteen. Sometimes younger. Teen moms, for sure, but not the ones you'd see on a reality TV show. Not the same kind of lives or experiences by a long shot. They usually live in multigenerational homes, and they're the backbone of the household, with some heavy expectations put on them for such a tender age."

Ericka frowns. "I don't know. That sounds a bit white-gazey, like those 'look at how oppressed I am' stories I always read as a teen."

It's true, I've seen far too many of those. She's probably right. Dulcie nods, concern registering. Which I appreciate.

But these kids, they're real. And they deserve to be acknowledged and heard, too. I take a deep breath and speak again. "It doesn't have to play like a stereotype. These are American kids, born and raised here, going to American high schools. But this is their community structure, and most of the time, they choose to stay a part of it. They know the expectations, and they abide by them. Am I saying it's not archaic?" I shrug. "I don't know. Everyone has their own take. But I know some of these girls. And I think maybe they'd love the opportunity to have their voices heard. Because I think that rarely happens."

Dulcie looks intrigued. "Do you think this is limited to California? The scope might be too narrow."

From across the room, Xander clears his throat. Becca looks stricken, but he plows full speed ahead. "Definitely seen some of this in Queens communities, and in Texas. I bet you'd find it in other ethnic enclaves, too—Filipino or Latinx, Hmong, Orthodox Jewish, certainly Amish."

Ericka seems more enthused now. "Seems like you could paint a pretty diverse, nuanced portrait—not just brown and Black kids bearing the burden," she says, sounding relieved. "We'd need some experts, but do you guys know any candidates we could feature for something like this if we did break out portraits along with the broad strokes?"

I know a few too many. But one stands out in my head as an obvious pick. "My friend Neela would be great. She's nineteen, studying biochem at Fresno State, and mom to Ravi, a very rambunctious and photogenic two-year-old. Her family is really old school, but she's balancing a lot. I think she'd be super quotable."

Dulcie grins, something sparking in her eyes. Curiosity?

Amusement? "Well, get her on board, and it's a little sticky, but you can do the breakout if that will make her more comfortable. Becca, you'll pull the threads." Then she turns toward Xander and the assistant contingent, who all look super nervous now. "And I'm thinking"—she turns back to me, then back to them—"we've got a pretty amazing pool of reporters here in the assistants and interns, people who are living these lives, who really know what's going on with teens and young people today. They're underutilized if they're fetching coffee."

I nod. It's true.

"Maya, you might be the right person to spearhead something I've been thinking about. A teen reporting fellowship. Something that gives kids real reporting and writing experience, and readers real access to these stories, stories that us older folks would have to stomp and shake out. What do you think?"

Whispers scatter throughout the room, and I can feel the stares, surprised and intrigued. "That would be pretty kick-ass. I'll pull together some thoughts and send them to you Monday. And I'll reach out to Neela today."

"Great. Okay. Next?"

I can feel Becca scowling. And it delights me.

Xander and I spend the next two days researching and sending out emails to find viable candidates for the new piece, which Ericka is calling "The Other Twenty-Five Percent: The Unexpected Face of Planned Teen Pregnancy Today."

But I'm distracted. I keep drifting, staring at the screen, thinking about Ranbir and his mom. And Roop and her mom. And all the things I've been hiding from my own mom. How she would feel if she knew. How it might just destroy her, us, all our trust.

But then I wonder how much of that trust actually existed in the first place if she took so long to tell me about the deal with Dolly's family, which is full speed ahead, "on shelves in September," according to Cherry's frequent updates, since Ma is unreliable at best. And she hasn't said a single word about the farm. But maybe that's because I've totally been ignoring her texts and not calling her back because I'm lying to her and Papa about pretty much every single aspect of my life. Like mother, like daughter.

"So what do you think?" Xander says, tapping my leg.

"Huh?" Clearly, he's been talking for a while, but I've been long gone.

He sighs. "Never mind. It can wait." It's almost four on a summer Friday, and the office is nearly empty. "We should do this Monday."

I shrug. "I could use a break."

"You doing anything fun this weekend?" He sounds weird again. Tentative. Unsure. So not himself. Definitely not the same assistant who had the gumption to chime in during the big Don't-Talk-to-Dulcie staff meeting yesterday.

"I don't know. Sleep, maybe. And there's this guy." It just pops out. Because I can't stop thinking about him.

"Rebound Dude?" There goes Xander's brow again, suspended, curious. "Didn't realize he was still around."

"I haven't seen him in a bit. And the last time was a mess. He's sort of maybe back with his ex." This just sounds worse and worse. "But I don't know. I miss him."

"He's in California?"

I shake my head. "Cow Camp." I swallow my stress. My mom still texts about it nonstop. And Guru and Ranbir and everyone. Clearly, Dolly hasn't spilled my secret. Yet. But I can't keep lying to her forever.

His face falls for a second. Then he puts the familiar Xander face back on, dimple and all. "Well, you should reach out." He shrugs. "Or not."

He's got his backpack slung over his shoulder, ready to go, when we hear the commotion.

"Then find someone else to write it." The voice is quiet but seething. And coming from Ericka's office. "I'm telling you. From day one, she's done nothing but undercut me."

"A—Calm down," Ericka says, her voice all business. "And B—I don't think that's true. She wants opportunity. Room to grow. The kind you had handed to you when you first got here. Lest we forget."

Ouch. "She's not messing around," Xander says, his voice low but excited. "Gotta love it."

I nod, and we lean in to listen.

"Not my problem," Becca says. "I'll hire someone, freelance it out. I refuse to carry an assistant. I have too much on my plate. I've paid my dues."

"You'll do it, or I'll talk to Dulcie."

"Go right ahead," Becca announces, standing abruptly and shoving through the door as Xander and I dive into his cube, hiding out until she storms off. He smells good. Crisp and a bit woodsy, like rosemary. I need to stop noticing these things. As his boss. And because he's in actual college. Off-limits, all around, in any scenario.

"Geez. Do you think Becca truly hates us?" I ask him. It stings, even though she's done very little to earn my sympathy. "I mean, maybe we should have—"

"Are you kidding me?" Xander says, standing and pulling me up. "We did amazing this week. I've done more reporting and writing in the last few weeks than I have in the whole time I've been here. You're going to leave with real bylines, and you're seventeen."

He shuts his mouth fast, because Ericka steps out then, her purse slung over her shoulder, her face composed. Like a bratty overindulged associate editor didn't just throw a tantrum in her office. Or maybe she's dealt with way worse. Which is probably the truth.

"You heard?" she says, and her voice betrays exhaustion.

I nod. Xander sort of hides behind me. Even though he's a head taller.

"Whatever. Maybe I can't fire her because of Jude and his mandates. But she doesn't get to tell me how to run things. She'll write it. And you and Xander will do your parts. You're earning those taglines. No ifs, ands, or buts." She starts to walk off. Then pauses. "Know what? This is a big effing deal. We should celebrate. So come on. Drinks and dinner on me. Both of you."

Xander frowns. He's being awkward again. "I've really gotta catch up on school stuff. But you guys have fun. I'll see you Monday."

Ten minutes later, we're seated at this fancy little steakhouse on Ninth Avenue. "I live in Hell's Kitchen, so this is my favorite local spot," Ericka says as the waiter walks up. My stomach's been flipping the whole walk over—what if they card me? What if they can tell it's a fake? What if everything unravels, right here, right now, in this moment? When I'm finally living my dream, and it's finally going pretty awesome?

The lies are going to be the end of me.

"Merlot for me," Rick says, then the waiter turns to me.

I freeze. Then breathe. "Do you guys have proscato, by chance?" I shouldn't even bring it up. But if Ericka likes it, she could put Bespoke Wines on the Best List. That would be huge for Ranbir and his family. And I'll just have the teensiest sip.

"You mean Moscato?" Rick says, grinning.

I shake my head. "No, proscato."

The waiter nods. "From Dhillon Estate Bespoke Wines, correct? They're quite lovely. We just got a shipment."

"Oh, I've never had that," Ericka says. "Maybe I'll try it, too. Let's get a bottle."

"Certainly, madame," the waiter says, then pauses, turning to me again. "I'll need to see some ID, though, miss." The moment of truth. I pull the card out—the fake, with my picture and Roop's everything else. He peers at it closely, frowning. But then lets it slide, no questions asked. Thank god.

We order food—steak frites medium rare for her, and roast chicken for me, and then the waiter's back with the wine. It's gleaming and familiar in his hands as he displays it, and I feel that little pang getting bigger. The waiter pours a small glass for Rick to taste before we commit. "Ohh," she says, taking a sip. "That's lovely. Like a floral fizziness. Tickles my nose. Where'd you discover this, Maya? We should put it on the Next Best List."

"I'm sure the family would love that. I know their son, Ranbir." I stare down at my burrata. "His dad owns one of the most eco-friendly wineries in Northern California. They have, like, twelve thousand acres."

"Sounds fancy."

"Yeah, it is. It's a funny little world. Like the celebrity scions, in a way. You don't think of farm kids as glamorous. But these Punjabi millionaires, well, they know their Prada from their Gucci, for sure. And the kids are a whole nother level."

Ericka cuts into her steak and leans forward, intrigued. "Fascinating. Almost sounds like a story to me. You're from this world?"

"Gilroy. Where the shooting happened." Am I sharing too much? Giving myself away? Maybe I should. The lying is exhausting. And I like Ericka. I wish I could just tell her the truth. To let her know me. The real me, seventeen and all. Maybe she'd like me anyway. But she'd have to fire me for sure. "Sort of the outskirts of it all. My family—my aunt's family, I mean—they've got a farm, much smaller, about twenty acres, in old-school garlic country. Like you can actually smell it when you drive through the town, wafting, and the sky's always streaked with fire at night. The colors are just incredible." My throat catches for a minute, and I grab my proscato, trying to compose myself. Just a sip. That's it. No more. Ericka can drink it, and I'll be good company. "It's beautiful."

"The festival was where the shooting was, right? You told me that?"

I nod. "Yeah. It's a tiny little community, a lot of brown people, green fields, fruit stands, an outlet mall. My friend Cherry, the designer, she's from Gilroy, too. It's changing now. A lot of tech folks buying in, since it's close to Apple and Microsoft, all those places. So the demographic looks different. In ten years, maybe it'll be gone. People are snatching up all those parcels of land."

Like maybe ours, I don't say. I can't bring myself to think about it, to accept that there may have been truth in Dolly's words.

"Sounds beautiful." She swishes the wine again, draining the glass. "This stuff goes down real easy. Do you miss California? I've only ever been to LA and San Francisco."

"I do," I say, and realize it's true, uncomplicated, unconflicted. "New York is amazing. But California is home. I miss it."

"It'll shift," Ericka says, wistful, "when you're here long enough. I'm from Michigan, Ann Arbor, and it's beautiful. Been gone ten years. It's not home anymore. New York changes you. Hardens you, maybe." I can tell from her eyes she's hoping it doesn't do the same to me. Worrying that it will. "And don't even get me started on dating here. It's like a waste of energy. Absolute." She pours another glass, and raises it. "But this wine guy—I saw the way your eyes twinkled when you mentioned him. You want him? Go get him. Because you're nothing if not fierce."

"I'll drink to that," I say, and we cheers.

20

THE TRAIN RIDE HOME IS TOPSY-TURVY, MY HEAD SPINNING the whole hour. Then I'm standing on the steps at the station, staring at Ranbir's building just across the street. I swear I only had a glass, maybe two, but it feels different from the fizzy effervescence of those little bottles I shared with Ranbir. Sloppy, uncomfortable.

I peer down at my phone, pondering Ericka's words, and wonder if I should actually text him. We took a photo, me, Ericka, and the proscato, glasses raised and clinking, in his honor. I can't post it, of course, because Ma stalks my social. But Rick said to send it. I can't bring myself to press the button.

"Maya," Ranbir's voice calls, and I must be truly wasted, because it's like I dreamed him up, standing there, right at the base of the stairs. I nearly tumble down them in my stupor. But he catches me.

"How are you here?" I say, cringing at the slur in my voice.

"You texted me. An hour ago. From some bar. With your boss?" He shakes his head, flashing his phone. The picture. The proscato. My head hurts. "Are you okay?"

I nod, trying to walk in heels, drunk, dignified.

He catches my arm. "You can't go home like that. Roop will literally murder you."

"And slice and dice up the body." I'm laughing. "She's a doctor. She knows how."

He leads me away from the station, his grip on my arm firm, not tender. I want to pull away, but I'm curious, too. And I miss him.

The elevator is not fun. Something sloshes in my stomach,

making me dizzy. Wait, can your stomach make you dizzy? I'll ask Roop. Ranbir takes the phone gently out of my hands, pocketing it.

Next thing I know, I'm in his room, on his bed. So soft, so familiar. Oh god, but the sloshing hasn't stopped, and the room—is it supposed to be spinning like that?

"Hey," Ranbir whispers, trying to get me to sip something. Not more wine. Water. Oh thank god, yes, water. Then my stomach lurches, and I race away from him, through the living room, and heave into the toilet.

I must be in there for hours, letting it all out, all the wine, all the anxiety, all the tears. Because then I just feel tired, empty. Like there's nothing left.

Ranbir stands in the doorway, frowning, running his hand through his hair like he does when he's stressed. Or nervous. "You okay?" he asks, and it's too gentle, too familiar. He kneels on the floor, close to me, looking into my eyes like he's a doctor with one of those little lights. But it's just his eyes. Staring into mine. He pulls me up by the arm, steadying, and gives me a toothbrush with a little squirt of paste.

I shake my head. "It's not mine."

He sighs. "It's okay. It's mine. I'll get a new one. You'll feel better. I promise."

I brush my teeth, letting the bubbles work up thick and lathery. Spitting and rinsing and spitting again. Then swigging the mouthwash in the little cup, minty and bright.

He's right. I do feel better. Sort of. I also feel really, really embarrassed.

But he's grinning at me in the mirror, all the way to his eyes. "Want to sit?" he asks.

I nod. But instead of following him to the couch, I head straight for his room.

Guru's in there, but he grumbles and bolts, annoyed.

Great, more stories for the aunties to share. I can't actually bring myself to care.

I throw myself on Ranbir's bed, absorbing the cool softness of his sheets, that familiar scent, lemon and mint and cardamom. Makes me miss him even more. He hovers close, kneeling, his palm on my back, unsure of what to do with himself. I wonder if he can feel my heart hammering, flinging itself around like a bird caught in a cage. I sit up, trying to steady myself, and pull him closer, trying to make him listen, understand. He stands over me, his eyes full of worry, but something else, too. Maybe hope.

Then he kisses me, long and deep, intense but not a raging fire, like it can be. A slow burn, one that might last, if we let it. But he pulls away, his breath a little ragged. A question on his lips.

"Sometimes I still think about what it would be like." He sounds far away, like he did when I asked him to tell me a story. Like he's seeing one in his head, and it just hasn't happened yet. "If it could be the two of us, here on our own individual adventures, maybe, but together? A little piece of home, even far away." I can almost see what he's saying, like that day at the waterfront. Music classes and story sessions and me running around the magazine. Celebrating bylines and concerts. A dream come to life.

But it can't happen. "We'd be so far away," I say, and he nods. Like there was no real hope anyway.

The farm, my family, the raging sun. I couldn't give it all up, not really. And he couldn't either. "Your mom," I say, shattering the illusion. That we could just chase shadows, run away.

He takes my hand, pulling me up off the bed. He kisses the top of my head again, familiar, and whispers into my hair, "Come on, Lachi. Think it's time for me to take you home."

He leaves me at the bottom of the stairs. The wine is long gone, but something heavy sits in my stomach like a stone, a pit of anxiety about to spiral. Launching myself up the three flights to the apartment takes an eternity. Then there's the yelling.

"She's gotten out of control." It's Roop. She's home. And upset. Which means it's probably pretty late.

"Whose fault is that?" Shenaz says. She's more composed, but has more bite in her pinkie finger than Roop does in all five-foot-eight inches of her. And she's not afraid to unleash it.

"Yours, obviously."

"News flash: She's not my responsibility," Shenaz says, and it's like a punch to the gut. "She's yours. And you suck at it, to be frank."

I push the door open, stumbling in, still a mess. "I'm nobody's responsibility."

And I thought it was gone, but I can't contain it. I race to the bathroom again, hoping to let it all out. But there's nothing left. Except tears. A thousand, a million, a whole damn river. Endless, endless tears. I can't stop them. I guess the sobbing is kind of loud, though, because then there's a palm on my shoulder, a hand brushing back my hair.

I turn, expecting Shenaz and softness and comfort. But it's Roop.

"You okay, Maya Memsahib?"

Shenaz has been calling me that endlessly, all summer, from day one. I thought she was just referencing that old movie, still on Netflix. But then it hits me. She got it from Roop. Who gave me that nickname when I was ten and trying on my drama queen vibe. The summer she spent at our house, gifting me *Fierce* and picking nimbus from the citrus tree in the yard, listening to Jagjit Singh records with my dad, and cooking with my mom. And fighting on the phone, endlessly and in tears, with her mom every night. The summer I was totally oblivious to what she was actually going through. How it would change everything. The summer I lost her.

Until I found her again, a different person in a different world, not my Roop. But there she is, when you soften the edges, trying to figure herself out, trying to claim who she wants to be, trying to stake her own space. Giving me the room to do the same, this whole time.

She puts out a palm. "I come bearing ginger ale," she says, her voice soft. "And Tylenol. Doctor's orders. You're gonna need it."

She helps me up, makes me splash water on my face, and waits patiently for me to change into pajamas. Then she plops down on the sofa and makes me sip the soda. "You heard, I'm sure. Shenaz is right. I have been, well, derelict in managing my responsibilities. She's not the only one who's noticed."

I nod and sip, but I can't quite bring myself to talk. I need to hear that familiar Roop voice for a minute. To absorb it again. It's been gone so long, I thought lost forever, so I won't chase it away. Not yet. Just listen.

"There's more." She sighs, leaning back, an arm resting lightly on her head, like when Ma has a migraine but still has to manage everything. Then she sits up and turns to face me. "Cherry's been complaining. And your parents called. They've been calling me a lot. You don't call Buaji; you don't text anyone back. For days at a time." She bites her lip. "That's a problem. You have to talk to them sometime."

And I can't keep lying. About camp. About Ranbir. About *Fierce*.

There's something she's not saying, and I want her to. But I also kind of want her to shut up, to leave it be, to not make me have to spin out any more lies.

"I'll call. I will. Tomorrow." I lean a bit closer, my head on her shoulder, almost making a little nook, like it used to when I was small enough to curl up and cuddle. When she'd still let me. She doesn't push me away. Not yet, anyway. Before I know it, I'm fast asleep. And definitely still dreaming.

21

I SLEEP THE WEEKEND AWAY, MOSTLY TO AVOID ROOP AND Shenaz and all the drama that I might have been too drunk to remember. Like throwing up my insides in front of Ranbir. And the conversation that keeps replaying in my head. How I shattered it, that fantasy. How I can't put it back together again.

And I sleep because I'm tired. Working for a living—even in something "fun," like magazines—wears you out. But Roop did leave a note saying I got paid—two weeks' worth, so far, dropped into a college savings account for future use. Sigh. She left me two hundred bucks on the table. I can hear the scold now: "Don't spend it all in one place."

But I probably will. In the Mac Media cafeteria.

I get to work bright and early on Monday, and on my desk sit final proofs of the inaugural How to Adult feature—my first one, on "How to Move to a New City." It's gorgeous, and I drop Marcie a quick note with a thousand exclamation points.

Then I comb through the emails to see what panned out for the pregnancy story. Lesson learned the hard way—clearly the way I choose to learn *all* my lessons, right?—Only promise what you know you can actually deliver. I open my email, and there's a response from Neela. With baby pictures. But that's about it for the good news. She says she thinks it could be an important story—one that she's never seen told. But she can't be a part of it. *It would kill me and my family to be seen as part of the problem, vague brown faces, statistics.* She says that they already get enough judgment, that she's tired of other women telling her how she's oppressed, that they're going to save her. And honestly, I know exactly what she means.

I write her back immediately, hoping to salvage this, hoping I can make her understand. I tell her about what I've learned in my short time here about point of view, and agenda, and nuance. About the *WHY* of the story. "Let me share our truths, your words, instead of the shorthand they assume." I hope that might be enough to change her mind.

But almost instantly, I get another reply. "Sorry, Maya," she writes. "I love you, but nothing is worth that much auntie drama."

Shit. There goes that. I scroll through my phone contacts, trying to figure out who else might be a solid contender. But if Neela won't talk—and she's the "bold" one—then I'm out of luck. Still, the scroll is soothing.

"You're here early." It's Xander. His hair is still wet, slick and black against his forehead, and I kind of want to reach out and touch it. Which is weird. "How was dinner with Rick?"

It's like words bring back the hangover, and my head throbs. "I got a little wasted. Bespoke Wine will do you in, if you're not careful."

"Bespoke Wine?"

"Proscato." The memory still makes me want to sob, but I manage to compose myself. "We're going to include it on the Next Best List."

"Cool." He grins, and I want to poke the dent. But I need to stop. I'm his boss. This would be actual harassment. And I'm seventeen. I don't need any more problems. Can't.

"So my tía Rosa found us a woman in Chicago who'll talk. She's Indigenous and Mexican, but Chicago born and raised. Wed at seventeen—not pregnant then, but a kid at eighteen. Her husband's twenty-two, and they live with his parents. I think it could work."

"Good," I say, spinning in my chair and instantly regretting it. "Uf, that was not smart. But Neela won't bite. She says she can't take the drama."

"What?" he says, tapping on the partition with his fingers.

I grimace, placing my hand over his again. "It's . . ." I sigh. "I'm sorry, my head. Just—"

"Nah, I'm sorry." He looks a bit stricken. "It helps me work the energy out." He swallows. "ADHD. But I'll try not to."

"Oh, I didn't mean it like that. It's just, it reminds me of someone."

There goes the brow again. Curious. Interested. Perched.

"Bespoke Wine."

"It reminds you of Bespoke Wine?" Confusion brings out the dimple.

"Ranbir. The guy from Cow Camp. His family owns the company."

"Rebound Dude." But he doesn't ask. So I don't tell him.

"Anyway, so let's dig in and figure this shit out," he says, handing me a bunch of files. "I pulled some numbers, and they're pretty solid."

"Good. Because I'm gonna put some together and try again."

"Try what again?" He's smirking. Why?

"Neela. I'm calling. And she's gonna listen. Then she'll do it. I know she will."

As I start combing through the research, highlighting certain facts, I can feel him staring.

"What?" I say. I don't mean to bite, but I can't take the tension.

"I was just thinking, I get that this is sort of a fluke—that you're not supposed to be here. Or maybe, you're supposed to be me."

"What?" I don't get it.

"The assistant."

Yes, that. Or intern, really. That's what I'm supposed to be. And he's supposed to be assistant editor.

He's leaning a bit over the partition between our cubes now. "But I wanted to say, I can see why Ericka would hire you. If you were twenty-six or an adult or whatever. Because I think you're good. At this. In fact, I think . . . I know that you could actually rock at it."

I'm too stunned into silence to really absorb the compliment graciously, and Ma would be terribly disappointed in that. But I'm blushing, and maybe that's enough, because Xander's grinning again. "And I'm not just saying that because you're cute."

He turns, abrupt, takes his seat, puts on his noise-canceling headphones, and stares at the screen, blocking me, the heat in my cheeks, and the weird moment we just had out completely. Maybe I should, too.

It's early, so I text first. Can I call you?

She responds right away. Sure. Ravi's nursing, though. You are forewarned: He's a slurper. I laugh, and I can feel Xander's eyes on me again, but I need to focus.

I dial, and it feels weird. She's a friend; I've known her since third grade. But this is different. There's something more at stake. Something big. I need to prove myself, yes, but I also think this is a story worth telling, worth sharing. I hope she'll let me.

She picks up right away. "Hey, Maya." Almost a whisper. "So you're in New York? Interning?"

Shit. I forgot the fallout this might have for me. Gossip. Drama. Aunties. What was I thinking?

"What happened to Cow Camp?" She lowers her voice. "I've been hearing things about you and Ranbir. And Dolly and—"

I take a deep breath. "Long story. One I'll tell you when I get back. But listen: Can you not—can you not tell anyone?"

She's quiet for a minute, contemplating. "Okay. If you don't want me to. But what are you doing there? Is it awesome? It must be awesome." There's a wistfulness in her voice, one I recognize. One I've lived through. Maybe I have the story all wrong. Maybe

I'm the one who's missing the nuance. I can hear Ravi talking and slurping as he snuggles, her mother-in-law shouting from the kitchen in Punjabi, and it's so familiar, it makes me miss home. And feel guilty for all the times I put Ma off with promises of tomorrow.

But I need to get this done. I need to lock it in. I know I can convince her. "Listen," I say, "Like I said, we're doing a teen pregnancy update, and I pitched them a different take. Your take."

"And what is my take?" Neela says, her voice amused.

"That's just it: I thought I knew. Because I know you. You're eighteen, a wife and mother. The backbone of a family. You're not a number. You're not a statistic. You're a story, like the millions of others that happen every year across this country. A specific, living, breathing story. A story that people need to hear. In your own words."

"So you're saying I can say what I want?" She sounds intrigued. "Like there's no real agenda?"

"I'm saying you set the agenda. It's your story to tell. I'll help shape it, but as an 'As told to.' You can control the narrative."

She's quiet again, and I can hear Ravi's breathing, soft and rhythmic. He's probably asleep in her lap, thumb tucked close to his mouth, the drool spilling out of his fat little pink lips. "How many teeth does he have now?"

She laughs. "Almost two. And he bites." She sighs. "But not enough to break the skin. Yet." She takes a deep breath. "You'd be the one to put it together?"

I nod, like she can see me. "Yup. Me. You know I won't do you wrong."

"Okay, then," she says, and all the anxiety that's been sitting on my shoulders falls off like shredded corn husks. "Let's do it."

"Cool," I say, trying not to betray my relief. "Tell me when you want to set it up." Then I pull off the Band-Aid, hoping for the best. "And maybe we can use some pictures?"

She ponders for a minute. Trying to figure out how much of this decision she can actually make, what the fallout might be. How much damage she'll do. Then she says, "Do you still have those ones from last summer? When Ravi was tiny and we posed in the fields with all the sunflowers."

"Yeah." I think they're still on my phone, actually. "Like the one of you and Sunny and Ravi in front of that whole field?"

"I think that one's perfect. It says what I want to say."

Just like that, it's done. I have my story. When I look up, finally, to tell Xander, he's beaming. Nosy bastard.

"You locked it."

"It's gonna be awesome," I say, envisioning it in my head.

The picture, all those words, telling a story we never get to hear.

"So, lunch?" he says, smiling over the partition.

"Yeah," I say. "And I got paid, finally. So today it's on me!"

We skip the café and head to a Japanese BBQ place down the street. It's a chain, and touristy, but they let you grill your own meat, and even make s'mores.

"Reminds me of the BBQs we have at home on the tandoor," I say, turning a batch of steak and shrimp on the grill as he watches me. The homesickness has been heavy lately. A lot to carry. "Ma makes these chicken tikkas with her famous garlic chutney—I should bring you some."

"Uh, yeah, you definitely should." His feet keep tapping against mine under the table. But I don't know if he's noticed. "We don't have a yard in Queens. Could you maybe make it in the oven?"

"Or even sautéed in a pan," I say, plopping grilled meat on his plate. "My fave is rubbed on fish and roasted."

"Maybe you need to invite me over for dinner."

I know he's joking or whatever, but I can't really imagine him there, with Roop and Shenaz, making small talk. Not the way Ranbir pulled it off, casual and familiar. Xander is New York and big media and snark. Nope. They're like two different worlds.

I think he gets it, though, because he changes the subject. "Have you thought about what you're gonna do yet?"

"What do you mean?"

"Well, it's August. The summer's almost over. And school."

I've been trying to unravel it in my head. How to give up this dream and go back to my reality. School. The farm and the aftermath of this summer.

But there are no easy answers. "I have to figure out how to tell Ericka. She's going to hate me."

He shakes his head. "She's going to be surprised. Probably angry. Yeah. But in the end, maybe down the line, she'll get it. Because she wanted it, too, and made it happen. She's one of us. And when she needs to find your replacement, I'll be right there to soften the blow." He grins, revealing the dent. "I can go with you if you want." His foot stops thumping for a second, his eyes intent on my face. "Just let me know when you're ready."

It's a lot to think about, a lot to sort out. The weight of disappointing her—and Dulcie—is staggering. "Maybe I can tell them it's a family emergency. Or something?" But that would mean more lies. And I'm tired.

He shakes his head, smiling. "You do what you need to. I'll go along with it. But honestly? I'd try honesty."

"What do you know?" I say, throwing my straw wrapper at him. "You're just an assistant."

That pulls up the dent, and he kicks me under the table again. "Well then," he says, awkward again. "Maybe we should get moving, boss. We've got a lot of work to do, and the clock is ticking."

22

FRIDAY NIGHT, AFTER I'VE FILED MY STORY ON NEELA AND edited my first front-of-the-book pages and done a hundred other tiny and important things for the September close, I look at my to-do list. One task left to tackle. But it's a big one.

So after Shenaz has locked herself away, I make a cup of haldi doodh—using the turmeric Ranbir brought over that night when we made dinner a million years ago—and curl up on the couch. I put on Netflix, setting it to *Mahi Way*. Then, finally, I video chat Ma.

She picks up immediately, the joy on her face bigger than I remember.

"Beta, finally!" She waves Papa and Dadoo over, and they hover, half heads on-screen, talking all at once, asking a million questions.

"How is the camp?"

"Are their bulbs supersized?" Papa asks. "That's what Bhullar Uncle keeps telling me."

"How is Guru?" Dadoo asks. "Seems like a nice boy, no?"

"How are Dolly and Ranbir?" Papa adds. "Do you get along with them? Did you celebrate the deal?"

The deal. "It's done?" The chutney. It's done.

Papa laughs, his belly jiggling with pride. "The first bottles are here," he says, shoving one toward the camera. "Dekh. Look at this fancy-schmancy label."

There's no Gera Garlic to be seen. Just Dolly's face, poised and plasticky, smiling primly along with the words SPICE GODDESS splashed across the top. "It's beautiful. I can't wait to see it in the stores," I say. But the words feel hollow.

Papa and Dadoo wave and blow kisses, then leave to go make haldi doodh, inspired by my cup. I think they know Ma and I need space.

And of course, my mom catches it, the pain that I let flicker on my face for the smallest second before putting on my brave front. "Don't worry, Maya. It's just chutney. Lasts forever. Licenses are temporary." Then she grins. "But it means we get to keep the farm."

"That's good," I say. "I'm sorry I've been gone all summer. I know how hard it must be, how much work you guys have taken on."

"It's okay, beta," she says. "You're doing important work, too. You're our future, and I'm glad you can have this adventure, absorb all this knowledge about the way the world works. Like Mahi, on her journey, making mistakes, falling, getting up again."

"Sort of, yeah," I say, wondering what she's heard—and whom she's been talking to. "I'm doing well, Mama. You'd be so happy to see it."

"I am happy. I'll be happier when you're home. This summer *has* been hard, beta. I've missed you a lot."

"I've missed you, too, Ma."

But this has been a dream come true, a minute to be myself, whoever that really is, and I had to take it. Because once reality sets in—in just a few weeks—it may be all I have to hold on to. Likely forever.

I wish I could say all that. I wish I could tell her everything. About Ranbir and Dolly, Shenaz and Roop, Ericka and Xander and Dulcie and maybe even Becca. About the amazing article Neela and I put together this week. About this thing I've found that I'm pretty awesome at. About dreams come true and living the life you want to live. But I can't.

So I just snuggle in, pulling the phone close and falling back on the familiar. "Okay, Mama, I'm so tired, and it's getting late here. But maybe, do you think, we could watch one episode of *Mahi Way*?"

"Of course, beta. I've paused it forever. I'll only ever watch with you."

And so we do, until I fall asleep, Ma's voice in my head and in my dreams.

* * *

The weekend is quiet, hours of Shenaz teaching me how to do a drop stitch, then coloring my hair with this new mehndi coat—a rosy sheen, she promises, but it does look sort of different. Then I work on pitches and respond to random texts from Xander. They're about nothing, mostly: links to articles. Funny, silly memes. Questions about pitches. Restaurants worth exploring. But then comes the question that I leave hanging.

Dinner maybe? You pick the place.

There's something about him that's intriguing—and I don't just mean the dimple. It's sort of the way his brain works, so fast, a bit chaotic, unexpected. The way our brains fit together. Better, faster, fiercer.

But I can't. It's not a good idea. The optics, of course. I'm seventeen. Younger than him. In actual reality. But in the world we live in, even if we're just pretending, I'm way older. His boss. It's just too much. Can't be done. No way. No how. And then there's Ranbir, who sneaks into my thoughts when I least expect it. The way his eyes crinkle, the salt of his lips, forever the scent of cardamom. All the words and dreams he put into my head.

But I still think about that text the rest of the weekend, as Shenaz uses me as a test dummy for her new quick curler, yapping

227

in my ear about Harleen Kaur's latest collection, her mama's nihari, the sneakers she's trying to convince Marcie to make her, and a zillion other things.

"I'm going to miss you." That's all I have to say. And it shuts her up good.

* * *

Xander doesn't bring up the text I ignored when I get to the office Monday morning. He's obviously been there for a while, pulling research for the next round of pitches, filing away the reporting from the September issue, making himself indispensable. Just the right person to fill in as stopgap when I bail. I can't even hate him for it. He'll be here. He's good. And he's not lying to anyone. Except on my behalf. Withholding or whatever. He deserves this opportunity. He does. He can make something real of it.

I'll be gone. I can't do it anyway. But still.

"So you did something to your hair?" he says, grinning over the partition. "It's cute." He doesn't mention the text. "But the old you wasn't so bad either."

"I know," I say.

"He's right," a voice says. "Much better. Maya, was it?"

It's Jude, traipsing through, probably here to drop off his pages. Because that's what he does. Drops them off. And no one edits a word. Or even fact-checks. That's what being the heir buys you in this world.

His voice makes my skin crawl, gooseflesh popping up like a rash. "Maya Malhotra." Cold, deliberate. "That's the name on the copy you filed." Which apparently, he's read. Then he taps the name tag on my cube, swapped out by HR, legalities or whatever. "RoopKiran Malhotra."

"It's a pen name," I say, stammering. "Maya."

"But why would you need a pen name?" He's leaning on the

edge of the partition now, and Xander hovers, overprotective. "Even if it is charmingly alliterative?"

"I—"

"Watch your step, little girl. I know Dulcie brought you on, like the others." The way Jude says the words, the way his eyes narrow, it makes me shiver. He looks from me to Xander and back again. "But she's got a lot to lose. And someone's always watching. Me."

What he doesn't have to say: *My misdeeds will cost her. Dulcie.* That much is clear.

Becca cackles at her desk as he drops a file on it as he walks by, stomping away in his red-soled boots.

"Correct me if I'm wrong," Xander says. "But isn't it weird that he wears boots *all summer*?" Then we both laugh, trying to cut the tension.

I lean close and whisper, despite the warning, "Do you think he knows?"

"About us?"

There is no us. "About me."

Xander shrugs. "You're overthinking. What's he gonna do? HR vetted your shit. Ericka hired you. You're an assistant. Like, in the grand scheme of Mac Media, does it even matter?"

"You're right."

"Usually am." He's grinning. Leaning. Too close. But I don't step back.

"Okay. Two weeks, clock ticking. Then it's all yours," I say, and his face falls a bit. "But I'm going to make it count. You down for something big?"

But I don't get to say anything else, because Becca's raging again. "What the hell is this, Jordan?" she shouts, stomping down the hall. "You ripped this to shreds. It was definitely solid."

Jordan peeks out of his office, catching my eye, making me cringe, as Becca waves the file in his face. "What?" he says, shrugging. "Newbie's writing definitely needs some work."

He's still looking at me, grinning. Like he's punishing me somehow. But I don't understand.

She follows his gaze, frowning. "Newbie? You think Maya wrote this? I fucking wrote this, and it's, like, bleeding. Who the hell do you think you are?" He pulls her into the office, shutting the door behind them. And I worry for a minute. Even about Becca.

"What do you think that was all about?" I ask Xander, who's still standing, staring over the partition. "Strange."

"He's too obvious. He was trying to show you how miserable he could make your life." Then he starts laughing. "He didn't realize that Becca ended up writing the reboots piece. Guess he tore it up."

I sigh. I should be enjoying this, too. But it kind of just sucks. I shrug. "All right, then, let's get to it."

We work all day and way into the evening, through lunch, through dinner, through Becca's endless, disdainful glares. Through Ericka peering over, somewhat concerned, as we don't even look up from the endless scraps of paper scattered on the main worktable, plotting, plotting, plotting. Xander lays out a spread, chips and salsa, more fajita wraps from home, a whole thermos of rose lemonade his mama made. But there it is again, that bittersweet floral. "Cardamom," he says. Lachi.

And then it starts. The nudging under the conference room table. His foot first. Then mine. Like a game. Teasing. Too easy. Too familiar. "What?" His eyes are on mine, his mouth a rosebud. I push away the thought. Ranbir's over, yes. But I can't let Xander into my head, not that way. It would be dangerous, no matter how much I might be drawn to him. I can't.

I need to leave a mark. Something solid that I can look back on once this fades like a dream I keep trying to grasp. Something to say, *Yes, I was here. I did that.*

And I know exactly what it needs to look like. But I need his help. So this—us—has to be what it is. Coworkers. Colleagues. Me being the boss of him. For as long as it lasts.

On Wednesday evening, after endless hours and all that research and ample use of Xander's stellar design skills, we have a real proposal. It's beautiful and meaningful, and I can't wait to share it with Ericka.

I want to bulldoze right into her office, to lay it all bare, but Xander holds me back a bit, literally. "Tomorrow," he says, minty breath buzzing in my ear. "When it's fresh." His arm grazes mine, electric. But I can feel Becca's eyes on us, too curious, speculating, intrigued. Nosy. "Come on," he says, his hand on mine as he leads me away. "I've got something to show you."

"What?" I wonder, following him into the copy room. The copy machine is going fast and furious, spitting out pages, and he closes the door behind us. I walk toward the machine, poking and peeking, wanting to gather it all up, days of work in beautiful form.

But he's right behind me, and then his arms are around my waist and his hands are pulling me up and close. His mouth is on mine, hard and greedy, my back pressed against the machine, no space between us. For the longest minute ever, I kiss him back. Because I want to.

Maybe it had to happen, because it's been there from the beginning, simmering. Maybe, if I went back to California, leaving this dream in the distance like a memory, I would have regretted not kissing him, too. Maybe I like it.

But I can't blow this, not now, and while his mouth is warm on mine, I have to end it. To step away. Because we can't do this, be this. Not here. Or now. It could cost us both.

For all the obvious reasons. But also because I still can't stop thinking about Ranbir.

"Okay, okay," he says as I keep shaking my head. "I get it. But I just couldn't let it linger."

"So it's out of your system now?" I say, a little too terse, probably.

"Is it out of yours?" His bite is worse.

"You know we can't. There's just no way." I take a step closer, and he flinches. "I hope we haven't ruined everything."

He frowns, faltering, but then pastes on that grin, complete with the dent. I stop myself from reaching up to poke it. Because I have to make it work, even if he's faking it.

I take a deep breath. "Tomorrow, then?"

He nods, gathering the pages, and we peer at them together. I can hear his heart thumping, loud and maybe too needy. But I make myself ignore it.

"There's no way she'll be able to say no," he says, grinning down at me. "Look at it. It's so very you."

23

I'M AT THE OFFICE WITH THE SUN, BASICALLY, THE NEXT morning, I'm that excited. I can't wait to share my story idea, and I can't wait for Ericka to see what Xander can deliver. Because that proposal is stunning. Even if she somehow does manage a no, I'll take it with me.

I push my way through the glass lobby doors, absorbing it all. Ride the empty elevators, savoring the swoosh and speed. I'll only get to walk these halls a few more times before I have to say good-bye. Who knows if I'll ever make it back?

Most of the cubes are empty, but there's Jude, skulking in his black boots. "You again," he says, his slink all sinister. "Intriguing creature, you are. I've been hearing things. About your ascent. Impressive." Then he slithers closer again. "But heed my warning, little girl. Upstarts would do best to watch their step."

I text Shenaz in my panic, spilling my fears, but she tells me not to fret and sends me pictures of new handbags.

> End game, dollface. Get those Gucci shades. No,
> really, please. Just snatch them right off his shiny
> face. K? Because the future is bright.

The future. Senior year and planting season and hair that smells like garlic. That's what I have to look forward to.

But I look down at the pitch document we made, the green of the rolling hills and the flame of the sky and Ranbir's smiling toothpaste-ad grin and even those endless jars of Gera Garlic chutney with Dolly's face plastered on top, and I know it's a world I can spend some time in again. A place I can go home to.

If I never make it back here, well, at least I'll have a few awesome bylines, a brief stint living my dream, and memories forever.

Becca's at her desk when I get to mine, which is weird. As soon as I settle in, she marches over and drops a stack of files on my desk, a smug smirk on her lips. "There go your plans," she says, the glee in her voice undisguised.

I start digging through, my eyes wandering to Xander's cube every few seconds, hoping he'll show up and we can plow through this mundane, boring busywork and get to our pitch. But then it's noon, then two, then four, and nothing's done and he still hasn't appeared. Or texted. Or responded to my what up.

Maybe I did ruin everything. Wouldn't be the first time.

The office is almost empty when Ericka swings by, curious. "What happened to the big pitch?" Her eyes float to Xander's cube. "I thought I was going to be wowed today."

"That was the plan." I'm fretting, but she laughs. "Do you think we could do tomorrow?"

She nods. "That works. Actually, Dulcie wanted to see you anyway, so let's do eleven thirty, her office. But we have a hard out at one thirty. Last few summer Fridays, you know?"

I try to read her face, wondering if I should panic. It's already setting in, either way, so there's that.

As she walks away, I stare down Xander's cube, willing him to appear. Then I walk to Penn Station, weaving through the crowds, staring at my phone, willing him to text back.

I can barely sleep that night, the bile churning, the nightmares fleeting and confusing, Xander and Ranbir and Becca laughing, a grumpy teenage Roop, the twins destroying my proposal by running it over with a tractor. A snowfall of garlic husks and Dolly and a wheelbarrow full of shit.

Shenaz shakes me awake, the sun glaring. "Maya. I'm catching the eight thirty. You going in?" I nod, bleary-eyed. "You need to stop stressing so much, dollface. It'll all be okay. It's not surgery." She heads toward the bedroom, then turns and tosses a new summer dress my way, sunshine-yellow eyelets, men's shirt collar, hits at the knee. "I heard about your meeting. Now go. Get dressed. We're going to be late."

When I finally scramble in—impeccably dressed, thanks to Shenaz, who totally missed the eight thirty because of me—it's almost ten thirty.

Xander's there, focused, his desk pretty much buried in paperwork. I stop at his cube, but he grumbles before I can say a word. "Becca's on a rampage," he says, shuffling from one end of the cube to the other. "I'm alphabetizing four years of files."

"She got me good yesterday. But I didn't do the pitch." I take step closer, and he takes a step back. "I wanted to wait for you."

He finally looks up. "Thanks. But I heard about your meeting with Dulcie. You should get ready."

"Do you think it's Jude?" I whisper. He holds my gaze for a second, an apology in his eyes. "Do you think—"

He shrugs. "I hope not. But he is a gossip columnist."

That makes me laugh, despite myself.

He grins. Finally. "Go. You're going to be late."

I look at my phone. It's nearly eleven thirty. I better hustle.

Ericka and I walk over together, the suspense killing me. But she won't say a word.

"Rick, I never knew you had such a mean streak," I say, finally, to cut the tension.

She looks down at me, confused. "What?"

"You gotta know. How can you leave me hanging for so long?"

"I wanted Dulcie to share the news," she says, knocking on her door and leaning in. "Ready for us?"

"Always," Dulcie says. "Come on in."

Her office is double the size of Ericka's, with floor-to-ceiling windows on two sides, like she's dangling off a cliff into Times Square. The actual, literal meaning of the word *breathtaking*.

She waves us toward chairs, clicks a few buttons on her keyboard, then takes a big gulp of water.

"So, Maya, you've been with us all of five weeks, and here we are."

"Yeah." I swallow hard. This doesn't sound promising.

"I've been reading the pitches and your copy, and I like hearing your voice."

I try not to let my jaw fall into my lap.

"You have a very distinctive take. It's young. Fresh. Unusual. Sort of 'not from around here.' Not so staid, stuffy old New York."

"Uh, thank you," I say. I still can't figure out what she's saying, whether it's good or bad. If she's about to drop a bomb.

"I'd like to see more of it. Of you. On the page, if you're open to that." I sit in stunned silence, which she takes as a negative. "I know Becca's been piling on. She thinks you're encroaching." She looks at Ericka, who nods. "Her behavior is a problem. But Jude won't let me fire her. I'd like to ask you to take a step in a different direction, a little bit."

She pushes forward a document, and it's a laid-out version of my piece on Neela. The picture bleeds across the whole spread, the yellow bright and beamy like my dress, while the text spills across it. Right there on top is the name *Neela Dham*, so she can own the story. And underneath, in small, dark letters, it says:

As told to Maya Malhotra

My first—and maybe last?—print piece in *Fierce*.

It's beautiful, stunning, all I ever wanted. And all wrong, too.

"I love it," I say, pulling it forward, taking it in. "But can I fix one thing?"

Dulcie frowns, sad to disappoint, then softens. "Of course. We've still got to fact-check it, but I wanted to show you." She hands me a pen. "Have at it."

236

"Thank you." I can't keep the smile off my face as I lean forward, crossing out one word and writing in the right one. My name.

As told to Maya Gera

That's better. Even though my stomach clenches as I hand it over, the beginning of the end. Because that's the thing I learned the hard way this summer. My words have consequences.

"Ah, great pen name." Dulcie grins. "So Maya Gera. We were thinking. Assistant editor is fun and all. But we want you to be able to focus."

"And not be under Becca's thumb," Ericka says, and I finally get what prompted this.

"You clearly want to do more writing, especially given the transition to web. So what do you think of a new title?" Dulcie wags those famously expressive brows. "How does staff writer suit you?"

This time, I do let my jaw drop. Because I can see it right there, on that *Fierce* masthead glued to the vision board stashed in my closet at home. The business card I made out of cardboard and markers, not long after Roop gave me my first copy, all those years ago.

"I'd take that as a yes," Ericka says, her voice beaming. "I know you have a big pitch for us. We're ready when you are. But in the meantime, we're thinking a feature story each week to start, then whatever else you can manage."

"A column, maybe," Dulcie says. "I like the How to Adult, but it's already been shared, with Xander and others contributing. So I figured, maybe something else youth focused? Your take always feels fresh. Like you're right there, living the life, tapped into youth culture in ways a lot of us aren't. So we thought we could call it From the Source."

She raises a very refined brow, expectant.

I almost can't take it. Maybe I should tell them the truth. I open my mouth, ready to spill it all, to end the charade.

That's when I hear the knock on the door. Xander. Totally eavesdropping. He's reading my face, wondering if we should be panicked. Relief flashes with that dimple, and he offers his excuse. A fresh copy of our pitch document, on thick stock and pristine, still warm from the printer. "I thought you might want this. To show Rick, uh, Ericka. And Ms. St. Claire."

"Call me Dulcie," she says, and waves him closer. "So come on, tell us what you've got."

I take a deep breath. Here goes. "I'm from Gilroy, the Garlic Capital of the World. It's a town that literally smells like garlic. There are a hundred towns like it, up and down the state of California, where brown kids, mostly Desi, but some Mexican and from other communities, sit on these looming plots of land, heirs to the thrones of these tiny kingdoms."

I pull out the document, bright and shiny. "Take Ranbir Dhillon here, for example. His father owns twelve thousand acres in Sonoma wine country, and their brand is Bespoke Wine. The specialty, proscato."

"Oh!" Ericka claps with delight and peers closer, curious. Then she blinks hard. Doing math in her head. Shit. But she smiles. "He seems charming."

That's it exactly. "Prince Charming in a pickup," I say. Dulcie leans in to look, too, intrigued, though Xander's frowning, like he finally gets it. "He stands to inherit a five-million-dollar estate. But he also has dreams of studying raag—an old-school form of Hindustani and Carnatic music—at NYU. Instead of taking over the family business."

"Conflict," Dulcie says. "Intriguing."

Xander taps the next box, happy to contribute. "Dolly Randhawa, on the other hand, fully embraces her role as the reigning Spice Goddess of California—and one day, the world. She's cute, perky, super marketable."

"And"—as much as it pains me to say it—"she's got the brains to match. Her agenda is to break the company out big, to take it to the next level, moving from Indian stores to grocery chains nationwide." I take a deep breath, trying to keep the edge out of my voice. "She plans to expand in other ways, too, seeking out strategic alliances, like smaller companies to buy out. But her softer side sets her up to meet more traditional family obligations. House, kids, career. All on her agenda."

"It's like a big, sprawling soap opera," Ericka says. "An enclave some of us would never get to see. Exactly what Legend loves, those simmering, insular worlds." She turns to me, excited. "The perfect way to kick off the column."

Dulcie's a bit more tentative. "Do you have access?" she says.

"I'll get it."

"And photos," Ericka says. "Do you think we'd need to shoot in California? How scattered are these heirs?"

"Actually, if we can get this moving this week, we can grab a lot of them together. Right here. In New Jersey."

Dulcie seems surprised. "Really?"

"Cow Camp. It's the Linden Institute Agricultural Summer Intensive at Rutgers." I purposely drop the precollege. Major red flag. "Step One on the Farm Kid Career Path to-do list. So they're all there now." Where I'm supposed to be.

Ericka takes a deep breath. "Okay, let me pin down the budget. If that works, you have a green light from me. Xander, you assist. I want at least five kids, preferably a group shot and some solos to pull out, a big picture graf explaining who's who—oh, and maybe a chart, linking them? And then the solo stories."

"Definitely Dolly and Ranbir," Dulcie adds, tapping their pictures on the proposal. "Actually, maybe we can pose them together."

I take a deep breath. "There's one I think we should fly in. Cherry Kaur Bhullar, the fashion designer I told you about. She's from Gilroy. Like me."

"I think we can make that happen," Dulcie says. "I loved the green dress. Get the pieces moving. If we can lock the art, this will go into the last print issue."

A dream come true. Xander and I lock eyes, grinning.

"On it." I leap out of the chair and out the door.

If this is going to happen before we all head back, I need to get the wheels turning now.

I know just where to start. If I can get Dolly on board, the rest will follow. Even Ranbir.

24

I THOUGHT IT WOULD BE EASY. THAT THEY'D TOPPLE LIKE dominoes. But I can't actually get anyone to text me back. Not Ranbir. Not Jiya. Not Dolly. Only Cherry, who's already booked her flight.

So I text Marcus, who, ever easy, actually responds. The last few weeks of Cow Camp are the most grueling, he reports. But there's a pool party tonight at the building next to Easton. I'm officially invited.

I ponder asking Xander to go, but then decide against it. Too weird, even for me. And it would be too awkward with Ranbir, no matter where we stand. So I have to fix it. For the story, yes. But also for me. Xander will just make things more complicated.

I show up wearing the sunflower yellow summer dress. Dolly and her friends will preen and judge and covet. I can deal. If I'm going to walk the walk, well then, I better learn to own it.

The poolside is crowded with kids from Cow Camp and all the other summer programs, too, I guess. I push my way through, hoping I don't ruin the dress. Wishing I'd maybe brought a swimsuit.

"There she is." Marcus's voice booms from the bar. He wraps me in a bear hug, and I can smell the beer on his breath, but I'm still happy to see him. "How ya been? Is that Tory Burch?"

He leans over and peeps at the tag. "I thought so. Nice."

I laugh. "How do you know?"

He grins. "Don't ask. I won't tell." He hands me a cup. "Bubbly only, if I recall correctly."

I sip, but not too much. "Proscato."

He nods. "I know what you like." He leaps away. "I'll find him for you. But in the meantime, if it's the drama you were looking for, well, here it comes."

He bolts, gone, as Dolly and Jiya make their way over. Dolly surprises me by clinking her plastic cup against mine. "Cheers, or whatever," she says. "I'm sure you've heard the news by now."

"About the chutney?" I say, trying to keep the seething in check. "Yeah, my mom showed me the prototype." I take a deep breath, swallowing air and pride. "She's really excited about it. And keeping the farm. So thank you."

Dolly looks floored, but does this little curtsy thing that's actually kind of charming. Ericka's going to love her. "I texted you guys." Jiya snorts. Some things never change. "I'm working on a project for my day job. I could use your help with it. And I think it could really help you, Dolly, and get the word out about Spice Goddess."

"Oh yeah?" Dolly leans in. I've said the magic words. "Tell me more."

"I'm doing a—an internship. At the magazine my cousin's girlfriend works for. *Fierce.* That's why I bailed on Cow Camp. Anyway, they want to do a cool spread in each issue on the awesome, amazing, and unknown lives of teens and twentysomethings across the country. The little pockets of culture no one knows about. Like us. Farm kids. I showed them your picture and told them about you, Dolly, and they want you front and center."

She looks suspicious. And pleased. But more suspicious. "Why would you do that?"

"Because you have a cool story. I want people to hear it. And see all kinds of kids. Kids like us. Kids like Neela Dham. I just did a story on her. Brown kids doing cool things, living amazing lives, writing ourselves into the narrative."

Jiya seems interested. But she hasn't said a word. I need to pull her in. "Jiya, they thought the idea of your family's cinnamon farm sounded intriguing, too. Do you think you'd be down?"

She looks to Dolly for her cue, and it's almost imperceptible, the exchange. But they're locked and loaded, forever in unison.

"Okay," Dolly says. Taking charge. As usual. "Tell me what you need."

I give them the rundown. The shoot needs to be on campus. Which means permission from Maxwell. "Easy-peasy," Dolly says. "I've got him wrapped around my little finger." She actually lifts her little finger to demonstrate. "Consider it handled."

She doesn't mention the slut-shaming. Or how she was an ass about my mom and the farm. But I have to let it go. To make this work. And because Ranbir needs her right now. Or forever. He clearly does.

And she'll make this part painless for me, happily, greedily, because of what's in it for her. That much, I'll take. Especially if it'll sell my ma's garlic chutney. "Awesome," I say, then pretend to ponder, as I don't have every bit of this laid out in my head. "So you, Jiya. Cherry. Guru. And one more."

"Well, Rana is the obvious one." Dolly's eyes flash. Curious. Maybe devious. Wait. "You've already talked to him, right? You know—"

I swallow hard. I remind myself that he's decided. That he has to do what's right for him. Because that's what I've been doing all this time, too. I shake it off, and try to focus. "I haven't seen him in a minute, actually," I say. "He'll be here tonight, though, right?"

"You haven't?" She seems confused. Annoyed. "All those nights, he said he was going to see you. I thought—"

The music class. He went back to it. I smile to myself, glad to hear he stuck with it. "Of course. I meant this weekend."

"When his uncle was here, you didn't go to dinner with them?" Jiya's so smug, I kind of want to punch her. But I need to let it go. I can't let the drama suck me back in. Get what I need and get out.

"Nope," I say, and leave it at that. "So next weekend. I'll text details. But be ready, probably ten A.M. Saturday. They'll bring wardrobe, hair, and makeup," and I can almost see them both squeal. "Get excited."

I see the flash of Marcus's head above the crowd. He's gotta have found Ranbir by now. "See you all then."

Jiya nods, satisfied, but Dolly turns back for a second. "Thanks, Maya," she says, cheersing my cup again. "This is cool of you."

They disappear into the crowd.

"Did you find him?" I say, tracking Marcus down at the bar.

He looks confused for a second—the liquor blunts him fast. "What? Oh, the proscato. Suite 605. You know it. Unlocked." I must look unsure, because then he barks it. "You got this, girl. Go."

I take the elevator up, staring at myself in the reflections on the metal. My hair's starting to frizz. My eye makeup's melty. The humidity and chlorine together take a toll. But a touch of lip gloss helps, and I dab, like Shenaz showed me. Perfect. Or, well, good enough. Because I can't waste any more time.

Marcus was right, the door is open. The apartment is dim, though, like no one's there, and I almost step back out, the nerves striking. Then I hear it. The raag from the Jagjit Singh vinyl the girls play sometimes. The one Roop loved from my papa's collection that summer she spent with us. He's been practicing.

His voice is clear and smooth, his breath controlled, but the emotion that fills it is what floors me, even though I can't quite understand the words. He goes through the sequence again and again and again, and I stand there, listening, the wonder of it, the surprise, filling me with something I can't quite name. Joy, yes, and affection. But it's deeper than that. Like I found someone, something. A little piece of home. That's what he said. That's what he's always felt like. What I've been missing this whole time.

The music stops abruptly. "Dude, knock at least." He barrels forward, then stops short when he realizes it's me. For a minute we just stare, caught in this vortex, unable to move. Like we need to get our fill of just looking before words and deeds break the spell again. But then he shakes it off, away.

"You didn't text me back," I say, shrugging. "I was hoping you might have a spare bottle of proscato." He's watching me again, his lips twitching, amusement lighting his eyes even in the dark. "Ask anyone, it's spoiled me for everything else these days." Then I look down. "I even introduced my boss to it."

"I remember." The grin splits his face, then, balm on a sunburn, all those Chiclet teeth, so neatly arranged, that toothpaste-ad smile. I want to reach out and touch it. But of course I control myself.

"How's the gig?" He's looking at the floor and not me. "I'm sorry about last time. This thing with my mom—it's a lot. But you know what she said? What she told me? That life goes on."

I must look confused.

"When I told her about you."

He flinches a bit, I see it. Cardamom pods in his palm. I take one and pop it in my mouth.

"You told her about me?" My voice is a whisper. "Is she okay?"

I step closer and he steps back, like a dance, familiar and infuriating.

"Not great. No. But she said I need to live my life. While she's here. When she's gone."

"So you went back to the music classes."

He nods.

But you didn't come back to me. The words hang, unsaid. He still won't look at me. So I take another step. And he backs away again.

"I feel like it's all my fault." He sighs, and when he finally does look at me, there's a sharp edge to his face. "Dolly, I mean. All of it. Everything she did was obviously about me. I didn't know what to do to fix it. So I stopped trying. Then I went back to her, even after that. Because I needed her. It was so selfish."

"Nothing she did—or I did—was your fault," I tell him, as soft as I can, as clear as I can, as firm as I can. "You can't control the universe or anyone in it. Just yourself and your actions." The words ring loud in my head as I step closer again, right up to him, closing the gap between us. "Got it?"

He nods, but I want to be sure.

"I'm responsible for me. You're responsible for you. Okay?" He looks down, his face inches from mine, and I don't think I can stand it another minute. "So I'm going to kiss you now," I whisper, quiet so he has to lean closer to hear. So quiet that his lips are on mine. So quiet that there's no room left between us. For Dolly, for doubt, for anything else.

As his arms lock tight around me, it hits me just how much I've missed home.

25

CHERRY GETS IN LATE ON THURSDAY EVENING, AND I MEET her at the airport. She hugs me for a million years, her arms wrapped around my neck so I can't escape, can't breathe. Then we get her little rolling bag and hail a cab.

"You better tell me everything," she's saying, fully shaking her fist at me, but then the cabbie opens the door. We climb in the back and whisper for forty minutes, and I tell her the whole story of my summer, all of it: About Ranbir. About *Fierce*. About Roop and Shenaz. Even about Xander. And we giggle. Like old aunties.

When we get to the apartment, I'm expecting it to be empty, the way it usually is on weeknights when Roop's got rounds and Shenaz is still working. But they're both on the couch, prim and patient, like parents whose kid sneaked out one time too many. Which I guess they could blame me for.

As soon as we walk in, they're hugging and hovering, serving up chai and even samosas. You'd think my mom was hiding somewhere in the corner, running the show, they've become such stellar Desi aunties.

And then there are the words—more than I've heard out of Roop's mouth all summer. Which pinches a little. "How was the flight? Did you eat? We ordered in. Thai, extra spicy. You said your favorite was drunken noodles, right? I got shrimp."

"Why don't we let her sit?" I say, trying to buffer. "Chai is good. And this maybe—" I reach for something on the table, passing it to Cherry as she grins. Chana chor and other old-school snacks. Where did these come from?

"It's so weird to be here," Cherry says as the girls stare. "Like, Maya kept telling me, but I have to pinch myself. The apartment, you guys, the whole *Fierce* thing. I can't believe I'm going to be right there in those pages." She squishes me tight. "And it's all because of you."

"Uh, and her," I say, nodding toward Shenaz. I don't think Cherry can quite bring herself to look at her head-on, like she's the sun and Cher doesn't have shades or something. "So tomorrow, you can come to work with me, and then we can grab a bite—maybe at Tamarind, this really fancy old-school Desi place, and then—"

"Actually, maybe Cherry could spend the day in the closet with me," Shenaz says, then laughs for a long time while we all watch. "I mean, no pun, or whatever. But I thought she might like to come check it out, show off some of her wares, meet LuLu and the team. And of course see the edit pod, too."

Cherry implodes with joy. "That would be truly amazing," she says. "LuLu Chang? The *Fierce* office? Surreal."

"And Saturday's the shoot," I say. "So I'll be prepping for that all day."

We all pile onto the couch and dig into our Thai food and weep about the spice levels and laugh too loud as we watch an old Amitabh Bachchan movie on the TV, like we did so many times that summer when Roop stayed with us.

Later that night, though, when I'm brushing my teeth, I hear the three of them chatting, voices low, and I have to admit, I'm jealous. This is the welcome I was hoping for. But it's for Cherry. That's okay, I remind myself. I can share. I'm happy we all get to hang together, and that I get to show her the little world I made this summer.

Way past midnight, I'm half-asleep, Cherry's snuggled close on the sofa bed—pulled out for two and lumpier than ever—whispering things into my ears, into my brain, familiar.

"Things will look different when you get back," she says, her voice a thrum in my head. "And that's okay, Maya. Things have to change for us to grow."

I wonder for a moment who filled her up with that nonsense. But she's probably right. I've had seventeen years to embrace my mundane—the farm, the family, the responsibilities that come with them. And now I'm on the brink of something. We all are.

"No matter what shifts, we'll still be able to hold on to each other," she says, words filtering into my dreams. "I'll always have you, and you'll always have me."

And as squished as I am, it's the best night's rest I've had all summer.

* * *

Friday is an absolute blur. We're late for the train, naturally, and race to the office, my casual Friday rocker tee soaked with sweat by the time I get there. I'm so behind on finalizing shoot chaos that I have to abandon Cherry at the elevator so she can head to the fashion pod with Shenaz. Then it's one thing after another with the shoot—the caterer canceled, the new one has to be university approved, one of the horses is sick, the photographer's team still hasn't verified insurance, and there are a hundred texts from Dolly and her crew asking about wardrobe and makeup and if they can bring friends and keep clothes. Like they're Beyoncé or something.

But Xander makes me pause and sit and we go through the to-do list, divide and conquer. "It'll all be over by tomorrow night," he says. "Then we can celebrate. I heard about this karaoke joint in New Brunswick. They even have Bollywood songs."

"Maybe we can take the whole crew out," I say, tentative. "I can ask Ericka if there's budget for that. A treat to celebrate."

"Maybe," he says, shrugging. "Or we—"

"Ranbir will be there." I don't know how else to say it. I stare at my computer screen, catching his reflection behind me. "On again."

249

"Rebound Dude." He sighs. "Okay." He frowns, shuffling through the stack. "Guess I should go find another Rutgers-approved caterer."

I watch him walk away, heading toward the copy room, a little pang in my stomach.

Four hours later, I'm in the closet with the girls, Cherry repinning the dress she made for me for the fiftieth time. "I want it to be flawless."

Shenaz grins, amused as she putters around gathering wardrobe and accessories for tomorrow—which have to be trucked to campus tonight. It's a lot. But she's got one eye on Cherry. "I have to say, Maya Memsahib, you may have a keeper here." She drops her voice low, ever cognizant of eyes overhead. "If you guys decide to come back next summer, Cherry might just have scored herself an internship spot, too."

She flutters away, leaving us squealing and dancing in her wake. Cameras be damned.

That night, as the three of us traipse up the steps to the fourth floor, we're exhausted, but I'm happier than I've been in—maybe ever. The whole shoot has come together flawlessly, and fingers crossed, as Papa would say, it will go without a hitch. A memory made and sealed in the pages of *Fierce* forever, something to remember my seventeenth summer by. Something to prove I've made a mark on this world. But tonight, it's just us and maybe some Middle Eastern food and a Bollywood movie—

And my dad? Weird. But that's definitely his voice booming from the apartment on the fourth floor.

Shenaz shrugs, but Cherry's face mirrors my panic as we storm up the last flight of stairs.

"I knew we shouldn't have trusted this trollop and her girlfriend," Papa says. It's Ma's fault, clearly. Because she's related to the trollop—Roop, in this case—and she birthed the other one. Me.

Although he doesn't know the extent of those damages yet. Does he?

When he sees me, though, standing in the door, slightly tearstained, a bit worse for wear, silence descends. Ma races over, wrapping me in her chunni and her bosom and that familiar waft of perfume and sandalwood talcum powder tempered with garlic. Who knew you could miss a scent like that? I must have, the way my tears just soak right through her chunni and onto her suit. She lets me sob for a minute anyway. Then I rise, stepping away, composing myself.

And ruin the stunned silence by opening my mouth. "Papa, I don't think you really understand the meaning of the word *trollop*. It's about being promiscuous, noncommittal. And I can promise you Roop and Shenaz are about as committed as you can possibly get. I mean, they might as well be old and married, because all they do is work and fight and order in and snuggle on the sofa. Except that I've been on their sofa for the past six weeks, at your request, because it's cheaper and safer than the dorms, and having been to the dorms, I can tell you that that's actually completely true." I take a gulp of air, and then go again for good measure. "Well, except, of course, if you count the 'leaving Cow Camp and traipsing through Manhattan pretending to be twenty-six and a magazine editor' thing. But obviously, Roop had nothing to do with that." Can't quite say the same about Shenaz, though.

"I couldn't understand what that dean was on about," Papa sputters. "Trying to refund some money. That you'd left weeks ago. What have you been doing?" He takes a deep breath. A refund would be nice, actually. "You ruined everything. And then this—" He's holding a copy of the newly released September issue. The one with Neela's story in it. My story.

Ma's trying to tuck me behind her, away from the wrath and the words and the blame. But I'm all of five two, and I still tower over her. So it's much too late for that.

Shenaz decides to help instead. "Isn't it amazing, Uncleji? She was like an actual, honest, paid magazine editor." She grins at me. "Not pretending in that regard. That's pretty huge."

"Maybe you both can just stop talking now?" Roop says. "Because this just went from bad to worse."

"But she's right about the trollop thing, babe. You gotta give her that."

"I don't have to give her anything," Papa says. "I gave her too much freedom, and look what a mess she made."

"It's true. It was a mess. I was miserable every day. I was bullied horribly. And I didn't want to be there." I take a deep breath. "Did I make some mistakes? Definitely. But I'm seventeen. If I don't make them now, when will I?"

Cherry nods sagely, and Papa glares at her.

"She didn't know, no one did, not everything. But in the end, I'm the one who made the choices I made." I take a deep breath. Here goes. "Yes, I lied to you all summer. That's absolutely unacceptable. I get that. You can ground me for, like, all of senior year. I'm ready to fly back, to pick up where I left off, to take responsibility. But know this: I'm glad it worked out this way, and if I had the chance, I'd do it again. Because I got to step out of the little box I've lived in and figure out who I am, who I want to be. That's what you really wanted for me, right, Papa? That's what this summer was supposed to be about. Growing up, fending for myself, learning from my mistakes?"

Papa sighs, caught, not quite sure what to say. It's what he and Dadoo have always instilled—deep end, sink or swim. But seeing it in practice is scary, I think.

"Because I made a lot. But Roop and Shenaz were my safety net. I won't let you blame them for my choices. So I'll go back to my reality. I'll learn to be okay with garlic-scented hair, if that's my lot in life. My dreams are big, but so were yours." I take a deep breath, hoping the words come out right. "Someone once told me there's a way to meet in the middle, a way to still embrace your past while building your future." Ma starts when I repeat her words, her eyes glistening. "I think I can figure it out, if you give me a little room to breathe, a little room to grow."

Papa nods, but I don't know if he's quite convinced. "I'm open—we're open—to hearing about your hopes and dreams," he says. "Within reason. But, beta, you can't lie to us and expect our support. If you want us to help, you have to share with us. How are we to know? No reason one can't be a garlic heiress and a writer, right?" How'd they get the magazine anyway? It isn't something they'd just grab from the shop preflight.

"It was Cherry," Shenaz says, unprompted. Which makes me think it wasn't *just* Cherry.

"I loved your story, beta," Ma says. "We all did. But you're in big trouble."

"I loved it, too. But wait," Roop says, turning to me. "I want to get a few things straight." She giggles, which is unlike her. I think Papa makes her nervous. "Are we being sued?"

"Not at the moment," I say happily. Though that could change, obviously, once I tell Ericka the truth.

"And the refund?"

"He sent it, that Maxwell." Papa grumbles.

"So no debt, no lawsuits, six weeks' hands-on job experience in a pretty viable field, and"—Roop lifts her phone, clicking away—"still six thousand dollars in the bank." She turns to Papa. "So you see, Uncle. Not bad for a summer gig."

Shenaz beams. "And she got quite an education. For free. Not bad, Maya Memsahib. Not bad at all."

Papa still seems gobsmacked, and less and less amenable to Shenaz's take, though I doubt it has much to do with her math. Except for the obvious thing: Maybe still, in his head, a woman plus a woman will never add up. Even though he loves Cherry. And Roop.

I don't get it. But I won't let it devolve further. "I think we've worn out our welcome here," I say to Papa. I note my packed suitcase—thanks, Mom—and gather a few knickknacks and keepsakes into my backpack quickly.

"You guys can take my stuff to the hotel, if you'd like," I say, "but I'm going to get ready for bed. I have a big day tomorrow—the shoot Cherry's a part of—and I need my beauty sleep."

That's when Ma speaks. Finally. "I'd—I'd like to come to the shoot," she says. "If that's allowed."

Shenaz claps her hands with glee. "Of course, Auntieji, and Uncleji, too, if you'd like. It would be the perfect way for Maya to end her summer, and you can see all that she's accomplished. It's no small feat."

Shenaz squishes me into a hug, handing me a small gift bag. "And while you're packing, dollface, here's the Le Labo. As promised." I squee, then shove it into my backpack.

Papa sighs, suddenly exhausted. "Chalo, let's go. And Monday, six P.M., we leave," Papa says. His tone is too even, which means he's just going to hold this against me for the rest of my life. "It's been a long day."

"The car?" I ask.

"Honda rental downstairs."

"You've eaten?" Cherry asks.

"If not, there's a great little kebab shop just down the block," Shenaz says, ever helpful. "I can go round up a few?"

Papa waves his arms, exhausted. "No, we'll eat at the Hilton."

"Text us about tomorrow?" Ma says.

"Oh, Buaji, we'll pick you up. Eight A.M. sharp."

"Cherry. Bag lah. I'm going down now, slowly. So many stairs." Cherry scrambles to grab the suitcase as Papa stops short near the door, where he sees Roop's Jagjit Singh records, including the one I got her. He turns to her one last time. "You are a doctor now. Take care of yourself." His voice is gruff, but there's a sprinkle of affection, like he still sees her as that kid he once knew. The one who'd lost her dad and hoped she might find a bit of one in him. The one who's been holding on to his old man music—*his* music—all those years later. The one who pushed us all away so she wouldn't get hurt. The one I've missed all this time. Now that we've reconnected, we can't let her go again. "You can do better than all these stairs. Live a little." He sighs, exhausted, and looks so much older suddenly than a summer away should make him. "And I can send the money, beta, if it helps. Call me if you need more."

He plants a kiss on her head, fatherly and familiar. He's hurt. Like I was. It'll take him a minute, maybe. He'll figure it out. I did. He disappears down the steps, and I know this conversation is far from over. But the expression on Roop's face, even without a hug goodbye, may have been worth it.

Ma takes Shenaz's hand, holding it to her chest, and her voice is too nasal, which means she was crying and she will cry some more later, but she's pulled herself together for now. "I'll see you tomorrow," Ma says. "And maybe, if there's time, you can take me to see my sister-in-law? Thank you so much for all your kindness to my daughter. She felt very at home here, and that is because of your generosity."

She stops for a moment, then pulls a small pouch from her purse. "I can't speak really for my husband. Or my sister-in-law. So this is a small token from me." It's a kangan, I know, the bangle that serves as a sign of a married woman, and this one is old and special, an endless spiral of peacocks dancing, their features carved in blue and red Meenakari work.

"It's stunning," Shenaz says, slipping it on immediately. "And this little Maya Memsahib is my favorite, Buaji." She's pointed when she adds, "She has a home here anytime," loud and clear, making sure we all hear it.

"And you have one in California," my mother says, squishing her in a hug.

Shenaz hugs me one last time, whispering, "See you in the

morning," then tucks herself away in the bedroom, leaving the three of us for a moment. Ma's eyes are going to spill again, but I don't think I can handle another breakdown. "I'll definitely see you before I leave," I say to Roop, and the words are familiar, like the beginning and end of something all at once, a cycle that keeps spinning. "We all will."

Roop nods, and my mom throws herself upon her again, a sob wracking her small frame. Roop lets herself be hugged, then slips her arms around my mother. "Buaji, Maya's had a big summer. A lot has changed. She has so much to tell you. But she's doing well. We all are."

Ma nods, and pats Roop's cheek, pulling her close. "So grown up now, but still Buaji's ladli. So you listen to me, too. Don't be stubborn, though that's a Malhotra trait. Your mother will see you and soften. Believe me. I did. In the meantime, you have us."

Having seen it close up, whatever happened between Roop and her mother doesn't seem like it can be fixed. I don't want that for us, I realize with a pang. I squeeze Roop once, just enough to make her squirm, knowing I'll be back. Then I tumble out the door and down the endless stairs behind Ma, watching her take them one at a time, slow and deliberate, just how she drives.

I promise myself then to give her a smidge of space, if she needs it, a minute to stop being angry. Then I'll share all my stories from this summer. Over and over again until she's addicted to hearing about my adventures. Just like she is to that one lonesome season of *Mahi Way*, never to be completed or repeated.

No single season for me, though. I plan on many more.

26

THE SHOOT AT RUTGERS GOES OFF WITHOUT A HITCH. THE sky is all pinks and purples, like it's showing off for my parents, who snack on chana chor and Shenaz's samosa spread as they watch the antics.

The green hills are vivid, the horses cooperative, the girls strutting in their Harleen Kaur and Suite Cherry Bombe gear, and Ranbir—though it took a minute to convince him to commit—all dashing and delicious, posing with a Mustang and a mustang, plus plenty of Bespoke Wine. He's the second-to-last shoot of the day, and it's amazing to watch Shenaz laughing as she readjusts his collar and deliberates a cowboy hat. Which I've already vetoed three times. "Way too on the nose," I say as it lands on his head again.

"Oh come on, spoilsport," Shenaz says, pouting. "Who made you the boss of things?"

"Ericka," I say, deadpan, and absolutely mean it.

She waves me off. "Let's just try a few shots with it on."

Cherry has followed her around like a lost puppy all day, completely smitten, comparing notes, helping with wardrobe and makeup, swooning, pretty much. Can't say I blame her.

"Keep the hat," Cherry calls out again. Suck-up. Then she leans in close, whispering in my ear. "Charming, sure." She winks. Then, too loud: "But I still say truckbois are trouble."

"I heard that," Ranbir calls, grinning, and the camera clicks.

Xander frowns, snatching off the hat again. "Nope, Maya's right. It's one thing too much. Ericka will nix those shots immediately. And we're losing light." He waves at the sky, like maybe we could reel it back somehow. "We've still got one more shoot to go, so we have to lock this one already." He looks over at me, dent properly in place. "And you're gonna have to redo their makeup."

"Well, in that case, give us a minute." Ranbir leaps off the horse and ambles toward me, but I gesture violently, and he notes the parents, and proceeds to sit instead, grabbing a samosa.

"Sun sets at eight," the photographer shouts. "You're up!"

Then it's our turn. Cherry's really. But mine, too. A hundred years of taking selfies together means we've got this down pat. We pose and click, pose and click, rocking the finest of Suite Cherry Bombe's spring line—for next year. She's put me in a cherry print dress, of course, and she's wearing a jumpsuit that shows off every curve. Chiffon scarves tie our hair back like headbands, old-school Bollywood and Bettie Page.

"Let's do bales of hay," the photographer says, and we settle on top, ready for the next shot.

"Wait," Ranbir says, waltzing up. "I've got just the thing."

He pulls out a bouquet—of garlic bulbs. Then he and Xander both dissolve into a fit of roaring laughter. Which probably says a lot about my taste in humans. The cornier, the better, I guess.

Shenaz kiboshes that quickly, and we get me sitting in a field of wildflowers, a picnic spread before me. And then a few shots of me and Ranbir and proscato and the garlic chutney for good measure. Tacky. Yes. But I need to claim it somehow, even though the Gera name is long gone.

The last few shots are of me and Cherry, a greenhouse of green garlic around us. Like home. Captured forever. For better or worse.

My heart drops a little when I think about Ericka opening the film. Seeing me there. Discovering the truth. But it has to be done. It's time.

"All right," the photographer shouts as the sun sets behind us. "We're wrapped. Good job, people." Then he calls to me. "Maya,

I'll send selects Monday. Pretty smooth for your first shoot." *And last*, I can't help thinking.

Xander helps me up. "Okay. Divide and conquer," he says. "Text Monday, then we're ready to go."

"I'm ready to go, you mean."

He frowns, wistfulness in his eyes. Or allergies, maybe. Either way. "I'll miss you for a minute," he says, leaning close. "Then I'll take your job." He grins, presenting the dent. "But you were a good boss. And other things."

As Ranbir steps forward, Xander grabs his bag, taking his cue. "Monday," he says, climbing into the Mustang with the photographer, ready to drive off into the sunset.

Ranbir leans down, dropping a casual arm around me, hyperaware of Papa. I have to say, I haven't missed Rutgers, though the cornfields aren't far behind us.

"Beckoning, don't you think?" Ranbir says with a smirk. But then Shenaz grabs him by the ear like an old auntie and drags him away as my mom laughs. "Lucha. Lafanga." If Shenaz had a broom, she'd beat him with it. Doing her Desi mother proud. "Maya's mum's right there, you besharams."

* * *

I spend the next ten hours holed up on the couch I've come to call home, piecing the whole story together for *Fierce*, going through it with Cherry, old Zeenat Aman and Rekha movies playing in the background as Shenaz plies us with food. Roop is spending the day with my parents, taking them to see some sights in the city. It'll be good for all of them.

And it gives me room to think. I definitely need it. It's like solving a puzzle, pulling the story together. The little profiles, a breakout on Cherry, a few grafs that sum up the big picture about the community, the images that complement and center without overwhelming. It should come together, but something's not quite right. A voice is missing.

Mine. It hits me like a punch to the gut. This whole time, this whole summer, I've been hiding myself, trying on different costumes, not letting it all just come out. But now it can't wait anymore. It all tumbles out in one fell swoop, like it's been there all along, waiting to break free, ink spilled like blood on the page.

And then there's that feeling again, that this is it. The beginning of the end. Monday morning, Dulcie and Ericka will know everything.

Homegrown

HED: Homegrown
DEK: Meet California farm country's mini moguls in the making

For the longest time, I was a princess in a fairy tale of rolling hills and flame-streaked skies, a world scented by garlic. We lived and breathed it, literally, growing small fragrant buds on endless fields of green in the swelter of summer in a land where big box stores and outlet malls meet the throwback of old-school farm families. Farmhands in overalls and work boots, children playing among cows and horses, and teenagers—like me—selling homegrown cherries, avocados, and everything garlic (even ice cream) to tourists driving through.

Mine is a story of a girl and garlic and community, safe and beloved. A story about fruit stands and cartwheels and one festival that ruled the summer every year, drawing thousands into this cozy little town in the rolling hills of Northern

California, where the sun could warm and scorch in equal measure. Where burnt garlic left a stench, and raging fires took their toll.

It's the story of a girl who just wanted to wash it all out of her hair, to leave it behind, to chase big dreams in the city. A girl who realized, in the end, that community can be anchor, yes. But sometimes that's what you need to ground you, to hold you firm. Even when you might drift away a bit. Something to go back to. A place to call home.

If it sounds idyllic, that's because it is. Or it was, for the longest time. Nearly forever. Until one day, at the town's most esteemed annual event, the Gilroy Garlic Festival, our peace was inalterably shattered. That's the day when, in 2019, a single gunman shot and killed three festivalgoers and injured seventeen others before killing himself.

My mother and brothers were at the festival that day, along with thousands of others, basking in the sunshine as they sold our family's inimitable Gera Garlic chutney. Before the celebration was all shattered in an instant. They got out unhurt, but not unscathed. None of us did.

The impact of that day has left a profound scar on the community. Like the other kids featured in this piece, I'm seventeen, a high school student, and a farm kid. I grew up harvesting garlic every summer with my family, who own twenty acres in Gilroy. I grew up trying to wash its scent out of my hair, trying to shake the loss off my shoulders. But that's easier said than done.

My father and grandfather have always been farmers—first in their native Punjab, and now among hundreds of other Punjabi and Mexican families in the heart of California, where, my dadoo says, "the soil feels like home." But as a wise uncle once told me, in a world where PepsiCo is patenting potatoes, resolving the plight of the farmer is a profound task. In Punjab. And in America. In talking to these kids, though—kids like me—I've learned that the future of our farms might be on solid ground, thanks to the next generation of farmers set to inherit their families' agricultural empires.

Here, I've gathered the stories of half a dozen kids who are carrying on their family traditions, including my own. And you'll be surprised, because we're not quite what you'll expect. In the very best way.

• Maya Gera, Gilroy, California, 17

27

SUNDAY MORNING DAWNS BRIGHT AND CLEAR, ENDLESS August sky above, the sun hungry to kiss skin.

Roop—likely against her will—has agreed to go to her mom's with my parents, and Cherry's off to *Fierce* with Shenaz for one last romp, to look at art from the shoot (and swipe some couture), so I leave her sleeping on the lumpy couch as I get ready.

Ranbir picks me up at the crack of dawn—which I've lost the taste for. Or maybe, let's be honest, never developed in the first place. But he insisted. He runs all the way upstairs, grabs my dinky bag, and leads me all the way back downstairs. He's got a rental, and I'm expecting a sensible dad-approved Honda or maybe a hot Mustang convertible like the one from the shoot. But instead, he's got this oversized, out-of-place pickup truck, shiny and obtrusive and familiar. They're everywhere in the Central Valley, but I haven't actually seen one all summer. I have no idea where you'd even find a monster like that in New Jersey.

I stand and stare and collapse into laughter. "Prince Charming in a pickup," I say, laughing, because that's the description Ericka loved, the one that encapsulates him, literally the caption in the story. I swear he'd tip his hat—if Shenaz had let him keep it. Thank god I made her take it back. "And you wonder why Cherry says—"

"Truckbois are trouble, I know. Nothing wrong with that," he says, opening the passenger door and scooting me in. He gets in the other side, then leans all the way over, pulling me close because there's just so much space in here. "This Raptor is nicer than mine." He shrugs. "Couldn't resist."

He's about to kiss me when I start laughing again. "Okay, wait, wait. Just tell me one thing. Is this even legal in this state?"

"What? Making out in a truck?"

"No, this honker. I mean, what does it get? Ten miles a gallon. Destroying the earth."

"You done?" he asks.

I nod. Then he kisses me, and we make up for lost time, not coming up for air till the sun's nearly full blaze.

We don't drive far. Just to Cook Campus, and then there are those familiar grinning faces as we walk to the stables. "You remember our pals Princess and Wilbur, right?" A little one ambles not far behind, and it's adorable.

"Who's the baby?" I ask, delighted.

"Markie." Ranbir beams. "Princess's colt. Two weeks old."

"That's amazing."

"You should have seen it. Marcus helped birth her. He decided to go to veterinary school."

We saddle up and ride in silence for a while, the horses—Wilbur and his pal Freddie—are neighing and braying and grinning up a storm. The campus is quiet, the tail end of the summer settling in before the fall rush. The greens are starting to fade, the bales are being turned into hay, and the garlic harvest is nearly complete, the waft pungent and familiar as we stroll past the greenhouses.

The homesickness is less sharp now that I know the end is in sight, and how much I'll lose before it's over. But I made the choices, so I'll deal with the fallout.

"Your class is wrapped?" I ask Ranbir, and he nods, his head somewhere far away, perhaps envisioning a false future somewhere here or there. "Did you like it?"

Did it change everything? How do you decide?

He shrugs, still tracking something in the distance. Something he can't quite touch. "I learned a lot. The music. The breathing.

The rhythm. All of that, of course. It was amazing." He takes a deep breath. "But maybe not enough. I don't know if I have the passion—or the temperament—to chase it. Not like you do." Because, he leaves the words unsaid, it would cost too much. Nearly everything. "Doesn't mean I won't find what I'm chasing one day."

I nod, finally seeing the flowers on the horizon as the sun rises even higher, casting long shadows. "But you can't give it all up."

"I can't. Not yet. Maybe not ever. I do miss it, home. Tending the vines, playing the piano for my mom, listening to my dad talk about all his big plans for the business—and for me. I'm excited to be part of those plans." He sighs. "I won't abandon them. Not until she's gone. Maybe not after. I have to stay. But it's okay if you don't. If you make other plans. And if I'm not part of your plans either." He pauses, breathing deep. "Though I'd like to be."

The horses trot a bit farther, the canter melodic, and I try to unravel what I want to say. What I actually feel. "I miss it, too." I know that much is true. "Not the harvest so much. But the way the skin of the garlic is papery soft, and how it mellows when you drop that just-picked clove into hot ghee. The hours Ma would put into the chutney, ordering me to chop this, sauté that, peel all those cloves. Making haldi doodh with Dadoo, then sitting near the firepit under a November sky, listening to his partition stories. I probably missed so much this summer. And I haven't thought about it for a second, I was so busy with my little adventure."

"Because you were soaking it in, like you should. So you'll remember every moment."

In case this is it. The end. And I never get another shot. Because that's probably actual reality. "When I get home, I'll have to soak it all up there," I say, my voice quiet. Because what if it slips away, right out of my grasp, and I didn't appreciate it?

"I know it wouldn't occur to you, but there might be a middle ground," he says, nudging his horse to stop. "A way to have both."

Like what my mother said. "Maybe." But I don't see it. "If you figure out how, let me know."

Freddie brays and honks loudly at that one, in full agreement. Because we drama queens don't do anything halfway.

Two hours later, we're at the dorms, and I hop into the shower so I can wash the horse scent off, while Ranbir pulls together a late lunch. The water here is strong and hot, and I scrub my hair with some of Ranbir's shampoo—strawberry scented, green bottle. Like the one I have at home. Weird.

"That smells good," I say, stepping into the living room. I couldn't find much else, so I just grabbed one of his T-shirts, which pretty much fits like a dress. It's the one that says PURE PUNJABI across the front, and I might just steal it if I can sneak it out of here without him noticing. I plop on the couch, pulling up a blanket, and scroll Netflix for a movie. He hands me a bowl—a simple yellow dal, spiked with hing and hari mirch, and rice. Old school. Classic. "Nanima's recipe?"

He swallows a bite, nodding. "She's pretty expert. But I've got a few things down."

Part of me wishes I'd known everything earlier. Part of me wishes I could unknow it even now. But I know that's not fair. "I told Dolly that my mom's cancer is terminal. She was pretty upset." He takes a deep breath. "She's been upset all summer."

It makes sense now. So much of it. "I only told her because I didn't want to come here at all. But Dolly wouldn't let go of it, wouldn't understand. Even though we weren't together. And Mom refused to hear it. This—you know how it is. They planned it forever. Her parents. My parents. If my dad had his way, he would have already had the wedding cards printed. Just so we could make sure—"

She'd be there. His mom. She'd see it all. Weddings, babies, business. And Dolly's perfect like that. She'd fill the slot, complete the picture. Take care of him.

It pinches, uncomfortable, no matter how I try to readjust it in my head. They all thought it was "meant to be," he said that day forever ago. Of course. No wonder she held on so tight, believed it so hard. It all clicks into place, like math or clockwork.

He sighs, treading carefully. "After we split up, things were really weird. This summer felt forced, and I definitely resented it. Her. Being here. The agenda. All of it. And there you were. Pretty and flustered and happy. Like a breath of fresh—"

"Garlic," I say, laughing.

"I just remember the strawberries," he says, and I blush, thinking about the shampoo in his shower. "And the way you laughed and mumbled to yourself and read your little quizzes, all serious, and wouldn't sleep even when your head was bobbing."

Oh. "You caught all that?" I thought he was asleep.

He grins, and puts down his bowl, then takes my small face into his giant hands. "You're so stubborn, Maya, no matter what it is—like you'd fight me for the remote, then put on what I want to watch anyway. Or make your chai the same way every time, because your way is the best way. And it probably is, though the kali lachi is an interesting surprise. Really clears your sinuses. But there's no convincing you of anything else. Full speed ahead, running over everything in your path, and then you look back and maybe survey the damage. Oops. With glee."

I want to argue, but I think about it for a minute, and realize, sort of, that's exactly what I did this summer. Some of it was not my fault, but a lot of it was. Ranbir was almost the damage. But maybe I can bandage us up, put us back together. It's worth a shot.

"You know," he says, slurping dal, "we never did get to have our dance-off this summer."

I grin. "That's one thing we can save for California." I slurp mine, too. "And get ready. Because I will kick your ass."

28

MONDAY MORNING. ONE LAST STOP. THEN I'M DONE. ALL the threads pulled free, all the lies unraveled.

I get on the train, now ever so familiar, and head into the heart of Times Square.

Ericka's expecting me, as I knew she would be.

"She wants to see you immediately," Becca says. "Like do not pass go, do not flirt with the assistant. Go directly to jail. I mean, Ericka's office."

I pause, gobsmacked. "Careful, Gemma."

"Becca." She is so very offended.

"Whatever. Watch out, because sometimes, when you're not looking, your racism is showing."

She rises from her seat, outraged. "Are you calling me a racist? I'm not a racist. I'll have you know that I'm the champion of the marginalized, having faced such hardships myself—you know I have two dads?"

"Oh, I know," I say, and keep walking.

Xander smirks from afar. Guess he agrees that one last low blow is always worth it in the end, when you're walking the plank, headed to your doom. And silently applauds me for it.

As soon as I step inside, Ericka stands. "Close the door," she instructs. Her voice serious. She beckons me to her desk, and there it is. My article, on her computer screen, a confessional.

"So I love it."

I frown. "What?"

"The story. I have to say, I had grand expectations. But truly, Maya, for a first-time feature writer, you really knocked it out." She runs her finger along the copy, pleased. "Like, especially this line. 'Farmhands in overalls and work boots, children playing among cows and horses, and teenagers—like me—selling homegrown cherries, avocados, and everything garlic (even ice cream) to tourists driving through.' I feel like I'm there."

For the first time, maybe in all my life, I'm at a loss for words.

I swallow hard. "You knew?"

She nods. "Not the whole time. But pretty quickly. Dulcie, too."

"And you didn't say anything?"

She sighs. "Honestly, I was waiting for you to say something. To fess up. But I guess that's expecting a lot." She shoots me that stern look, the one Becca gets all the time. "From a teenager."

"That sounds like something my mom would say."

She laughs, and a tiny bit of the bile gnawing at my stomach settles. Just a bit, though.

"You're not off the hook," she says. "Not by a long shot. I need you to understand something. This magazine—the one you've told me a million times has your heart—is in a precarious situation, you know?"

I nod.

"What you did could have caused a lot of problems," Ericka says. "But Dulcie and I, once we figured it out, we started fixing it. Making it right. To protect you, yes. Because I like you, Maya, and will protect you. But to protect *us*, too. Me and Dulcie. And the future of *Fierce*. Of what it could be." She takes another deep breath, and the look on her face sort of kills me. "I really wish you had told me the truth to begin with. Maybe I would have shut it down right away. Dismissed you as a child. Which is so obviously what you are."

That stings.

"But if there's one thing I have to give Dulcie—and Legend before her—credit for, it's knowing how to twist things. To make them fresh. To make them work." She grins, and I can breathe again. "So four weeks ago, when we first found out, we made a plan. And fixed it."

"How did you figure it out?"

"Well, Maya Gera, when it comes to identity fraud, you kind of suck. As soon as you sent HR your cousin's ID, I knew something was off," she says, pulling out a file. Of course she has a file. "Close enough, maybe, but not quite right."

She pulls out a sheet of paper and pushes it toward me. It's an image of my ID. My real ID. Maya Gera. Gilroy, California. All of seventeen.

"Then Jude—you know Jude—kept sending me and Dulcie little missives, veiled threats. He does that sometimes, gossip column overload. Thinks he's a badass detective. Sent me this."

She leans closer, her voice even lower. Oh yeah, cameras everywhere. "So I went to HR weeks ago and told them there was a mistake. Inputted RoopKiran Malhotra as a freelancer, a medical consultant on the Saira Sehgal story. Which she can be. Legally. Have her read the story before you turn it in."

I'm confused. "You knew the whole time." I still can't quite believe it.

Ericka smirks. "Yeah. Pretty quickly. I mean, the ID, the baby face, the boy problems. I was so curious what you'd do at the restaurant—that surely you'd say something then. Or politely decline. But kid, you took three sips, and the way that wine hit you." She laughs. "It was quickly unraveling. Then I overheard you and Xander. By accident." She takes a deep breath. "In any case, according to McIntyre-Scott HR, RoopKiran Malhotra simply consulted at *Fierce*. We don't need to talk about who she is or where she came from or her documents or address or age. Ever again. Got it?"

I nod. My phone buzzes. I ignore it.

"A blip on our records." I can almost feel her glee as she hit delete, delete, delete.

"That said, I have to give you credit."

I frown. "For what?"

"It was a lot to pull off. For a seventeen-year-old," she says. "Being assistant features editor. You did a good job. But you're still a teenager. A student. Whose family owns a small garlic farm. Whose boyfriend—ex-boyfriend, whatever—is a teenager who's charming and the future heir to a winery. And not allowed to drink." I nod. "Whose best friend is a pretty kick-ass designer. Who is also seventeen."

So she really does know. Everything. I press my lips together. "If you're worried about Roop, don't be," I say. "She's my cousin. She knows. You're not going to get sued by her." I can see the relief in that, at least, instant. "And I do actually have a social security number, and I didn't steal—"

"I know. I already processed your paperwork." Ericka pushes forward another folder. A freelance contract. Under my name. For my piece on the farm kids. For three thousand dollars. "This has already been invoiced and processed for the December issue. The last issue. Byline, Maya Gera. It's really good. Sometimes I forget you're a teenager. And other times it's so obvious." She beams. "I mean, I have to hand it to Dulcie, too, when she called you out in the meeting, when she said you'd run the *teen* fellowship—like, blatantly, and"—she makes a whooshing motion over her head—"you still didn't get it. You totally make me laugh, kid."

I scan through the folder, and I can feel her watching me, pleased.

"It'll announce this week. A press release that will include your name. Your real name. If it's okay with you. And your parents." The press release announces the *Fierce* Teen Fellowship Program, naming Xander as the managing editor for the program and me as one of the inaugural members, citing my Homegrown feature as the first commissioned piece. "It'll be all over the media. I hope you're ready for that."

I don't want her to see me cry. But the tears fall anyway. "Thank you," I say, my voice going all nasal like Ma's. "I'm really sorry I lied. There were a million times I wanted to tell you the truth, honestly, right from the beginning, but I wanted to work here, be here, even just breathe the air, so badly, and then it was like a miracle, meeting you, and all mixed up and everyone and everything kept reminding me how hard it was to even get in the door, and once I was here—and I thought I'd applied for an internship, really, ask Xander—I just couldn't give up my shot."

"I know," she says, passing me a tissue. "We're trying to fix that. You know, the big-picture problems."

I nod. "And the magazine will be better for it."

Ericka pauses and takes a deep breath. "I know you have to go home, back to school. But I meant what I said. Talent is talent, and I think you're good. You are what the future of this magazine should look like—what we picture when we push forward. Dulcie wants you on the team. I could use you—Maya *Gera*—as a freelance writer. And if you apply to intern next summer, I'd hire you. In a heartbeat." Then she says it again: "As an intern."

Her voice drops. "This is probably my fault a bit, too. I don't like résumés. HR said it looked okay." She shrugs. "And like I said, I didn't care. Your test was strong. You were so excited. And I liked you." She shuffles papers, smiling. "But if you ever, ever lie to me again, you're disowned. Got it?"

I nod.

"So go finish high school or whatever. Maybe I'll see you next summer." Ericka sighs. "If you can arrive with a proper note from your parents. And swear not to make out with assistants in the copy room. Becca made that shit up, right? Because, girl, if that was real, even Dulcie wouldn't be able to save your ass. Could not, would not. Got it?""

I just sit there, tears at the ready again, barely holding it together.

"What? Why are you not moving?"

"Thanks again, Rick. I learned a lot—maybe too much—this summer."

"And you have a long way to go."

"Thank you for all of it."

She nods. "Don't worry. Xander will email you about the fellowship stuff."

"Okay." Then I stand, still hovering.

"Yes, you can hug me," she says. "Thank you for asking."

I pretty much throw myself on her, and maybe the tears stain her emerald silk blouse a little bit, but she doesn't complain—not today, anyway, though I'm sure she's filing it away for future reference.

"Good luck, Maya. You've got a big year ahead. Try to be a kid and actually enjoy it, okay?" I see another light bulb go off in her head. Because everything is content, and I wait for it to spill. "I'll email you. Now leave the building. And when you say bye to Xander, make sure it's not on Mac property. Clear?"

"Clear."

I march right past his desk, willing him to pick up my cue and follow.

He does, of course. Once we're two blocks away from the Mac Tower, he grabs my arm and pulls me close, talking into my hair.

"Done?" he says.

"For now."

I kind of hope he might kiss me. But I know it would be all wrong. So we just stand there for a minute before he lets go, flashes one last dented cheek my way. "I'll email you. Because I'm your boss now."

Then I watch as he heads back into the building to officially take my job.

29

As the sun sets on my summer, I stare out the airport window at the darkened city skyline, New York City all lit up in the distance, glittering and beckoning on the horizon, beyond an endless runway of airplanes.

I can't believe I got to live and breathe and work at the center of it all, even for a minute. To finally write myself into the story, at least for a little bit.

"It's beautiful," Ma says, resting her head on my shoulder for a moment. "Maybe we'll go back one day to visit. You can show me the office where you worked."

I point at the window, right to the middle of the skyline, poking at the glass. "You see that purple building, lean and tall, shooting right up?" Ma squints at the skyline, trying and failing to pinpoint it. "That was mine." And still might be, someday.

"When you're ready," she says, the way Shenaz does, reading my mind.

"When I'm ready." She leaves me standing there, staring, wistful. "Never gets old, does it?"

I didn't get to tell Ranbir what happened with Ericka, to unravel the end of the story. Wasn't quite sure when I'd get to see him again at all, really. But he's standing right there, a T-shirt, baseball cap, and, wait—"Are those pajamas?"

"What? It's a long haul. Midnight by the time we land. You'd totally do it, too."

If I'd thought of it. "Cherry's going to hate them." I'm pretty sure she's not going to be thrilled to see him. "She and Papa went to go get one last pizza. But she'll be back in a second."

He leans in close, and I think he's going to kiss me, but I can still feel Ma hovering, so I step back a little. "I might have a spare pair in my backpack," he whispers. "If you play your cards right—"

"Wait, are you on my flight?"

"Yes, doofus. Your parents booked my ticket."

"They did?"

"I'm sitting right next to you." He laughs. "Don't get too excited, though. It's not first class. And Cherry's got the window, so you're stuck in the middle."

I can't even—

"I think your mom called my mom, and I was headed back anyway, and you know what?" He's laughing, pulling me closer. "Look, they have good taste. And high hopes. No pressure."

"Okay," I say. "No pressure."

I'll just relax and embrace it. If there's anything I've learned this summer, it's that I have it in me to make my own path. And—I realize as I sneak Ranbir behind a giant pole to steal a kiss— sometimes, quite by accident, it might be one my parents and I happen to agree on.

And if they don't? Well, guess that gives me plenty more to write about.

Acknowledgments

WHEN I WAS ALL OF SEVEN YEARS OLD, I TOLD MY PARENTS I wanted to be a writer. Specifically, a journalist. Even then, somewhere in my scattered little head, I think I knew I wanted to tell stories—but back then I was afraid to acknowledge what some small part of me knew deep inside.

Little brown girls couldn't become writers, right? Over the years, slowly, I learned that I was wrong. First, when my sister and I wrote a very strongly worded letter to one *Seventeen* magazine—published in the fiftieth anniversary issue—about their own appropriative Indian Stunner spread, which left us out of our very own story. Seeing my name in print, that was it. I was a goner. I had my mission.

So, as always, first and foremost: to all the little brown kids—the dreamers, the schemers, the overachievers, and especially the underachievers. I see you. This story is for you. I write so that maybe you can see yourself, too. To Kavya, to Shaiyar, to all of you: You can be whatever you want to be. It's okay. Thank you for chasing your dreams and changing the world.

This book, in so many ways, is an homage to the girl I once was, the one who was so desperate to see herself as the hero of the story, the one who wanted so much to write herself into the narrative. Because that girl still exists in kids like my daughter, to whom this book is dedicated.

Thank you to S. Mitra Kalita—the first editor I ever had, and a fellow (pigtailed!) brown girl at that, for leading the charge first at the *Daily Targum* at Rutgers, and then as part of the team of brown journalists in the early SAJA days, alongside Sree Sreeniva-san, Aseem Chhabbra, Jyoti Thotam, Deepti Hajela, and so many others, who taught me two very important things:

a) Punjabis are known as the party people with good reason.

b) If you can see it, you can be it.

Because of the mentors I had—in magazines, in book publishing, and in life—I got to write myself into the narrative, to tell my own stories. And there's no way I could've gotten here alone.

Thank you to my amazing mentors during my formative years at *People* and *Teen People*, including Liz McNeil, Maria Eftimiades, Natasha Stoynoff, Irene Neves, Steve Dougherty, Lori Majewski, Laura Morgan, and Meaghan Murphy. And especially to my forever work wife, Ericka Sóuter. (Yes, Ericka Turner is based on her.)

Thank you to my publishing team at Imprint—the brilliant Erin Stein, Weslie Turner, Natalie Sousa, Katie Quinn, Dawn Ryan, and the rest of the Imprint crew. Thank you also to the amazing team at Feiwel and Friends, who embraced this book with enthusiasm as the whole world shifted beneath our feet—Kat Brzozowski, Lelia Mander, Aurora Parlagreco, Kelsey Marrujo, Kim Waymer, and the whole F&F team. Thank you, too, to the tireless and amazing Clay Morrell, keeper of deadlines, schooled in the art of the graceful nudge. Thank you, too, to early readers like Priya Arora, and to my fashion guides Alla Plotkin and Meena Memsahib.

I'm forever grateful to the awesome team at New Leaf Literary, especially agents Joanna Volpe and Suzie Townsend, Jordan Hill, and Dani Segelbaum. You guys are far more amazing than I could ever actually express in words.

Thank you, too, to the awesome Clubhouse Crew for endless sprints and chats, to my Desi writers group for cheering me on and letting me vent, and to my faves on the WNDB team for all your efforts, always, to make the world a better place.

And last but certainly not least: to my heart and soul, my

family. The Charaipotras, the Dhillons, the Bhambris. You are my favorites, and so very loved.

To my first and favorite collaborators, Meena and Tarun Charaipotra: I'm so glad I grew up sharing stories with you both. To Navdeep, Kavya, and Shaiyar, my beloved little band of storytellers. Thank you for always being patient, always being present, and reminding me to do the same. I can't wait to see the stories you will share with the world.

And to Mommy and Papa. I know my path wasn't exactly the one you were hoping I'd take. But everything you've taught me has led me here. Thank you for believing in dreams, and in me, no matter what direction I went off in. I hope I can make you proud.

Thank you for reading this Feiwel & Friends book.
The friends who made *How Maya Got Fierce* possible are:

Jean Feiwel, Publisher

Liz Szabla, Associate Publisher

Rich Deas, Senior Creative Director

Holly West, Senior Editor

Anna Roberto, Senior Editor

Kat Brzozowski, Senior Editor

Dawn Ryan, Executive Managing Editor

Celeste Cass, Assistant Production Manager

Erin Siu, Associate Editor

Emily Settle, Associate Editor

Foyinsi Adegbonmire, Associate Editor

Rachel Diebel, Assistant Editor

Aurora Parlagreco, Associate Art Director

Lelia Mander, Production Editor

Follow us on Facebook or visit us online at mackids.com.
Our books are friends for life.